I0578015

ADVANCE PRAISE
FOR *WATER & EARTH*

"Unique world-building coupled with an exciting story make this YA novel hard to put down. A.L. Mundt is definitely an author to follow!"

—Lisanne Norman,
Author of the Sholan Alliance Series

"*Water & Earth* is a non-stop fantasy adventure beginning in the prologue and continuing into the realms of magic and possibility. Fascinating characters with super-human abilities in tandem with the elements of the Earth!"

—Lori Hines,
Psychic Medium and Author of *Visions of Time*,
Award-winning Finalist in the International Book Awards

"A.L. Mundt puts you in a post-apocalyptic winter wasteland on a very changed world. Humanity is barely holding on. Gods and demons use what's left in a war for control, and one family is torn apart by these forces."

—Brian Oppermann,
U.S. Marine Corps Combat Veteran of
Desert Storm/Desert Shield

WATER & EARTH

A.L. Mundt

WATER & EARTH

BOOK 1 OF THE
MESSENGERS TRILOGY

A.L. Mundt

Green Bay, WI

Publisher/Executive Editor: Brittiany Koren
Proofreader: Callie Trautmiller
Cover Art Designer: Sunny Fassbender
Illustrator: Mark Shamlian
Interior Layout Designer: Amit Dey
Ebook Layout Designer: Amit Dey

Category: Post-Apocalyptic Young Adult Fantasy
Description: *Battling many different evils, two siblings may be the last hope for human civilization.*

Hard Cover ISBN: 978-1-951375-50-8
Paperback ISBN: 978-1-951375-51-5
Ebook ISBN: 978-1-951375-52-2
LOC Catalogue Data: Applied for.

First Edition published by Written Dreams Publishing in December, 2021.
Ebook Edition published by Written Dreams Publishing in December, 2021.

Green Bay, WI 54311

To Sunny always, for the use of your galaxy of characters, your plot hole superglue, and for humoring me when I laid on your floor and complained about weather motifs.

To Mom and Dad for rereading and rereading, and to Grandma (again) for the titles.

Lastly, to everyone who's stuck around since I wrote this thing in high school—I promise, Messengers has never been bigger and brighter than in this moment.

PROLOGUE

A high-pitched whirring shook young Letty Skylark from her dreams. Where imaginary friends and unconscious fantasies had woven their threads through her sleep before, a tall figure in a sweeping gray cloak now stood.

The world around her was unbridled chaos. She could hear thick voices, muffled by the dense fog that spiraled around her and the stranger. There was no visible sky, though the air spun with glowing specks of light—some sort of odd, twinkling stars.

Letty looked down at her bare feet, shocked to find no solid ground beneath them. She was standing on emptiness. Between her toes stretched a void of mottled azure.

She stared in horror, her tiny hands balled into fists. Was she still dreaming?

"Are there others?" the stranger asked. It was a cavernous voice, like an echo into an uncertain sky. The face it belonged to was inhuman and strange, with blank lapis eyes and streaks of blue and red painted across silver skin.

"Others?" Her voice came out far too frail. "Where am I? Who…who are you?"

The man blinked round, alien eyes. "My name is Komi," he said.

She repeated his name under her breath. *"Komi? Komi."*

"Many years ago, a humming world thrived on this land, Aletta Skylark," Komi said. His voice was a powerful web, strings she couldn't untangle from.

"It was a time with roads beneath shoe-shined feet, when humans worked in smoky factories and toppled whatever rose in their way—before the End, the Final War, when they tore it all apart."

"The End?"

Komi looked at her gravely, as though he pitied her for not knowing. "The gods intervened to halt this human war, but when gods come to your vulnerable Earth, demons are sure to follow—to fight and prey on the weak. We managed to save the last scraps of humanity and banish the demons back to Hell to lick their wounds. The planet had to rebuild, accelerated under the blanket of our postwar dust—have you never heard these stories?"

Letty wrinkled her nose. "My parents were born in the time before mine. They fled from that war; they never told me *gods* were involved, or *demons*. Is that what you are? A god? What do you want from me?"

"Enough. This talk is not what I came here for." Komi's hands lifted and his eyes closed.

Letty watched with incredulity as silver wings lifted from Komi's back and ascended to a full, stunning height. She was positive she was dreaming—and if she wasn't, she was beginning to wish she was. She'd give anything to blame this on an unsettled meal.

"Bring me the other," Komi said.

"Other...?"

"Your kin." Komi's brow furrowed in a rather humanlike gesture. "Family your age."

Letty was still young enough to not understand everything said by her elders, but she was old enough to know right from wrong. Was he asking about her siblings? She had two: her older brother, Majest, and a much older sister, Lunesta. But Komi had asked about someone *her age*. Only Majest was still a child, but with the appearance of someone a decade old like herself.

"My brother..." she began.

Komi dipped his head. "Bring him to me."

Before Letty could form a reply, she felt the invisible ground give way beneath her, and she was sucked into an endless void. She couldn't hear, she couldn't see—all she could do was scream, teeth rattling and hair whipping.

With a gasp, Letty resurfaced in a small bedroom. A dusty dresser stood to her right and straight in front of her was a small, fur-covered bed. Various sketches lined the walls, dotted in her father's foreign script, and on the floor sprawled an old spruce slingshot.

She froze. This was her brother's room.

Bring him to me.

Majest was asleep in bed, his hands tucked against his chest, breathing slow and even. Chestnut hair dangled around his face; his evergreen eyes were closed, but his eyelids twitched with the inklings of dreams.

Letty put a hand on his shoulder. "Maji," she whispered.

Majest's eyes fluttered open, his face contorted into a tired stretch. He blinked groggily at his sister, whose head didn't even reach the pillow. "What?"

"I had a dream," Letty whispered. "About a god. He wants me to bring you to him."

Majest made a face. "Go back to sleep." He pulled his seal-fur blanket to his face.

"No," Letty protested, yanking it off. "Please— He was saying all these strange things."

Majest turned his head to glare at her. At most hours, he was good-natured and humorous, but interrupting his deep slumber was like waking a bear from hibernation. "You can tell me about it in the morning. Mother wants me on an early hunt with her."

"You hunted yesterday," Letty said. "And to be frank, repeating yesterday's *'success'* wouldn't exactly fill any of our stomachs. Come with me *now*."

"Bossy. You're sure about this?"

"Yes."

"All right." Majest heaved himself out of bed, the wooden frame creaking in protest. Still in his sleep-clothes and with his hair sticking halfway toward the ceiling, he was barely presentable, but it didn't matter. Probably. Hopefully.

Letty turned to the doorway in relief, then pursed her lips. "Um," she stammered, looking this way and that. "I don't know…how to get back."

At once came laughter in her head that wasn't her own. Then, Letty was falling again.

This time she didn't scream. She flew through the patchwork folds of darkness and light in silence. She heard Majest cry out, but before she could reach for him, they landed on their feet—as though they had never fallen, as though they had been in this starry chasm all along.

"Wow," Majest breathed, his eyes huge and green as he searched the nothingness on all sides. He wasn't afraid, he never was, but his gaze faltered. "What is this place?"

Letty opened her mouth, but was cut off as Komi reappeared, his wings a satin cloak around him.

Majest gasped. "Letty, what—?"

"Aletta Skylark, welcome back," Komi said. "I see your brother looks just like you."

It was true. Majest and Letty both had the same square jaw, the same angled nose, and the same faint spray of freckles. If Majest's hair had been coppery, they could have been twins.

"Komi," Letty said, his name still foreign on her tongue. "What are you, really?"

Komi spread his wings wide, blotting out several feet of darkness. "I am the Deliverer. My duty is to bestow power in times of strife, in the hope it will fight against the dark and bring the message of peace."

"Then how could you allow the world to be destroyed in the first place?" Letty realized her tone and winced, but Komi did not look offended.

"I was forbidden by my superiors to intervene directly." He shook his wings, sending stardust flying.

Looking at Majest, she mouthed, *"Forbidden?"*

"The gods have given me another chance," Komi continued. "And so, as Deliverer, I have come to make the two of you Messengers. The elements' chosen. You will bring the truth of how humankind is intended to be—free of darkness. You will bring this frozen land a new beginning those before you were unable to."

"Messengers?" Majest echoed. "What does that mean?"

"Majest Skylark."

"Yeah, that's my name. You know, like 'majestic'—not like 'majesty.'" His lip trembled, though he clutched his casual tone close. "Spelled like it sounds."

"Do you believe you can contain the force of what I am about to bestow unto you?" Komi asked.

"Sure? I mean, I can handle anything."

Komi fixed him with unnerving, jeweled eyes. "Then, with the power of years long gone and the four earthly elements, I present to you your gift. You are gifted with the force of the land that runs under your feet. The force that spreads across your meager planet to keep life in balance, to understand all who dwell inside it, large and small, plant and animal."

As Komi spoke, a glowing green light rose up around Majest, whose eyes were wide and just as feverish in color. His whole body shook.

Komi turned to Letty, who was beside herself. *If he can make Maji shake like that, what's going to happen to me?*

But Komi's endless eyes went soft on Letty's face.

"Aletta," he began, "you are gifted with Earth's greatest force. The force that can quench all others in a single breath. While thought to be uncontrollable, you will have its strength at your beck and call whenever it presents itself to you."

A blue-black light shone around Letty with his words, and she shuddered as all thought dissolved. She felt as if she were being poked with needles, pinched and sewn from the inside out. Something dark and strange wove between her seams; all she could hear was a wild, mad roar—the beat of the world's heart.

Then Komi was gone, the swirling world was gone, and most frightening of all, Majest had disappeared. Letty had never been so afraid. She had never known less about who she was and what she might become.

And then, she awoke.

1

It was dark. Darker than it had been since Majest could remember. Even in the dead of a sunless winter, he could usually rely on a pale slice of moon. The cold habits of Cognito often bit out his fire, but Majest always searched for light on the horizon—for the smallest ray of hope.

Tonight there was nothing, just the vast, eddying black clouds pounding a thick crust of snow into the treetops.

The Skylark siblings watched the storm from inside their cottage, hearts pooled in their stomachs. Majest couldn't untangle himself from thoughts of Komi and the land of stars that weren't quite stars, the godly words of element and power—and the idea it all might have followed them to the waking world.

That thought gave him the biggest stomachache of all.

He sat in the kitchen, Letty plunked next to him. She picked at the ends of her hair, taking fidgety sips of water. Their mother stood outside, a winter coat pulled over her nightgown. She kept this vigil every night her partner went hunting, stubbornly ignoring the frozen tips of her ears and the drowsy tug of her eyelids. She would wait for him to come home.

And tonight, Majest and Letty waited with her, cloaked in darkness.

"Should we tell them?" Letty whispered, holding her cup between her hands.

"About Komi?" Majest fought the urge to fidget along with her. "I mean, Father always wanted us to be believers in that sort of thing—the gods, the heavens, prophecies."

"Do you think Komi would *want* us to tell?"

"Who cares, if it was only a dream?" he asked.

"You know it wasn't. We both saw it."

"I don't have the processing power for something that insane, right?" Majest tried out a grin, but Letty's glare yanked his mouth back down.

"Be serious," she said.

Majest tried, but *really*. They were too young for any real responsibility, let alone a magical one. Letty was only ten years of physical age, while Majest was twelve—time flew by at double the rate in this restarted world. He had been born six birth-years ago, though he was indistinguishable from an old-world boy twice his age.

"We might have magic in us," Letty insisted, still fiddling with the cup. "And what if it turns out to be dangerous? What if Komi's an evil spirit using us to do his bidding?"

Majest snorted. "Now, *you* be serious."

"Serious about what?" a voice said from the doorway.

Majest turned and saw his older sister leaning in the long shadows of the doorframe, just out of reach of the sputtering candle. Her short blue-black hair curved around her face.

Letty paled. "Nothing, Lunesta."

Even in the dark, Majest could tell Lunesta gave a sour face at that. "Why aren't you asleep?"

"It's hard to count sheep with you two banging about in the kitchen," Lunesta said.

Majest rolled his eyes. "Count howling wolves. They'll drown us out."

A soft thud came from outside—then shuffling, then a soft cry.

Their mother.

All three siblings turned toward the sound, stiffening.

"Get a lantern," Majest told Letty, as Lunesta vanished into the hall. "And my slingshot."

But when they yanked the front door open, Majest found a familiar pair of eyes that glimmered with all the stars the night sky was missing. The tangle of dark hair, the ice-caked beard—it was a sight of home.

"You're back," Majest cried, and flung himself into his father's arms.

He got a low, surprised *oof* in response. His father held him, swinging him like a bag of market grain, before plopping him next to Letty.

"We thought you might not make it back until tomorrow," Majest said, breathless.

His father hadn't stopped chuckling. He pulled a sack of meat from his shoulder, depositing it in the icebox on the porch. "I keep telling you, we from Ísland, we do not feel so much cold. Canada—as it is called now—is nothing in comparison. No storm can get the better of me. I have seen worse." He winked at Letty, who giggled. Majest had missed that rough accent.

"Even Icelanders can lose a toe or two, Dagur," their mother reprimanded, though she was smiling, too. She shivered, her boots poking out from beneath her thin cotton nightgown.

"Maxine, *elskan*, you worry so much. Are you not happy to see me?"

She swatted him with her sleeve. "Oh, get inside."

"Yes, ma'am," said Dagur merrily, and followed her in.

Alone on the snow-covered porch, Letty caught Majest's eye. He could see a question gathering behind her pursed lips.

"Okay," he answered as they went inside. "Let's tell them."

Maxine had a cheery fire started on the stovetop, warming the room. Dagur had discarded his gloves and boots in range of the heat, shaking ice from his hair.

He looked so young when he did that, Majest thought. But everyone in Cognito was just another bug caught in amber, stuck at whatever adult age their body said, *"Stop right there, that's old enough."*

It was evolution, Dagur preached—Earth knew nothing could survive this climate for long besides the hunkered-down trees and anemic sky. So, people in this new time grew quickly, made a family, then froze. Boom-boom-boom. Dagur, uprooted from frigid Iceland before the End, was a rare exception.

Maxine watched Majest and Letty come in, strands of her red hair fleeing its knot. "You two look dreadful," she said. "What's wrong?"

Glancing at Majest, Letty said, "We…have something to tell you." Her hands kneaded one another, as if trying to form something between them. "We had a dream. Both of us, the same one. We want to know…if you think it means something."

"All dreams mean something," Dagur said.

They gravitated to the table, and after they sat, he patted Letty's hand. His eyes were soft. Maxine's were the same—green and orange in the firelight, her freckles like sparks.

Of course Majest and Letty could tell them. That was family—trust in its most intimate form.

And so they did: of Komi and his wings that shimmered like starlight and smoke, his war of humans and magic, and Messengers. Elements and power they could not even imagine.

Majest expected a lecture from his mother, a "you should stop stuffing yourself with lemming before bed and quit reading your father's mythology books." But Maxine was quiet. Only the smudgy shadows on her face moved.

Dagur, on the other hand, said, "*Messengers?* You are serious?"

"Yes?" Letty said, her voice small.

Dagur's chair gave a startled yelp as he stood up. His eyes shone like Majest had never seen them before. "My children are *Messengers?*"

Maxine swung a sharp gaze toward him. "What does that mean?"

Something unknown fluttered in Majest's chest, something that must have been in hibernation his whole life. He saw it on Letty's face, too.

"I have heard of it—of them," Dagur said. He sat again, scooting closer to the fire. He was stammering; his English couldn't come fast enough for his thoughts. "Messengers—four chosen by the gods—four elements—just as prophets are chosen, and guardians, and—"

"Dagur," said Maxine. "Don't."

"But we know it's real." His fire-bright eyes never left Majest's. "It's all real."

Real. The word gusted through Majest's head as if on a particularly impressive wind. It was hard to feel any uncertainty or fear when his father was staring at him like he had found a path to the heavens. *Had they? Maybe they did.*

"Maji, Letty." Dagur reached two callused hands out to them, and they each took one. "I only know so much, but if you have power, can I help you…what is the word…unlock it?"

Majest grinned. "What, right now?"

"It's the middle of the night," protested Maxine, scrubbing at her eyes. "If you want to explore the inner corners of your subconscious, or whatever, you can do it when there's a sun in the sky and a full night's sleep in your bones. I love you all, but *please.*"

For the first time, Dagur hesitated. "All right, Max."

Majest craned forward, suddenly unable to bear a whole night of not knowing. "But—tomorrow?"

"Tomorrow," his father promised.

"You really believe in what this god told us?" Majest asked, hoping it didn't sound as though he were searching for a way out. He had told Komi he could handle anything. He wanted to mean it.

What he found in Dagur's voice, in the infinite blue of his eyes, in the firm squeeze of his father's weather-roughened hands when he said, "I believe you," was certainty and trust.

During Cognito's winters, the sun was not only fleeting, but deceiving. It shone with all the fierce slant of summer but did nothing to ease the bitter northern winds that cut straight through the bone.

Today, Letty had three extra layers under her fluffy fur jacket, feeling less like a potential candidate for heavenly power and more like a waddling seal. She stood shivering in the front yard with Majest and their father, whose enthusiasm was equal parts consoling and unnerving.

Letty smacked her gloves against her thighs until feeling crept back into her fingertips. Power, responsibility, *control*—she didn't know if she wanted any of it.

Dagur's rumble cut through the worry brewing under her ribs. "There is a key to focusing," he said, positively glowing under the cold sun.

"What is it?" Majest asked. He had on fewer layers than Letty—all the bouncing he was doing would keep him toasty enough.

"To focus," said Dagur, "is to reach inside your mind without worry, without fear. Without feeling."

Letty sighed. *All I've done for two days is worry and fear and feel.*

"It is much easier to find what you are looking for if you cannot see it," Dagur said. "Close your eyes."

Letty frowned, then obeyed. Behind her eyes was black and frigid—a space beyond where anyone could find her. She didn't feel focused. She felt the chill; she felt alone.

"This is an old family trick," Dagur said. "Used for meditation, or an attempt to reach spirits. I thought it could be of some help to you."

"How come you've never told me about Messengers before?" asked Majest. He was the one Dagur taught about his language and history—he soaked it up like a tree soaked up the sun.

"It is not a well-believed part of history. Letty, please keep your eyes shut."

She hadn't realized she'd been peeking. Her cheeks burned.

"My country heard many stories," Dagur continued. "Stories of gods picking sides in human wars and fighting alongside them. There were those who claimed to be prophets. Rumors of elemental power in remote lands. My family did not believe, but I read all the news anyway."

Letty tried to imagine faraway strangers with star-spun dreams like hers. She wondered if they had wanted them to be true—or if they had felt the black pulse of fear, too.

"Now, focus," Dagur implored. "Open new doors. Break them down if you must."

What if I don't want what's on the other side? Letty wanted to protest, but she kept her mouth clamped shut. *Maji, are you getting any of this?*

She cracked one eye open. Majest certainly looked focused: his brow thick and furrowed, jaw taut as a drawn bow. Still not scared.

Letty bit her lip and tasted copper.

"Try moving your hands," Dagur said.

Majest's breath plumed in front of him. After a moment, he struck a pose with a low grunt. His hands pinwheeled, body twisting like a fish. "Nothing," he pouted.

Thankfully. Letty covered her mouth with her glove.

Dagur chuckled. "Well, it is a rare thing for success on the first try."

"Rarer still when the goal isn't possible," said Majest.

"*Reyndu aftur,* Maji. Try again."

Majest sighed, then retreated to his former position, hands open and still at his sides. His face shuttered. The wind passed dry and unforgiving overhead.

Dagur's eyes went canyon-wide. "Did you feel that?"

"Feel what?" Majest and Letty asked—Majest with hope, Letty nauseously.

"The trees. They're rustling."

Majest let out a long, grumbling breath through his nose. "It's the breeze."

"You said Komi gave you the force of the land." Dagur's words were firm. "*Large and small, plant and animal.* Yes?"

Letty watched Majest's heart set off.

"If I have an element, it's Element Earth, isn't it?" Majest asked.

Dagur beamed, and Letty's chest caved in.

"Here." Dagur found a rock on the ground, shaking the snow free and holding it out to Majest. "Try this," he said. "Smaller object. Smaller focus. See what you can do."

Letty watched for a third time as Majest turned to marble in front of her. The wind seemed to carve out his gangly stature, the stone-sure lines down his arms, across his face.

This time, when Majest lifted his hands, he pointed in one direction.

The rock fractured in Dagur's hands.

Majest whooped, breathing like he'd run the forest end to end. "It's real! I did that!"

"I knew you could," said Dagur, clutching him around the shoulders.

Majest's eyes swung to Letty's, and she fought the sudden, terrible urge to look away. "Letty, you *have* to try. You were right about that dream."

Dagur turned. Waited.

Letty crushed her hands into fists, her nails digging half-moons into her palms.

Her eyes fluttered shut. *Okay. Okay.*

"I'll try," she decided.

She burrowed deep. Her mind was a lightless tunnel and she was digging blind without a lantern, but Majest had crushed a rock without even touching it—so she kept going. Focused down to her fingertips and the balls of her feet.

But she didn't have the right tools. She couldn't hammer away at the sick pulse in her veins, the quake of her knees, the panic fogging up the spaces behind her eyes. Letty was lost in the dark, hitting walls, scuffing her hands. As if from a distance, she heard herself scream.

Then—a hand on her shoulder, pulling her back to the surface. Majest. "Hey."

Letty opened her eyes slowly, allowed her throbbing fists to unfurl.

"It's all right," Dagur said. "It was a good try."

Letty shook her head to clear the last of the darkness, glaring at the blinding snow under her boots. "It's not all right."

"Of course it is," said Majest. He was smiling. "Now we know this is real—"

"*You* know it's real," Letty said.

"It's tough the first time, but you'll figure it out," Majest insisted. "I did."

"You…" For a moment, incredulous fury overtook disappointment. "You didn't think any of this was real thirty seconds ago. Now you act like you're an expert because you broke a rock? Anyone can break a rock. Don't talk down to me."

Concern and hurt splintered his expression. "I was just—"

"Don't worry about it. I need a break. Have fun making pebbles."

With that, Letty marched herself to the door, stomping snow onto the patio. She ground her teeth so she wouldn't hear the encouragement straining behind her—she was water boiling in a pot, and steam was seeping from under the lid.

She couldn't take having power, but she couldn't take *not* having it, either. How wretched was that?

Flushed crimson but thankfully tearless, she went into the kitchen, boots and gloves and coats thrown every which way. Her nose ran, ears burned, and somehow, the more layers she shed, the more overheated she felt. And the sillier.

"Aletta Skylark." Maxine caught her by the arm. She sat at the table, surrounded by her half-sharpened hunting knives. Lunesta lurked next to her, pretending to read an old book.

"Are you all right?" Maxine asked. "What in the world is going on out there?"

"The powers are real," Letty burst.

Lunesta's pale face snapped up, her hands tightening on the book's binding.

Maxine only blinked. "So, Cognito's people are ageless, hungry, and mutated, and now we're magicians, too. Okay."

"Just Maji." Letty felt short of breath. "I don't know…what mine are… He broke open a stone. He can focus. He can do *anything,* and I can't."

Lunesta opened her mouth, likely to discharge something nasty, but Maxine cut her off.

"Sit," she told Letty, nudging an open chair. "Let's talk about this."

Letty sat, Lunesta's gaze pinching at her skin.

Maxine slid one of her knives back in its sheath, tracing the seam in the leather. She said carefully, "Snow so often falls in gentle sheets, you forget how wretched blizzards can be."

"What does that mean?" Letty asked.

"It means you might be sad you can't make snowflakes, but you certainly don't want to make a snowstorm. Is it so bad this new gift does not come naturally?"

Letty tucked her chin to her chest. "You think our powers could be dangerous."

"Not just the powers, but the fear those powers can put in others." Maxine's gaze had a quality like a single flame in the dark; Letty couldn't look away. "Before you were born, Dagur and I sheltered a woman who was always running from enemies because of what she could do."

"Why?" Letty asked, though she thought she already knew the answer.

Lunesta scoffed. "Your friend sounds more *guilty* than afraid. Only the guilty run."

Maxine silenced her with a harsh look. "I've seen many types of power— used for good and used for the opposite. Maybe we don't know what your powers mean, but you should be careful. And you should not be discouraged."

"How can I not be discouraged when it'll be trouble for me whether I can unlock this gift or not?" Letty felt her temperature rise again.

"If you're meant to get this right, you'll get it right." Her mother said nothing more on the subject and went back to her knives.

Lunesta, with one last sneer, turned a page in her book.

And Letty let herself wonder how it would feel if her power could coat the land with something bright and beautiful.

2

Despite her mother's encouragement, the more days Letty begged her mind to clear her a path to untold magic, the more her focus slipped. The sun and moon traded places again and again, but Letty felt as though she were trying to catch the sky in her bare hands.

She followed Majest to the woods each withering winter day only to watch as her brother made Element Earth his personal assistant. He moved stones, bent branches, all while Dagur hooted at him with excitement.

No matter how firmly Letty gritted her teeth and balled her fists, she pulled nothing from between her own ears but a raging headache.

Quitting practice sessions with Majest didn't make her feel any better, because she still had to hear about Majest's victories every night over dinner. She tried to be happy for him, though—unlike Lunesta, who only congratulated him for all the mud on his clothes.

Majest hadn't batted an eye when Letty had skipped out again today. She'd made up some lie about sewing her torn nightshirt, but she was far too distracted for needles and thread. She wanted adventure: dirty crescents under her nails and ice crystallizing her lungs.

Outside it was foggy, the trees soaked through and blurred into one another. As Letty set off on her usual walking path, she blinked up at the sky, which was so stuffed with clouds it might have burst. She wondered if Komi were up there. Why he didn't *say something*.

The fog thickened as she walked, each step practically into the unknown. Letty couldn't stop thinking about Komi; he was stuck frigid to her mind and she couldn't thaw him off. Was he not human enough to understand how much she needed his help?

Suddenly, she halted. The trees had grown unfamiliar. There was no way she'd mis-stepped—she knew these woods better than anything.

Letty squinted. Everything was grayed-out ahead. When had the fog gotten this bad? It glistened, too, mirage-like and floating.

Her feet picked up again, almost of their own accord. Something lapped against her thoughts, a murmur just out of reach. She shook and shook her head—it didn't clear.

She wanted to turn back, but her boots kept moving through the glittering woods. Forward. Forward. A shape began to split the fog ahead, taller and darker than the fuzzy trees—a cliff face, Letty recognized, even with the low visibility.

Rock formations were anything but uncommon around here, even this far from the mountains, but Letty was certain she had never seen this one before. She was even more certain she had never seen the gaping cavern that plunged straight into its heart, beckoning her inside.

Her feet halted. Letty had arrived at the cave entrance.

It was beyond tall, its entrance a jagged, fanged mouth. She had to crane her neck to see where the cliff clasped the foggy sky. She knew she shouldn't be here, wherever she was. Not by herself, and not when an unintelligible voice itched at the far end of her thoughts.

Inside, she saw nothing but mist. The darkness was so poignant, it stirred something under her skin. This place was terrifying, yes, but it was also an undiscovered mystery—a place that could be *hers*.

Letty crept inside, consumed by the vastness, tiptoeing as though she might wake a great beast if she stepped too loudly. She fought off glittery fog and found enough light to see the feeble patches of moss, the striated rock, the icy roof high overhead. It was strangely warm in here, like a living thing.

She stumbled on. Something buzzed inside her ear, and she clapped a hand to it. Then froze. The cave seemed empty, but what if something had heard?

Dazed and helpless, Letty reached the end of the tunnel. A domed cavern greeted her, bare and black as a starless night, its ceiling climbing to impossible heights.

Behind her, water dripped and she startled. Shapes waved from the walls, blurs and blots of shadow, and they pressed down onto her as though hoping to force her to her knees. She couldn't think.

Droplets plinked on and the darkness took on new horrible forms. She could no longer tell if she was imagining them.

It was time to go—but the same way her feet had forced her into this place, they now held her captive and let the cavern swallow her whole.

Letty was ensnared. Her bones sagged against invisible pressure, her body going limp and see-through. As her eyes widened, the cavern appeared to expand, growing eternal and dizzying before her. It was still murmuring in her ear, loud enough she wondered how she could not make out a word of it.

Of all things, jealousy brewed in her gut—this place was limitless, and she was powerless.

She thought of Majest and his element. Did she feel like this standing next to his power? This small, this far from control?

The ceiling drip-drip-dripped on until her feet remembered they were attached to her. She pivoted, but the toe of her boot caught on a sharp claw of rock on the floor. Her arms reeled for balance, a shout ripping from her throat before she could stop it. Its echo was deafening.

No. She'd broken the silence. She couldn't see—couldn't breathe—as she hurtled toward the cave mouth, heart under her tongue. She heard something rumble in warning behind her, and pushed her legs faster—faster—not fast enough—

Letty emerged into the blinding fog. The world hissed and glowed as she crunched through the snow, unable to shake the sensation that something was behind her, snapping its jaw at the tail of her coat.

Thankfully, her previous footprints could guide her home, but nothing could remove the image of that cavern between every panicky step. It was crushing blackness, a tightening vice, everything she was not.

She feared she had awakened a beast between its stone walls. But perhaps she should have feared that something hidden had awakened in her own cavernous mind.

Letty felt like she was still shivering the next day, long after stumbling home, long after a new morning had rinsed the fog from the trees. Last night her body had rested, but not her mind.

She found Majest alone at the front of the house, lacing up his boots. He looked up at the sound of her footsteps. "Morning, Letty! Missed you yesterday."

Letty shifted her socked feet. "I needed the walk. Where is everyone else?"

"Hmm? Oh, they're all out, like I'll be in a second." Majest raked hair out of his eyes. "Father's hunting again and Mother's grumpy she can't join him and leave us unsupervised, or something, so she's getting water. No idea where Lunesta went."

"Where are *you* going?"

"Practice." Majest tugged on his fur-lined gloves. "Want to come?"

Letty lowered her gaze. "Oh, well—"

"I learned something *really* cool," Majest hedged, like he could sense the incoming *no*. "Please come?"

Letty hesitated, the rejection on her tongue, but something in his face did her in. It was earnest—he wanted to spend time with her. He missed their time together. And going with him might help get that cavern off her mind.

"Okay," she said, and couldn't help but smile when Majest's face lit like a match.

"Great!" He grabbed for the door, then paused. "Should we invite Lunesta?"

Letty imagined the curled lip, the brooding, belittling eyes. She made a face.

"Fair enough," said Majest.

They got their coats and headed for the frigid yard. The sun slunk low across the gray clouds, already at its maximum height. Watching Majest skip over to his practice clearing lightened Letty's spirits—she couldn't help but be excited for him.

"What miracle will you be performing today?" she teased.

"A baby miracle. A teeny one." Majest tossed her a wink. "I've thought more about what Komi said, and it gave me an idea."

Letty ignored the dark shiver of envy that went *plink* in her chest, and she smiled. "Show me, then, or I'll think you're all smirks and no action."

Majest's grin swelled. "Watch *this.*"

Letty prepared for him to slip into his concentrated trance, but instead, he spun to the forest and put his hand to his mouth. From between his fingers, Majest let out a stream of loud, high chattering sounds into the forest.

Letty knew better than to ask what he was doing.

Majest trilled again, the sounds of springtime, of new life and unfamiliar wilderness. Letty wasn't sure how her brother had learned how to make noises like that, but they ripped effortlessly from his throat and deep within his chest.

She waited for something magical to come of the ludicrous chirping, but as Majest fell silent, the forest remained stoic and cold.

"Maji?" she asked.

"Um." Majest rubbed his neck in embarrassment. "Sorry. That was, uh…supposed to… Hmm. I'll try again."

This time, Letty was prepared for the various clucks and sighs. She figured enough weirdness had happened recently; this might as well happen, too.

Movement between the tree trunks made them turn. A small snowshoe hare shivered at the tree line, pink nose jittering. Letty couldn't remember the last time she had seen a rabbit this far from proper grass to graze on.

"It worked," Majest whispered in glee.

"What worked?" Letty matched his soft tone, one eye on the hare, who had one eye on her. "You summoned a bunny?"

"Exactly," said Majest. "I don't quite have the sounds down, but look— this guy was curious enough to check us out."

Her jaw went a little slack. "You—*huh?*"

"The forces of nature and all who dwell inside it, large and small, plant and animal," said Majest. "Animal! Okay, let me try something else."

Letty laughed as he squeezed his eyes shut, letting out a soft, huffing sort of grunt. He thumped his foot for good measure.

The rabbit cocked its head, but responded in turn, beating its hind leg against the snow.

"Are you talking to it?" Letty asked.

At the sound of her incredulity, the rabbit scampered off, its footprints tracking in the snow.

"Oops. Sorry," Letty said.

Majest spun around, practically shining out of his skin. "Wow. I can definitely understand what it's saying, but it's a *lot* harder to sense how to talk back."

"What did it tell you?"

"It outran a fox this morning. I guess congratulations are in order."

Letty poked him in the shoulder. "You're learning a whole new set of languages—you're the one who should be congratulated, Maji."

That wobbled Majest's dimple. "I wish you were learning with me," he said.

Letty forced another smile, pushed the pang of darkness further down into her ribs. "Oh, don't worry. I have no desire to make friends with the lemmings."

Majest shook his head. For once, he didn't seem to be joking. "It's not right doing this alone. Where were you yesterday, really? I wanted you to be here, learning with me."

Letty evaded the question, tensing. "I found a cave and went exploring. That's all."

"Look." Majest wet his lips against the dry air, crouching to Letty's height. "I've never felt freer than when I use this element. It's something that's *ours*. We might not know what it means, but it feels like these gods are giving us a fighting chance to survive out here. To be happy. Don't you want that, too?"

Their gazes met, blue and green.

Letty remembered her mother's words about snowstorms, how suffocating it had been to stand before the cave dome. "It's not a fighting chance if we end up creating more danger," she said. "It's not surviving if we threaten anyone else's survival."

"If there's danger, then we'll figure it out. Together, like always. Letty, I'm not leaving you behind."

Letty dropped her gaze to her boots and felt Majest press one of her small hands between his own. She shuddered and allowed herself to ask, "Even if I can't use my powers?"

"Even then. You're my sister—your headaches are my headaches, just like your leftover dinner is my leftover dinner. Right?"

"Oh, sure." At the word *sister,* a new thought weaseled into Letty's head. "But why do you think we got powers and Lunesta didn't? She's our family, too."

Majest shrugged. "Ask Komi. She's always been the odd one out."

Letty knew what he meant. Lunesta's quiet malice was only one facet of the strange shape she was. She was years older, and had red, spotty scars lining her arms and shoulders instead of freckles. No one had ever spoken of those scars. Letty had never known whether it was the story behind the scars or something else entirely, but Lunesta had never asked to join her siblings' world long before a word of elements had ever been breathed.

"Letty," Majest said.

She realized she had been staring blankly at the snow.

"Hey, don't worry about Lunesta. Don't worry about anything. When Father comes back from his trip, come and train with us again. It'd mean a lot to us both."

Don't worry. Fear still clung wetly to her skin, refusing to drizzle away. "All right," she made herself say. "If it'll make you happy."

He waggled his brows. "It always makes me happy to have more people to show off to."

"You can show off to the squirrels."

"We can show them together, once you've got your power, right?"

For once, Letty basked in his confidence, let it warm and dry her heart, let it make her smile. "Right," she told him.

She purposefully did not look at Lunesta's scowl the rest of the night.

3

It was difficult to trudge through the thick snow that followed a heavy storm, but after three days of pounding white with nothing to do but wait, Majest didn't mind the added challenge. He let his boots crunch into the powder, burying him up to his knees.

He was grateful for the protective layers of logs and tundra moss insulating the house against the screaming wind, the wooden shields over the windows, but he had missed the trees.

He had missed Dagur, who was out here somewhere, on his way home.

The thought of seeing his father made Majest's blood sing, and he tore through the snow with high bounds, plunging into the full, nose-tingling forest of conifers.

He needed to be a safe distance from the house because he wanted to practice another type of power—one that was not elemental at all.

Majest pulled a small, neatly packed ball from his pocket made up of mosses and leaves. In the center was a bundle of explosive powder, something his mother's old-world people had created in their former home.

Now, it was Majest's favorite new-world way to hunt. He snatched his slingshot from his belt, rolling the grass-bomb into its seal-skin pocket. After checking his surroundings, he pulled back on the strings and launched the green bullet into the mingling trees ahead.

He tore after it, feeling the *whoosh* as the winter air nibbled his face. The bomb's small explosion thudded against the thick-packed ground, and green smoke plumed out before him.

Majest whooped. Then, he activated his element. It was simple, now: an inhale, a molded thought, a direction. Without his slingshot, without touching a thing, he scooped a rock from the ground and sent it sailing between firs and spruces.

Alive, alive, beat his heart. This was home. Majest charged freely over roots and stone, safe under the forest's high-rising crowns. He kicked up snow; he howled to the clouds; he flung his second grass-bomb and tunneled straight through the smoke, spluttering as he laughed the gas out of his lungs.

He stopped, still chortling, to catch his breath. The explosion had disrupted the snow and now something stuck out of it. White and red and brown and blue. When Majest arrived at the scene, fighting back breakfast as it inched up from his stomach, he hardly knew what he was looking at.

A corpse, his brain clicked together. A large one.

His expression freezing on his face, Majest crept toward it. The sun caught the figure's edges, and Majest recognized the part closest to him: a human hand, blue and swollen.

The hand was not connected to anything.

Something had torn this corpse apart—birds, maybe, or desperate wolves. It had clearly once been a person, but now it was open like a book: sinew, bone, blood gone slushy. Ribs poked up from a frozen soup of organs, and the framework of limbs was inside-out.

Horror closed a fist around Majest's own insides. He was grateful, at least, that the frozen body did not smell. The sight was bad enough, showing everything that didn't need to be seen.

This poor person. Their poor family. Majest itched to turn, to run, but then he caught sight of a coat's edge poking out from the snow and carnage. Dark fur. Careful, familiar seams.

Majest had seen this coat a thousand times.

He had seen this coat three days ago, headed out the door.

It was as if a mountain had landed on his chest. Majest's knees gave out, his eyes roving without permission, following the line of the coat up to the snowy place where a face should've been.

Majest went cold—as though he too had been opened up, split right down the middle for the wind to sear through. He moved closer. He brushed the snow aside.

He found the face hidden beneath and remembered how it had looked when it had smiled at him. When it had told him there was no storm that could ever get the best of it.

It—him—Dagur.

"No..."

He was all blue now, the same blue of his eyes. Nothing had touched his father's face—it was preserved in this pristine icebox.

Majest didn't know how he got to the ground, snow seeping into his skin through a tear in the knee of his pants. He didn't know how his hands lost their gloves or how they wound up at his father's frozen cheeks.

He only remembered screaming high to the treetops, the cold that became his blood and his bones, the way his tears froze to his face before they had a chance to reach the ground.

Letty was still crying, long after her eyes had first dried. She had cried when Majest had burst ice-covered and haunted through the door. Then, when her mother had collapsed over the table. And when they had retrieved the solid parts of Dagur's body and set them ablaze down the nearby stream. She continued to cry while she watched the flames die from a high-flying yellow to the most solemn blue.

And Letty cried now, as she packed Dagur's shirts and socks into neat sacks, knowing full well they would be traded for food at the market the first chance they got. With their best hunter gone, they would need the extra rations. It was such an unfeeling, cold knowledge. But starving by clinging to memories would not bring her father back, and it would not keep their family alive.

Letty hated it; she knew Majest and their mother hated it, too. They hadn't stopped crying, either, and that was even worse. Majest never cried. Maxine cried less than never.

The only face without tears was Lunesta's. She sat at the edge of their mother's bed calmly boxing a set of furry hats.

Maxine dug through the back of the closet, hands wobbling, hair trailing from its knot. She looked like an earthquake waiting to happen. The room had been silent so long, Letty was beginning to forget what it felt like to hear anything but the soft brushes of wind against wood.

She watched as her mother pulled out something small and bright: a piece of jade on a necklace that would fetch a high price at the Kartho market. Instead of placing it into a sack, Maxine slung it around her neck and stood.

"I'm going to get dinner ready," she said, her head bowed. Her voice was tight, as though she were embarrassed to be crying even now.

Majest looked up, his expression miserable. "You don't have to do that," he said.

Letty could hardly dream of eating with her stomach in this many knots.

Lunesta, though, just blinked. "Do we have any market bread left? I'd like some."

Maxine made no indication she had heard the request. She clutched the stone around her neck, disappearing into the hallway.

When she was gone, Majest whirled on Lunesta. "How can you be thinking of *bread?* How can you pretend nothing's happened?"

Lunesta didn't even look at him. She folded a pair of pants. "Don't get all defensive. I wasn't close to him like you were."

"You aren't close to anyone," Majest spat in a manner so unlike himself. It was a terrible thing, what grief could unlock. "He was my best friend. He taught me everything—he was *still* teaching me—and now he'll never get to teach me again. That's no more night-hunting, never another word of Icelandic, no stories for Letty and I when we can't fall asleep—and no more practicing our powers together." His words broke at the end. Letty watched them fall through the air before her, realizing their truth as they hit the ground. *Never again.*

Lunesta's face brewed with fury. "You're grieving because he can't help you with your *powers* anymore?"

"What? That's not—"

"Everything's about you and those elements now, isn't it?" Lunesta stood, towering over her siblings. "Both of you."

"This is about our father," Majest snarled. He met her anger step for step and rose to his feet to face her. "He's dead, don't you care?"

"I care that in this family, the planets and the stars revolve around *your* dreams and what *you* want and what *your* father meant to *you.*" Lunesta's mouth was a thin, white line that made her eyes seem even darker. "I won't listen to it anymore."

Majest's mouth wobbled painfully, as if he was trying to form words, but Letty saw them die in his throat. He looked absolutely devastated.

Lunesta turned to Letty. "Just remember," she said darkly, "it was a snowstorm that killed him, all right?" Then she stomped into the shadowed hallway.

Majest tore after Letty as she followed Lunesta into the hall, feet lost and unsteady.

"Lunesta!" Letty cried. "We didn't ask for these powers, and we didn't ask for you to be left out. Is that why you're angry? We have them and you don't?"

Majest felt sick. How could this be happening on the day of their father's death?

They pooled together at the front of the house, where Maxine was bent intently over a steaming pot. She didn't look up as the three siblings entered the kitchen.

Lunesta whirled on Majest and Letty. "Of course I'm angry," she answered. "Even the gods themselves think I'm second best to you. I've never felt like a Skylark."

Majest blinked. Though he had been inside for hours, he was frozen solid. "When have you ever showed that you *wanted* to be a Skylark? Letty and I have tried to be your family. You never let us!"

Maxine looked up from her cooking, her eyes red-rimmed and glazed. "Don't be cruel to each other," she whispered. "Not today. Please."

Majest couldn't have agreed more, but a whole new fire exploded behind Lunesta's eyes.

"That's *it*," she snapped, her words crackling. She stormed to the kitchen cupboards, dug through soup pots and oversized plates and pulled a stuffed-full sack from the very back.

Maxine paled. "Lunesta, what—what is that?"

"Supplies. Enough to last a month." Lunesta's bitter gaze wove around the room. "I packed it the morning after we found out about their powers."

"*Why?*"

"Because all those elements will ever be is a burden. It's just getting started, and already, look what it's done to us."

"You're running away?" Letty demanded. "Do you think this is *our* fault?"

"If Father hadn't been so busy training you, he would have gone hunting earlier in the week. He wouldn't have trekked out in a storm."

"Lunesta, *enough*," said Maxine. "Put that bag away and go back to packing. All of you." She reached for Lunesta's arm, but Lunesta backed away toward the front door, her eyes wild, hair everywhere.

"Don't *touch me!*" she howled.

In the six life years he'd been alive, Majest had never heard her voice at such a ferocious volume.

"I'm full-grown. There's no reason for me to stay here," Lunesta went on. "I'll find a place where I'm wanted. I'll tell the whole land about these powers and how dangerous they are. Maybe someone will stop you!"

Her lips were wet with saliva, her eyes hidden by the shadow of the door. She looked like a monster—their own sister, a monster. Majest was stunned into silence. How could flinging rocks into trees hurt anyone as badly as the skies had hurt his family today?

"Stop," Maxine tried again. She was so weary. "No one's going anywhere. We'll figure this out."

"You can stay," Lunesta snarled, and whipped open the door. Wind smacked away the warm kitchen air instantly. "Good-bye, Mother."

Maxine's face caved in for the second time that day.

Majest met Letty's eyes. What were they supposed to do? All he knew was that snowfall was seeping into the room, and Dagur's stone was around their mother's neck, and Lunesta was stepping out into the night, clutching her bag like it was all she could trust.

Their family had shattered.

Lunesta turned back, her eyes dark. They were Dagur's eyes, but hers didn't twinkle with the starlight like his had; they put out the moon. "This is a warning," she said.

"What warning?" Letty asked, extending both hands. "Lunesta—"

"You'll never bring anyone peace," Lunesta hissed, and then she was gone.

4

Nearly two years passed in the way they always did—quickly; it was dark, and then it was light, and then dark once more.

The only difference was that there were three sleepless bodies in the secluded cottage, not five anymore. It made the house less of a home, especially at night when the forest shuddered with cold and creatures whispered behind rocks and tree trunks.

Majest, awake too late as usual, felt more like he was hovering over the kitchen counter than standing next to it. The dark passed through the walls, through the insulation, stopping only to cling to his skin. Two years gone, but he still thought often of the body in the snow, his mother's half-hidden tears, and Lunesta vanishing for good.

Moving forward was inevitable but forgetting was impossible.

"What'cha thinking about?"

Majest startled, turning in the dim room to see Letty's faint outline. She had grown. Before the world was altered, they would've said she had the physical demeanor of someone twelve or thirteen years of age, though now, she was barely past six. Her red-brown hair was in tangles on her shoulders.

"You should be asleep," Majest told her.

"So should you, Maji."

Majest shrugged. "Tried. Can't."

"Me, neither," Letty whispered. "Every time I close my eyes, I remember Mother still sitting out in the cold, waiting for the rest of our family to come home. I remember Komi's face—he must be so disappointed that all this time has passed and I still can't use my power."

Majest tried to smile, even against the miserable truth in her words. *"Það er í lagi,"* he told her, as if his father's language would make him more convincing. "We still don't even know why Komi gave them to us. I'm sure there's no time limit."

"I know," Letty murmured, and Majest knew she did.

"Chipper up. Practice your knife skills or your sewing. You don't need powers to be strong."

Letty rolled her eyes. "Easy for you to say. You're outside all day long chatting up squirrels and tossing trees around. Sometimes I like to think you've forgotten me."

"Maybe it's because the squirrels are nicer to me than you are," Majest teased.

Letty smacked him and they both laughed, but Majest had to wonder if his sister would ever be able to dig out what Komi had buried in her mind. Surely it had to be powerful if it was that deep.

"You really should try and sleep," Majest said.

"With Mother still out there?"

Fair enough. Majest looked to the front door and pictured Maxine beyond it, in her nightgown and boots, her eyes fixed on the trees. She had always waited for Dagur to come home. Now, she waited for two people and they would never come. Every night would end the same—alone.

"Want a cup of water?" Majest asked. "I boiled some from the river earlier."

As he poured them each a few mouthfuls, Letty sat at the table, pressing her lips into a pensive line. "Sometimes I wish we lived down south," she said. "You know, in a town or a pack. It's warmer there, and they have fresh food and water all the time."

"Yeah, but they have to worry about theft, and feuds, and everyone in their business all the time," Majest said. He set the cups down, and they both drank. *"Faðir* built this house here for a reason. It's safer hidden in the heart of the woods. Besides, we can still reach the markets."

"Maji, we haven't been able to get to the market in months. We can't make a life out here anymore, not without our best hunter. Can't you use your powers to catch animals?"

Majest sighed. They had this conversation often—more so, recently. "You know Mother won't leave his house," he said. "And I'm not going to make friends with something just to kill it. That has to be wrong cosmically."

Letty's brow furrowed as she frowned into her water. It rippled suddenly, as if she had dropped a pebble into it. Then again.

Majest lifted his head. He had heard something—something that wasn't his mother's boots scuffing the wooden porch or the *crick-crack* of wildlife moving under the secrecy of the moon. It had been high, sharp, alien.

"What?" Letty asked.

Before he could answer, it came again: swelling, shrieking, bringing with it a strange violet light that smashed against the windows and walls. Majest and Letty covered their ears as the scream passed through them, grating against the floorboards and furniture—and then stopped all at once.

The house flashed, then went black. The candle on the table blew out in a rush.

Majest heard Letty breathing hard, scrabbling toward him, tripping over the nightgown she hadn't quite grown into. They both grappled into their coats and boots because they both had heard it: a new sound outside. The sound of running, a terrible heartbeat over the ground.

"Mother," Letty cried, and they leaped for the door.

It only took a step or two into the still night before Majest saw her.

Maxine was dangling in midair, untouched, as if the darkness alone held her in place. Her arms were bound behind her waist with invisible rope, feet and nightgown flying.

"Put me down," she howled.

"Where are the children?" a voice responded. It was high, piercing. Majest couldn't see where it was coming from.

Maxine's face whipped to something below her, and then they appeared—two identical figures, long and lean as shadows, wearing dark brown uniforms and sickening yellow grins. They were women, but they did not look human. Not the curve of their catlike eyes, not the violet glow of their unkempt hair, not the predatory hunger of their stares.

They were something out of a nightmare. Majest pinched his arm, but the women did not vanish as dreams did—they became more vivid as his eyes adjusted to the night.

One of them held up a faintly glowing hand, aimed at Maxine. Holding her in place.

Magic? Majest's throat swelled.

"I told you," Maxine spat, hair whipping around her like an open flame. "There are no children here."

The strangers laughed, high and tinkling. "And yet," one said, "we aren't leaving."

Terror whittled Majest's thoughts into sharp spurs. Whoever was here, they were here for him and Letty. He had heard from his parents the stories of rogue travelers raiding houses for food and treasures and children, but always to make servants of them, never to kill.

Majest didn't waste a second. Heartbeat thudding in his ears, sky closing in overhead, he ran toward the woman holding Maxine in midair. He clawed his way into his element, snapping rocks from the ground and hurtling them at both strangers.

"Drop her!" he screamed. Letty's steps pounded behind him.

Two white faces whirled to Majest, lips curving in delight. They sidestepped his assault with a twitch of their legs. As simple as a yawn, a blink.

"Majest and Aletta Skylark," a voice said.

Majest could not tell which woman the words had come from, or if they were speaking in perfect piercing unison.

"There you are."

Majest gritted his teeth and tried not to tremble. He grabbed harder at his element, but panic suffocated his focus. His power slipped. The world reeled; Maxine's boots swung. Letty's nails grabbed hard at his sleeve.

The strangers' amber eyes narrowed.

"Stop!" Maxine cried from above, hands out in a plea. "Maji, Letty run! They—*they know what you are*—"

Her body thrashed through the air, scooped from the sky. One of the women snapped her glowing hand sideways, and Maxine smashed into the front of the house. It was over so quickly, Majest was half-convinced he'd blinked and missed a shooting star.

Then, he heard the crunch. The snap.

The scream.

Letty ran for the crumpled figure on the ground before their mother had even stilled.

Majest stared into the empty air where his mother had been—numb, flooded, hyper-aware of the two women turning to him. They prowled closer, hands continuing to glow.

He tried to remember what his father had taught him about fighting. Tried to shout a warning to Letty or help her shield their mother's body. Tried not to throw up. His racing heart was in command of his body, pounding his processes into nothing.

Sparks flicked between the women's fingers. If Majest didn't find a way to tear his feet from their roots and do *something,* he would join his mother's corpse in the snow.

But when the women thrust their hands forward, the sparks stuttered and died at the clawed ends of their fingernails. Their magic, somehow, was gone.

They whirled to each other in horror. They looked naked and helpless without that violet glow. Absurdly human.

"*Chami,*" one of them hissed. "Fall back!"

Just like that, they fled, fluttering into the distant trees. Majest watched them, heavy and horror-struck, thinking only *why, why, why?*

The strangers were gone. Any hope of discovering their motive was gone with them. And Maxine, still as youthful and beautiful as she had been years ago when she had given her life and name to the children she'd sworn to protect, lay on the frozen ground, gone just the same. Blood pooled from her split-open skull, freezing into scarlet crystals.

Letty sobbed into Maxine's nightgown—the pale pink one Majest had once traded his best coat to gift her. It was ruined now.

Why, why, why?

Majest stood there in the heaving silence, panting, the world hanging around him, suspended on thin strings. It was the same feeling of floating that had come from standing in the nothingness of Komi's realm.

No—not only the same feeling. The *same,* because sudden stars sprang to life behind Majest's eyes and he heard Komi's voice burst from within them.

"*The other gods do not permit this,*" Komi said, "*but in light of your absent Protector, I have temporarily drained the twins' magic so you may escape. There is not much time, Majest. They will hide away to recharge, but they will return. And you will be at their mercy."*

"What? I—" Majest gasped a breath. He and Letty hadn't heard a word from Komi in over two years, and now this? "Who are these twins? Why are they hunting us?"

"They are proof of the evil that comes from your gifts, the kind that always festers. And you are not ready for it. At my own cost, and once only, I give you this time. Use it."

Majest heard the words a thousand times echoed. They came from everywhere, nowhere.

Their mother, he managed to think. She had said something—before the crunch.

They know what you are.

This was about their powers. Those haunting, catlike women had somehow discovered them and determined them a threat. And Komi's bodiless voice had known, as if it had been prophesized.

Reality snapped back together, and Komi's voice was gone. Majest could see the trees again, hear his sister crying, feel the weight of loss pulling his heart to his knees.

"What am I supposed to do now?" he whispered.

But he knew, of course he knew.

Time—use it.

He and Letty had been sleeping these last two years, unwilling to open their eyes to what was coming for them. Maxine had known. Lunesta had known. Komi, too, had known.

They would have to wake up now.

And they would have to run to survive.

5

Seti Sinestre was running. He was out of practice—he hadn't needed to move this fast in years. And after spending centuries with the face and body of a child, years to Seti were both an unbearably short and hopelessly long span of time.

He tried not to pant. Not only would that give away his location, but it was a sign of fatigue. Weakness. Right now, he could not afford that stamp to his name.

Behind him chased two women in brown uniforms, violet sparks flying off their fingers. Their bodies rippled as they ran, teeth yellow and bared. Two lionesses after a gazelle.

"You can't get away, Seti," one voice called. The woman it belonged to was in no mood for games. "The Organization needs you."

They seemed closer. He was running out of time—the one thing he'd never lacked.

But despite his size, Seti was fast. His thin legs were swift and agile; his sleek black hair spilled behind him as he dodged the hazards of the northwest forest, known as the Frozen Roots for the way the trees clung to the ice in the rocky ground.

The trees, like everything else in Cognito, were new to being immortal. Seti, on the other hand, had been stuffed full of Heaven-and-Hell energy long before the End's squabbling of gods and demons when they had shed it all over every hemisphere. It was that dust, coating forests and seasides and long-fallen cities, that was breathed in and digested and passed down for generations that had sped and skewed human aging forever.

Seti didn't know if this new species of human was more god or demon. He only found it ironic that after nearly three centuries the rest of the world had finally caught up to his curse.

Today, he refused to be caught up with it again. He tore on, an odd sight in his tailored black coat and wool pants, which would've cost a fortune and a half in wilderness resources. He was grateful, at least, he looked native: Cognito-black hair, Cognito-milky skin. He'd even changed his name to make it ordinary for this country.

"You're one of the best trackers on the continent," one of the women yelled. "We need you to find the Powers. By the time our magic fully returns, they will be gone."

Seti knew who they were talking about. He'd heard the wildfire whispers running rampant through local villages, spread by a stranger with a bitter tongue. Rumors that dangerous powers had infected the wilderness.

Seti also knew the rumors were likely true. He had seen it for himself, what sort of chaos came about when gods left their fingerprints in the hearts of children and let them brew wars powerful enough to strip the landscape. He'd presumed the gods didn't interfere anymore, that they had learned their lesson about letting humans handle the world's fate. Apparently not.

"I told you, I have no time to get involved in something like this," Seti shouted back. He'd hit his stamina's limits and struggled to hold his pace. "I'm only on this continent to avoid the nonsense happening across the ocean. If you want a worker bee, you can search elsewhere. I have no quarrel with those children."

"It's not just them," the other voice said, shriller than the first. "To create an equal world and build back the past as the President designed, everyone with the gods' gifts must go."

Cold air seized Seti's lungs and he coughed. "Just because you were able to track me down, Chami, Shayming—" He broke off, wheezing. "Doesn't mean—"

The twins made a delighted sound. The higher voice—Chami's— replied, "You know who we are?"

"Everyone like us knows about everyone else like us," Seti snapped.

"True," Shayming agreed, not at all out of breath. "We know you're the perfect candidate for this position. You're skilled, cold, cunning—a hunter."

"Shay's right," Chami said, and Seti didn't need to turn around to know she was smiling. "You're the one. And you know what we'll do to you if you refuse."

"So, your Organization is dedicated to destroying those with powers, but your magic is overlooked because you joined the cause? You're nothing but hypocritical cowards." Seti was tiring now, gasping as he lurched onward.

It wasn't enough. Shayming had a burst of speed and flung herself in Seti's path, cutting him off with a glittering grin.

Seti hissed in frustration, trying to dart to the side. Shayming mirrored his every move in a crackling, electric blur.

They had him now. Chami snatched Seti's shoulder from behind, pressing her other palm to her forehead. Seti pulled against her claws, but she dug in, and the world began to slow. Thoughts seeped from his head, traveling right into Chami's. Her eyes narrowed.

"I thought…your magic was depleted," Seti choked out.

"I thought we said it was on its way back," Shayming crowed. Without laying a hand on him, she backed Seti into a tree's trunk, knocking the rest of his breath from his lungs.

"His mind is impressive," Chami reported. "He's thinking of nothing but escape. No emotional ties to anything or anyone."

"It's calming to absorb," Shayming agreed. Her gaze on Seti was almost fond.

"Psychics," Seti managed to spit. "You have no right to—"

Shayming lifted one hand, a flick of fingers and wrist, and Seti let out a howl of agony. His blood was molten, his head on fire.

"I'm very sorry, Seti, but you have to learn some manners," said Chami. She and her sister watched with acidic satisfaction as he slipped to the ground, face hot against the snow. "Defy the Organization, and this is what will happen. The Powers might be strong, but our power is stronger. Stronger than you, too, demon boy. Don't forget that."

Seti looked up enough to shoot her a look of excruciating malice. "I'd rather be dead than be a part of this madness."

Shayming leaned down to him, head cocked, breath reeking of metal. Into his ear, she said, "Dead is exactly what you *will* be, right here, if you refuse."

Chami held up a glowing hand, the threat clear.

Seti knew he was defeated, but it still hurt as he bit his lip and rasped, "Then, I impolitely accept your offer."

An explosion of colors greeted Majest as he and Letty returned the next morning to the spot of their mother's murder. A normal sunrise in Cognito was a simmering, watery yellow, but today, the sky seemed to mourn the Skylarks' loss alongside them. It was a deep red, with fistfuls of violet-blue bruises. The sun crawled beneath the clouds, already near its peak.

Majest hoisted a wooden shovel over his head and swung it at the icy ground, grunting with effort. He'd been at this for hours, his hair damp and sweat-sticky, and the hole he and Letty had dug earlier was now almost refilled.

Letty, who had gone inside to wash up, re-emerged with two sad-looking sandwiches. "You should eat something," she said. "Your hands are shaking."

Majest took another whack at the ground, ignoring her. "If I'm going to fill this grave, I'm doing it right. No powers, no slacking off. I owe our mother that much." He left out the part about how the rhythmic pound of the shovel took away the sounds of a body breaking. "Besides, there's no time to waste if we're heading out this morning."

"This *morning?*"

"Why wait? Those women know where we live."

"I know, but… It feels wrong, leaving Mother and Father."

Majest squinted through the sunlight at her. "You were the one wishing we lived somewhere else. Besides, you can't leave people who are already gone."

"That's an awful thing to say."

"Komi told me if we stay here we'll die, all right?" Majest didn't look her in the eyes, didn't acknowledge the hurt in her words. If he thought too hard about any of this, he would collapse into the grave alongside his mother.

Finished digging, he wiped his filthy hands on his shirt and grimaced. The disturbed patch of earth where they had lowered Maxine looked so ordinary now. Guilt rubbed into Majest, more painful than the blisters on his hands.

Letty took a few steps toward him and stared, waiting.

"Come on," Majest managed. "Let's get our things."

They went inside the house, tracking footprints over the old wooden floors. Down the hall, Majest followed the lived-in marks in the walls, the scuffs in the ceiling. Letty's bedroom was the first door on the right.

It was cozy but bare inside, the same clean-cut cedar as the rest of the house. The blankets on her bed were thick seal furs bought from a passing trader, and the rug on the floor was caribou. A few collectibles—mostly stones and owl feathers—sat on a small table, and two piles of meticulously-sorted winter clothing were packed against the bare walls. That was all.

"You have far too many belongings," Majest said lightly. "How will we ever be able to carry them all?"

Letty, clearly in no mood to be livened by a joke, knelt on the floor, gathering her clothes into her arms. She said nothing.

"Take a minute," Majest told her, squeezing her shoulder. "I'll be right back."

Leaving Letty to her thoughts, Majest crossed the hallway to his own room. It was much less organized, and he had to kick aside several sketches and socks to reach his traveling pack. Into it, he stuffed extra gloves and two sets of clothes. The drawings he left to litter the floor, proof of his life here. Then, he grabbed his remaining grass-bombs and slingshot.

He had other weapons—a bow, a smattering of hunting blades—but none of them fit into his hand like they were made of home itself. Hand-carved when he was younger, the wood wasn't uniform, as though it hadn't grown into itself, and the leather pouch wasn't correctly cut and tied. But it was his.

Majest attached the slingshot to his belt and went to the kitchen, gathering the parcel of food and water he'd laid out earlier that morning. Then he rejoined Letty, who looked up from the floor when he entered and made an attempt to smile.

"Surely you want to take more than that small pack?" she asked, her voice tight.

"I have everything I need," said Majest, shuffling his bag onto one shoulder. "And by that I mean, everything I'm willing to carry. Are you ready to go?"

"I guess," said Letty. "What direction were you thinking?"

"East, maybe, toward the bay. It's a few weeks' walk, but it'll be easier to hide near the water. I don't want to risk heading for a village only to find out we have enemies there, too."

Letty pulled a thick jacket on. "The Hudson Bay? I think you're right."

"Let's get a move on, then."

The future was mapped, home strapped to their backs like turtle shells. They walked to the front door like it was that simple, an adventure rather than an escape. As simple as the east, the sunrise, the day cracking open and shining a light ahead.

Majest opened the door and was greeted by a chilly day like any other. The house already felt less like home, with nothing and no one left inside to make it so.

The protest had left Letty's eyes. She knew it, too.

And so, they walked away from their woodland cottage and their mother's grave, their private, nestled world that had been something out of a children's story. And turned the page.

6

“Are you sure we're still going east?” fretted Letty, her hair a cloud against the harsh wind. “I can barely see my own fingers.”

“My internal compass says so,” Majest assured her despite his own misgivings. “Though it's, uh, been a while since I calibrated this thing.”

“You should've bought the *real* compass you saw at the market last year.”

“They wanted an entire pelt for it!” Majest raised his voice over the pounding snow.

A storm had blown in shortly after they had set out. It wasn't much compared to the sky-shattering blizzards they'd faced in the past, but it was enough to stunt their progress straight from the start. Luckily, it would at least hide the footprints trailing from their house.

“Sounds like wolves howling out here,” said Letty, clutching her hood over her face. “Remember Mother complaining about how loud they used to get?”

Majest frowned and said nothing.

They trudged onward, snow piling above their ankles. The wind was at their backs, running east to west, but its persistent assault still slowed their steps and slapped at their clothes. Normally, they would have sat inside watching the snowflakes swirl during a storm like this.

“This is getting ridiculous,” Letty called after a while. “Should we find shelter?”

“We still have daylight left, I think,” Majest said. “We shouldn't waste it.”

"You don't know for sure?"

Majest turned his gaze upward, shielding his eyes. Dagur had taught him how to tell time by the sun's position, but he faltered on his own, especially in this thick of a storm.

"There's a drop-off near here," said Letty, sounding frustrated. "If we keep going blind, we might walk right into it."

"What else can we do? How are we supposed to find shelter?"

"Mother would know," Letty snapped. "She could follow her gut anywhere. And Father would know where the sun is."

Majest heard his own voice swell with irritation. "Well, they're not here, and wishing they were isn't going to keep us alive. We have to do this ourselves."

"Mother *died* yesterday, Maji. You're already so willing to leave her behind? Maybe no one lives for long in this awful wilderness, but that doesn't make it okay."

Majest stopped in his tracks, stung. In his mind, he saw his parents at the dinner table, laughing with deep rolls coming from their chests. He saw himself, sitting and watching and feeling the deepest form of love right in front of him. Now, it was behind him.

"That's not what I meant," he said. "You sound like Lunesta."

Her eyes went wide with hurt. Then wild.

"I'm sorry," Majest said quickly. "That's not—"

Letty whirled, her fury almost as tangible as the slap of the wind and marched away.

"Hold on," Majest called after her. He clenched his gloved hands into fists, feeling the leather pull taught. "We have to stick together. Like Mother and Father taught us!" He hoped his words offered an olive branch.

But Letty's reply was still frigid as it drifted back on the wind. "Our parents taught us to hold our roots in the ground and refuse to budge for anyone. And now we're running away, hoping we survive long enough to get caught by whoever is trying to kill us. This is insane!"

Majest barely heard her. Letty had somehow gotten farther ahead of him, her colors a smudge in this world of white. He began to run after her, unsteady and half-tripping, but it was no use. In seconds, he could only see the crash of ice and snow.

"Letty," he called desperately. "Letty, where are you? Come back! *Letty!*" She was gone.

Seti was blindfolded and gagged, and dragged through hallways blaring with violent sounds. Under normal circumstances, he would have been listening for information that might help him design an escape, but these were not normal circumstances.

Once Chami and Shayming had used their psychic abilities to transport him to what he presumed was the Organization headquarters, they had thrust Seti into the hands of two strangers he could not see. A man and a young girl.

Seti didn't pay much mind to the man—he was gruff and silent, more brick wall than person. He grunted as he walked, feet clanking on the floor as though either his shoes or the floor itself were made of something hard and metallic.

But the girl interested Seti. He could tell she wasn't much taller than him, which was rare. When she spoke, it was in breathy tones of someone not yet sure of who she was.

"Just a little longer," she said to Seti, her breath tingling in his ear. "I promise she won't hurt you as long as you do what she says."

Seti, unable to talk with the foul-smelling rag in his mouth, stayed silent.

They moved onward, Seti dragging between them like a prize buck. Their footsteps echoed in hall after winding hall until at last they took a sharp right and halted.

Something beeped like from the press of a button. Then a motor's whir, and the *ching-kick!* of gears. Seti was intrigued; he had presumed electricity was dead in the ground like the rest of the continent. Perhaps he had underestimated the Organization. If they had the resources to recreate old-world technology, they might have other tricks up their sleeves.

"I see you've brought the boy."

The voice crushed Seti back into the moment. A woman's. Her electric tone was familiar, but Seti couldn't place it blind. He could, however, place that its owner was in a nasty mood and sounded older than ten birth-years old. It was rare for someone to age past childhood before physically freezing, but the immortalizing Heaven-and-Hell dust settled over everyone differently.

"Lady President," said the girl holding Seti's arm. "Seti Sinestre, just as you asked."

"Excellent," the woman—the President—responded. "He looks even younger than I imagined. Precious, really." A pause. "Don't just stand there. Untie the boy and let him speak."

Hands roved over Seti's face, freeing him from his blindfold and gag. Color and light flooded him, and he gulped down his surroundings without missing a beat.

He was in a stark-white room with no windows or furniture, save for three stout desks piled high with foreign devices and a plastic chair dead center. The President sat there, her slim legs crossed in an almost bug-like manner. Her hair was too long and shining to be real, half-hiding the displeased crescents of her eyes.

Seti's nerves stood on end. He knew immediately who this woman was.

The duo who'd brought him here—the man and the girl—stood off to the right, their heads bowed in respect. The man was tall and nondescript; the small girl had messy butter-blond hair and darting, animated eyes. They wore snug white suits, each with a haphazard "O" stitched into the breast pocket.

Everyone was staring at Seti.

He cleared a thin layer of bile from his throat. "Lady President," he began, his voice soft. He was beginning to piece the connection together— the Organization, the Powers, the President. "I understand you've brought me here to play bloodhound."

The President smiled. It was not a nice smile. "Now, Seti, I know you're more than that. You're a killer, aren't you? And your curse is one of a kind."

Seti swatted away the praise. "You don't know what I am."

"I know you can take care of dangerous magic-users," said the President. "And I need you to take care of the elemental Powers: Majest and Aletta Skylark."

At that, the girl who had brought Seti to the room pricked up in surprise. "But President," she said, "with all due respect, Seti's troubles aren't necessary. The twins are more than capable—"

"Shatter, I have other uses for Chami and Shayming. It's Seti I want on this hunt."

Seti's toes curled in his shoes. He had no desire to kill innocent children. It wasn't worth his time. Besides, this was exactly what the gods wanted—for their chosen ones to draw out the dark forces in the land so that their heavenly power might stamp it out.

"Aletta is your primary target," the President continued. "Majest's abilities are hardly a threat, but no one knows what darkness is knitted under his sister's skin. Surely, it's dangerous."

That, Seti thought, was the fault in the gods' logic—power was *always* dangerous.

"How can you know so much about these children yet have such a bloody hard time finding them?" Seti challenged.

The President did not answer. Instead, she pulled a golden object from her pocket and held it toward him. Its presence hit Seti like a mouthful of black water, and for a moment, he had to remember how to breathe.

"This is for your journey," said the President. "It's a pocket watch infused with demon energy. You'll see for yourself what it can do, but for now, I order you to wear it at all times."

Seti was teeming with demon energy himself, but he still recoiled, dread caught in his throat. It was only a watch, but the thought of touching it made him cold down to his fingertips. It winked from its metal shell, ticking audibly.

"I was involved in the watch's testing," said Shatter from where she stood, not taking her eyes off Seti. "It's safe. As long as you're the one wearing it, it can't hurt you."

"Thank you, Shatter," said the President, silencing her with a look. To Seti, she said, "Take it." It was not a suggestion.

Seti swallowed. He didn't trust it, but he was outnumbered. Holding his breath, he reached out a pale hand and took the watch. It felt cold, but otherwise seemed ordinary. That did not put him at ease.

"The twins put a psychic tracking signal in it," the President added, pursing her lips. "So they can...check in with you." There was a knowing glint in her eyes that said, *Whatever sort of beast you are, this is now your cage and I am your ringmaster.*

Seti sighed. This was going to be a miserable week.

"Go, now." The President waved a hand at him. "I will see you soon."

Majest's cries faded as Letty stumbled on through the storm, shivering and furious. She did not stop or slow down. She did not look where she was going or where she had come from.

He doesn't understand. He's too stubborn to see how much we still need our parents' help because he's always insisted on doing things his own way.

The snow gained momentum, chasing her down and beating against the back of her coat. Letty couldn't see an inch beyond her hood anymore. Couldn't even see the treetops.

Cold gusts tugged at the corners of her eyes, teasing them until they watered. The wind-whipped tears froze on the tops of her cheeks, and she paused in her staggering to swipe at them.

She realized it, then: how rash she'd been. How childish. She would not survive if she lost Majest.

Letty pivoted, reluctantly turning back. But all ways were white.

"No," she gasped, lost to the storm. "No, no, where am I?"

One reckless act, and she might have dug another Skylark's grave. She tried finding her footprints, tried calling out for her brother, but got nothing back except the smack of the sky.

She crouched for a moment, shuddering. Majest, she knew, would be fine on his own. He could use his earth powers to secure wood for a fire. He could build a log shelter with his mind, convince animals to cook themselves for dinner.

Beside herself with panic, Letty's stomach still found time for a stab of resentment. Komi's second Messenger was still a useless mystery. She wouldn't deliver any *message*—couldn't even keep herself alive.

I want my own power, her mind hissed, and it didn't sound like her own voice.

Frustrated with everything—Majest, Komi, herself, this *storm*—Letty stood and kicked at the ground, sending a huge chunk of stone flying. She noted with dull interest that she didn't hear it hit the snow. Curious and blind, she stepped forward.

And then, there was no ground.

Letty remembered the night she'd received her powers from Komi, the land of stars she had fallen through—dark, swirling, and utterly bottomless. That feeling returned, wrapping its formless claws around her feet and *yanking.*

She tumbled down and down, arms thrashing as she tried to regain a sense of direction. Just as she thought she would never hit the ground, it struck her, clattering her teeth. It was cold and wet—a snowdrift. It filled the sleeves of her jacket, smashed into her eyes and nose.

The drop-off, Letty thought in a daze. Her head began to throb.

Although the drift had softened what would have been a fatal fall, it had still knocked the wind out of her and brought shooting stars across her vision. She realized with a jolt how close she was to losing consciousness.

She fought her aching body, forcing her way into a sitting position so she could look around. She was lost, but as the storm thinned enough to see through, she realized her situation was so much worse. The sight of the five-hundred-pound grizzly bear standing across the clearing, gazing at her with exhaustion and not at all with sympathy, because she had fallen straight into its winter home.

7

There she was, Seti thought, as he peered out from behind the boulder he had chosen as his vantage point. Aletta Skylark.

He leaned forward on his knees, enough to see over the cliff's edge as the storm quieted. He had been searching the northeastern woods all day after the twins had dumped him at the Skylarks' stripped-bare cottage with a pathetic bag of supplies. Majest and Aletta's footprints had been smothered by hours of snow, but he'd still found a steady trail to the east.

After pursuing the Skylarks for miles through unpleasant conditions, Seti had begun to hear their voices drifting, his demon-charged hearing cutting a line through the wind.

They'd been in a shouting match by the time Seti had caught up, and he had ducked behind a line of trees when Aletta had suddenly charged in his direction. He had slammed into a fir and brought down a bough's worth of snow onto his head.

Why anyone wanted to live in this ice-smothered, godforsaken wasteland was beyond him.

But now, his luck was turning. Aletta had managed to hurl herself over a hidden precipice, landing with a plop in the drifts below. Like a baby bird fallen from its nest.

At best, she would die here, battered and weak, the gods' great and powerful savior bested by a common snowfall. At worst, she would be easy enough to discard in this condition.

Seti peered down from the lip of the cliff, squinting against the fluff pounding into his face. He could make out Aletta's form as she sat up, then clutched at herself in horror.

"What's the matter?" Seti muttered, following her gaze. The pocket watch in his belt pressed into his side as he leaned closer hard enough to make him hiss. The *tick-tick* of the thing pulsed like a second heartbeat.

Or, like the beat of an animal's footsteps. Seti's brow rose as a bear's face appeared in the mouth of the cave. The great brown mass attached to it moved in Aletta's direction.

Hmm. That's the matter, then.

Aletta and Seti both held their breath as the grizzly swayed forward, sniffing the air with its drowsy chapped nose. It must have been in the process of beginning hibernation, and a stranger on its doormat would be at the bottom of its wish list.

The bear stood to its hind legs. It huffed out a challenge, eyes on Aletta's frozen face.

Seti was ready—for the blunt trauma of paws, the blood on yellowed incisors. Gore and screams and unfeeling claws, the stringy pieces of a body torn apart. The sight would be ghastly and the stench dreadful, but Seti had known worse, and suspected he would know worse in the years to come.

He could only think: if the girl died here and now, perhaps the Organization would set him free.

This is it. This is my way out.

There's no way out.

The words orbited Letty's head as she backed herself up against the cliff face. Her head pounded from the fall, but her heart throbbed harder as she stared up at the beast before her.

She had never seen a bear before. Dagur had told her stories of them; they were hulking terrors made of thick fur and endless bulk, with dull claws that tore, serrated teeth that destroyed. They could be brown, black, or white, but Dagur had always warned that a livid grizzly was the worst of all.

And one was looking down on Letty like an angry god, its eyes black and merciless. A rumbling snarl came from deep within its gut.

Letty shuddered, goose bumps rubbing against the interior of her coat. The coat was wolf's fur, but she was no wolf inside it.

I'm going to die, she realized.

Letty struggled into a standing position. Time skidded on its heels as bear and girl stared at each other, blue eyes and beady black in one weighted moment.

They began running at the same time. Letty knew it would not be for long, but she at least wanted to die on her feet. She staggered through deep snow, dizzy and lurching, as the bear pounded the storm's drifts into glitter behind her.

Fractions of seconds passed, each one bleaker than the last. Letty could feel pain from her injuries from the fall and her mouth already tasted like blood. Summoning the last candle-flickers of energy in her, she leaped for the downhill slope ahead and rolled herself into a taut ball.

Her momentum carried her into a gentle valley, where she landed at the foot of a white pine, panting and empty, arms tucked around her neck.

Maji! Her mind screamed as she heard the bear's approach. *Maji, I'm so sorry I'm leaving you alone. Please, please, run far away from this place.*

She didn't dare open her eyes. She wanted the last thing she saw to be the blank snow, her brother's face in her mind. She didn't want that washed away in her own blood.

But the attack never came.

Letty heard a soft cry and a low *thwack*. The bear roared once, twice, then went quiet. The air stilled, leaving Letty with the wind, and her breath, and her fast pumping heart.

She uncovered her eyes.

A woman stood before her, paces away from the corpse of the enormous bear. A curved blade stuck from its back, pushed through fat and sinew and the knobs of its spine. It had pierced the bear's heart, killing it near-instantly. A trained, impossible maneuver.

The threat of death dissipated as Letty watched the bear bleed dark rivulets into the snow. The woman, meanwhile, retrieved her blade and wiped it off on her rabbit's fur coat. Her hair was one long, black sheet, eyes the precise color of the nightgown Letty had worn on the night of her mother's death—eerie blue, like the untouchable sky.

"I almost didn't get here in time," the woman said. Oddly gentle. It was not the voice of someone who had slain a bear seconds ago. "But I couldn't fail you again. It's lovely to finally meet you."

Finally? Letty sat up on her feet, relief fading into dazed curiosity. "Did you just…wipe blood on a white jacket?"

The corner of the woman's mouth twitched upward. She knelt next to Letty, a rabbit's foot poking from her pocket. "Are you all right?"

"Yes," Letty said. "Or…no?" Her throat went dry. "Who are you?"

"A family friend, you could say. What are you doing so far from home, Aletta?"

Letty, despite everything, was taken aback. "You—you know my family? How?"

A sound in the forest yanked their attention. Letty hunched her neck, too numb to feel any new fear. What now—the bear's mate, come to take revenge?

At once the woman shifted protectively over Letty, terror rippling over her face, as if expecting something or someone. "Is someone there?" she called. "Show yourself."

To Letty's utter disbelief, the order was obeyed. A boy stepped from between the trees, hands in the air, a bow strapped to his back. His expression was nowhere close to menacing. In fact, it was shy and peeping, all lashes and angles and gold-brown hair.

"My apologies," the newcomer said in a sheepish tone, as if embarrassed simply to be there. His voice lilted at the corners. "I'm from Inertia Pack. Raizu Capricorn. I was tailing a few foxes, and they, um, led me here. I can—I can go."

The woman was still filled with tension, but she stopped reaching for her weapon. Raizu was clearly not who she'd been expecting. "It's all right," she said, relaxing. "You startled me, that's all."

"O-oh. Okay." Awkwardly, Raizu stared around the clearing. He looked younger than he sounded, and Letty guessed he wasn't much older than her brother.

As he stared at the bear, Raizu went pink. "Did you—did you kill that?"

"She did," said Letty.

"And now I have to go, before I lead your enemies to you," the woman cut in. Her eyes darted from Raizu to Letty and back again. "It was dangerous enough to interfere at all out here. But I couldn't let her die. Raizu, will you help her? You have such a kind face."

Raizu took a step back. "Huh?"

"I don't need help," Letty objected. "I need to find my brother. I lost him when the storm hit."

"How do you lose an entire brother?" Raizu asked.

Letty glanced at the sky. The clouds were parting, enough to make out the setting sun. "I ran off," she said. "I shouldn't have."

She paused, then added, "I'm Letty Skylark."

"I guess I can help you find him," said Raizu, the words coming out like a question. "I mean, there's an *entire bear* I can piece apart and take home so Kallica won't have my head—I'm part of the Inertia pack—did I say that already? And if you think your brother's close by…"

"Definitely," Letty said. "He couldn't have gotten far." Guilt nagged at her stomach. Majest was probably tearing apart the woods looking for her.

"Then, we'll find him," said Raizu. "It won't be far out of my way."

"Thank you," Letty said, bewildered. She didn't know whether it was his self-conscious lip-biting or the cautious light he radiated, but something about Raizu told her she could trust him.

"My thanks as well." The black-haired woman whirled to Letty, eyes huge, hands splayed. "We will meet again, Aletta. May I always get to you in time."

Then she rose to her feet, turned tail, and vanished without ceremony, taking a thousand unanswered questions with her. Letty could hardly imagine all the ways she could have asked them. For now, she decided to simply be grateful for her life, and for two complete strangers.

"Um. So," said Raizu, turning toward her. "Where do you want to start?"

"Impossible!" Seti spat, kicking at the unsympathetic snow. He didn't usually let emotions loose from their binding, but this was an exception.

Everything had been perfect. Aletta Skylark had been about to be out of the picture on day one—but Seti's Aunt Soti had materialized for the first time in a century and saved the girl's life.

Seti kept kicking, hard enough that his toes went prickly and numb. It had been Soti's name he had taken after the old world had rolled belly-up, using her disappearance to create a convenient new identity. But now, here she was again—a bent gear that had stalled his whole machine.

Soti, his mother's sister, had been the anonymous type. Seeing poltergeists between the boards of the walls and demons under the stairs in a time when witchcraft had been cause for execution, she'd been in the shadows longer than Seti. After years dipping her toes into alchemy and afterlives and heavenly magic—the opposite path of her elder sister—it seemed she had finally gotten a position among the gods.

A position protecting the *Skylarks*, of all people. The exact children Seti's freedom depended on disposing of.

Seti's patience was thinning. "Let's see how long she lasts before the Organization gets a hold of her," he snarled aloud, clenching his fists. "I bet they're on their way to her right now."

He paced, hands on his head, coat whipping behind him. Centuries-old anger blurred his vision. Soti could have stopped her sister from learning to conjure demonic energy, stopped her from flooding her own son with it. But Soti had run away, as she always had, returning only at the most insufferable times—

Stop, Seti ordered himself. The pocket watch swung at his side, ticking with the constant reminder his time was not his own. Anger would get him nowhere.

As long as Soti and her effortless magic were around, the Skylarks would be difficult to pick off. He would have to do it under her nose, before she knew he was here. His escape from the Organization depended on it.

With no ticking time to waste, he could not afford to wait until dawn to try.

Night came quickly, but Letty and her new travel companion were still able to make good time under the soapy light of the moon. It had been Raizu's idea to start where Letty had last seen Majest and branch out in a circle from there. He was smart, Letty decided. The kind of person who could have worked his way out of a room with no doors or windows.

Despite his bright ideas, in the dark, Raizu's earlier uneasiness became full-on jitters. He jumped at every snapping branch, cringed every time an owl crooned. Letty didn't share his fears, but she felt for him; the dark woods were unnerving. It was nice to travel with someone cautious for once. She did not feel weak or childish for her careful steps.

Raizu was leaner and shorter than Majest, too, so he understood how Letty felt when shallow-looking drifts ended up swallowing her to her waist. He was fast and nimble and restless, allowing for quick travel, and though he had only met Letty that day, he was sacrificing his own travels to bring her back to the only family she had left.

"This place needs more people like you," she told him. "I don't think I've ever met anyone who'd willingly help a stranger."

Raizu flushed, but he laughed, too: a breezy, springtime sound. "Oh, where I come from, it's pretty normal. Inertia doesn't raid towns or abandon those who can't hunt. We aren't like the other packs up this way. We help anyone we can because the forest is everyone's home."

Letty had never heard of anything like it. "Where is Inertia?" she asked.

"South of here," Raizu said, seeming happy to change the subject from himself. "A week's travel or so. They always send me north to hunt because I don't mind the cold."

"Will this be the first time you've brought back a bag full of bear meat?" Letty teased.

"Ha—to be honest, this will be the first time I've brought back anything bigger than a hare in an embarrassingly long time."

Letty grinned, imagining the camaraderie of a place like that. If Inertia had been closer to the bay, maybe she and Majest could have visited. But an escape over water made the most sense. The waves left no footprints, and with Majest's powers, he could build a boat to sail over them. The southern forests had less protection with their village-dotted slopes. A known center of civilization would be a screaming target.

"So," said Raizu, his voice faltering as a cloud hid the moon, "tell me about you and your brother. Why are you traveling? Don't you have a town?"

"We lived west of here, in a cottage with our mother," replied Letty. She knew she shouldn't have been exposing her family, but she doubted Raizu was a threat; he could barely meet her eyes without stammering. "She was— she died in an attack last night."

Raizu gasped. "What— You're serious? I'm so sorry. How did you escape?"

"The murderers ran off," Letty said. "They told Mother they know what we are, but then they disappeared. We left before they could come back for us."

"They know *what you are?* What does that mean?"

Letty paused, catching her tongue before she spilled their secrets. Raizu couldn't have been much older than Majest but was already chasing down foxes and roaming days from home by himself. What could she really know about someone like that?

But Letty *wanted* to tell him. Not even Majest understood the pain that spiked every time she watched him toss his element around like a third arm. She needed to confide in someone, and there was no one else here but Raizu.

"Two years ago," Letty began, feeling uncertain, "a god visited my brother and I in our dreams who called himself Komi the Deliverer. He gave us both elemental powers."

Raizu stopped walking and turned to stare at her. "That's not possible."

"It's true—he said the world needed gifts like his to put things back together. Somehow, our mother's killers found out about them, and came for us."

"Gods aren't—they aren't *real,* though."

"When we find my brother, he'll show you what he can do. He's amazing—he can move the earth with his mind, speak the language of trees. He always has a plan, and no matter what, he never gets scared or gives up, even when his own sister can't—" She broke off, reluctantly setting aside the jealousy in her voice. "Sorry. He's my brother. He does a lot to protect us."

Raizu looked thoughtful, lip worrying between his teeth. "Sounds like… Sounds like quite the guy," he said, tentative, as if searching for the least confrontational thing to say. "What's his name?"

Letty sighed. "Majest. I call him Maji."

Raizu seemed to sense her discontent. "I'm sure your powers are incredible, too," he said, slowing his pace as they walked. "I may not believe in the gods, but I'll believe in your element if I see it. What can you do?"

"I…don't know."

"You don't?"

"Komi never said what our powers were, only hinted. Maji figured out what he could do right away, but I haven't learned about mine yet."

Raizu tilted his head. "Well, tell me your hint! The answer must be in your subconscious, if your subconscious was able to take the form of this Komi person and tell you about your power in the first place."

"Okay," Letty said, and didn't bother trying to understand Raizu's god-free reasoning. She had Komi's words memorized to heart. "He told me I was gifted with Earth's greatest force. A force that can quench all others."

"You said the powers were *elemental* gifts, right? Do you know the elements?"

"I don't—there must be hundreds."

"Only four," said Raizu. "Take out earth, and that narrows it down to three. Wind, water, and fire. Out of those, only water can quench, don't you think?"

"Water?" Letty was doubtful. Even someone as smart as Raizu couldn't solve a two-year mystery in a single breath. "We hardly had any water around our home. It was a day's walk to the closest stream."

"Maybe that's why you couldn't figure it out," Raizu urged. "You can't use something you don't have."

That lit something deep in Letty's stomach. Maybe. *Maybe.* "We *are* going to the Hudson Bay," she said. "Can't get much more water in one place than that."

"You and Maji will have to check it out."

"If we ever find him." That thought slumped Letty's shoulders back down.

"Hey, the one thing I'm good at is tracking animals. People are just weird-looking animals, right?" Raizu continued chewing at his lip. "Have you seen anything around here you recognize yet?"

"I'm not sure," Letty confessed. "Everything looks so similar. Though I do remember a patch of dead trees with no needles. Maji pointed them out because he couldn't get a reading off any of them. That was a little while before I lost him."

"Like…those trees?" Raizu gestured ahead.

Letty followed his gaze. It was much darker now, the sky holding the sun hostage below the horizon, but she could still see the harsh edges of wood stretching nakedly into the air.

"Yes," Letty breathed, her voice filling with excitement. "Those trees. We're getting close."

8

Seti enjoyed the dark. In Cognito, the night brought solitude, as most preferred to spend the wee hours engulfed in warm, woodsy slumber dreaming of a life beyond this wasteland. He knew what lay beyond this place, and it wasn't worth dreaming about. Since his gears churned fine with minimal sleep, he headed out under night's black veil, keeping watch for any sign of a white coat.

He would only have one chance before Soti recognized him and realized his plans. Attacking Aletta was risky when Soti already knew her location. And Seti had yet to figure out what his aunt's bond to the Skylarks was exactly—he only knew he had to outrun it.

Tick-tock, tick-tock sang the watch on his belt.

Majest was easy enough to track down, and easier still to spot with his bags dripping from a white pine like laundry out to dry. The boy himself was an unnatural shape sagging between two branches in a hammock that would've been obvious even to someone without Seti's night-proof vision.

Idiot. Though the boy was innocent enough, Seti was not sorry for what he was about to do.

In the pack the President had given him among the stale bread and a rusted water canister was a knife. It was the Organization's, nothing close to the finesse of the one they had confiscated from Seti, but it would have to do. It was an accurate sentiment, anyway. The Organization was killing the Skylarks in the ways that mattered.

Gripping the gawky thing in his palm, Seti approached the base of Majest's tree. Cold conviction focused his mind as he began to climb. His toes bunched, pressing into the ribbed spine of the trunk as he passed through rings of branches.

This was it. Majest's hammock swayed in his sights, Soti nowhere to be seen. One quick throw right to the throat and Seti would be—

There was a hard *tink,* and then Seti was no longer holding the knife. It fell to the ground, a small stone landing beside it.

For a moment, Seti could not comprehend what had happened. Had he somehow dropped the blade? No, the rock had struck it clean from his grasp. Too precise to be coincidental.

Seti climbed down cautiously to the ground and took up the knife once more, his breath a sharpness in his lungs. This time when he ascended, he clenched the blade hard enough to indent his hand.

He hauled himself up until Majest was within arm's reach, his pale neck exposed where his scarf had sagged to his shoulders.

With no hesitation, Seti swung the knife forward, a blur of starlight as precise and impatient as Seti himself. It happened so fast, he could not miss.

Tink.

A growl burning in his chest, Seti whipped his head around in time to see a sliver of white disappearing into the black woods. Another stone had joined his blade in the snow.

Soti wore only white, and *only* Soti wore white.

Damn it. Seti gnashed his teeth. *She's found me already.*

Majest's breathing filled the air with soft sleepy breaths, the boy completely unaware of his rinse-and-repeat jeopardy and salvation. He rolled to the left in the hammock, branches sighing.

Seti debated leaping atop him to see if he could smother or strangle him before Soti intervened. He decided he valued his life too much to risk being bowled from the tree like an acorn, or worse, obliterated by the same magic that could perfectly aim a pebble through a breezy midnight forest.

Before he killed the Skylarks, he would have to kill Aunt Soti.

At his top speed, Seti hurtled himself to the ground, scooped the knife between his fingers, and chucked it javelin-style toward Majest's hammock.

He expected another failure, but it still made his toes clench when hardly a moment later, the blade plopped back down to the ground.

"Show yourself," he hissed into the trees. "Let's settle this."

Only Majest's dreaming mumbles answered.

"I'm coming for you," Seti told the spruces and the junipers. "You can try and protect your Skylarks all you want, but I am coming for you."

But no one is protecting you.

Dawn cracked its shell, spilling yellow over cypress and pine, nudging animals from their slumber. Majest joined them, groggy and miserable and alone. It took several minutes for him to blink away the crust of ice on his lashes and unknot his aching back. His body throbbed from the ache of yesterday's storm, but the tightness in his lungs was worse. Losing Letty was like losing his breath.

At least he'd had his leather hammock stored in his travel pack. At night, it was important to stay up high if you couldn't find proper shelter.

"*Hímin,* you never know with these woods," Dagur had told a much younger Majest. "Wolves, bears, magic folk like elves. They tell you such people do not exist, but in my land, we hear them laughing in the rocks. You want safety, stay as close to the sky as you can."

Majest wanted safety. He wanted *Letty's* safety. It was why he had made his shelter easy enough to see from the ground. But she hadn't come.

He took a moment to narrow his focus, and a thrilling *snap* came between Majest's brows: his element. He moved his hand, and the branch he'd tied his supplies to bent into an arc, sloping toward the ground. It was an easy enough scoot down once he'd untied the hammock.

Once on the ground, Majest let the branch spring back and took in the morning. A line of dead trees interrupted the green woods to his right, and to his left were caribou paths.

But on the ground in front of him, Majest saw a handful of small stones…and footprints.

He bent for a closer look. Some of the prints were his own, but there were smaller sets, too. A petite precise set, then a set of pointed prints nearly as long as Majest's, and lastly, the same markings as his own boots, but smaller.

"Letty?" Majest said, baffled. The prints were pointed in the opposite direction he and his sister had been walking. Had he gotten himself turned around?

A thousand and a half new fears overwhelmed him. He was practically startled out of his skin when a red squirrel darted in front of him, scurrying into the tree he had slept in. It was chattering something fierce—as if telling him something.

An absurd idea came to him and Majest grabbed for his element a second time. He focused on the squirrel, now squawking its head off from a low branch, and grappled for meaning until he could understand the noise as words.

"Oh, oh, oh dear," the squirrel trilled. "Oh, oh, no, the nuts, the nuts!"

Perfect. "Excuse me," Majest called, doing his best to match the pitch.

The squirrel's tufted ears pricked in obvious astonishment.

"I won't hurt you, little guy," said Majest. His tongue fought the unfamiliar sounds, and his jaw cranked at the effort. "I want to know if you've seen anyone pass through here. In particular, a girl dressed like me."

The squirrel's rosy nose twitched. "A *girl?*" it burst, leaping to a higher branch. "Oh, what does a *girl* matter? I cannot *eat* a girl! Oh, the nuts, the nuts. Where have they gone?"

"She's my sister. I'm trying to find her."

"The nuts, the nuts, the nuts," the squirrel driveled on, pitching itself to the next tree over, then the next.

Majest followed it, desperate. "No, the *girl.*"

"The nuts! The nuts!"

"The girl!"

"The nuts!"

"Fine! I have nuts," Majest cried, throwing his hands out in frustration. "I can trade you."

All at once, the squirrel stopped scrambling. "Nuts?"

Majest thanked every star in the sky that he'd collected acorns off the oaks this summer and had brought a handful along. He stomped closer to the squirrel, whose black gaze shrank Majest's scowl into a grimace.

The squirrel stuck its head toward him. "Nuts?" it repeated. "For Amitu, to eat?"

"Not until you tell me if you've seen my sister."

Long, stubborn seconds passed before the squirrel scrunched its face in exaggerated disdain, climbed down the tree trunk, and said, "Fine. A girl was here. Yesterday. With a boy."

Majest sighed. "Are you sure that wasn't me?"

"Foolish nut-creature you are. A different boy! A much *quieter* boy!"

Majest refused to be offended by the squirrel. "She was with someone else? Who? Where did they go?"

"He had a weapon, many weapons, sharp little weapons. Oh, but not as sharp as the hunger in my belly! The nuts, the nuts—"

"*Amitu,*" Majest demanded.

The squirrel sat in front of him now, and Majest could see his own desperation reflected back at him in those black eyes.

"Oh, the girl and the sharp boy went where their footprints lead," Amitu said. "Did you really need me to tell you that? Happily, they went. The weapons were not for her. Maybe for Amitu, though! Oh…"

Majest was half-tempted to get out a hunting knife instead of a handful of acorns. But the information left him too shaken to be properly irritated. He knelt down and held the nuts out. "Don't lose them this time," he said.

Amitu squeaked and ran forward, guzzling three acorns down before stuffing the last few between its teeth. It said something that might have been gratitude, but it wasn't paying Majest attention any longer. With a tail-wave of delight, the squirrel vanished.

"I liked animals better when I didn't know how rude they were," Majest grumbled.

Still simmering, he returned to the footprints he'd found earlier. He eyed the thin, pointed toes of the largest set. The sharp boy, huh? Who was he— and who had he become to Letty?

Majest set his feet in the same direction, covering the smaller prints with his own. Almost reflexively, he tightened the belt around his waist and felt his slingshot at his side. He'd walk until he found out.

Soti hunched into herself, head in her hands, hair spooling through her fingers. She had reached safety again that morning—this time, a small cave system with enough condensation to clean some of the filth from her coat.

Seeing her nephew again had reminded her of her life before this one. Of southern London and the lightless tunnel running under the reading room of her estate. Two sisters, their magic hidden, feigning innocence. A game. A secret. That memory was a nuisance now, dangling in the back of her mind like a stray thread she could never reach to snap. She didn't like to think of her sister, the fork in their road to immortality, and how Soti had climbed to the heavens while Sira had sunk down into demon-summoning books.

Soti had met the End resolutely, at the side of the gods. She had pitied the humans—their lands finally looked the same on the outside as it had always been on the inside.

Scoping out the newly-born Cognito for the gods had left Soti drained, unused to this kind of cold. A young couple—Maxine Skylark and Dagur Sigurðsson—had caught her as she'd fallen. They had offered her their home as refuge and taught her the ways of this new world.

They had treated Soti with kindness she had never known on the other side of the ocean. She had loved them—Maxine with her red curls and grit, Dagur with his quiet determination and thickly-accented English.

"I come from far away," he'd told Soti. "Ísland. Plenty of snow, but not trees like this. I do not know of this new place. I only want our children to be at peace, to be Skylarks and fly."

Dagur had soaked up every last one of Soti's stories—gods and demons and the crossroads between—and even Maxine had rolled her eyes and played along over the light of a warm fire. They'd shared their food when they'd hardly had the means to keep their little girl and boy from going to sleep hungry.

Soti hadn't wanted to leave them, even after she'd learned her way around the woods, but she couldn't have burdened them any longer. Not with their third child on the way.

Then, Komi had told her, *"You don't have to leave them."* He had whisked her from the Skylarks' house into the swirling, barren heavens. The familiar stars of the gods' realm.

"I have a job for you," Komi had continued. "A job that will tie you to this family forever, if you choose to accept it."

"Anything for them," was Soti's immediate reply. She and Komi had never met, but she knew many gods sneered away his dreams for Earth's future. They knew only of his past failures, his present desperation. "I am in their debt, and in your service."

Komi's wings had shaken out from his back, cresting and rolling. "The Skylark boy and girl will play an incomparable role in years to come. I ask you to protect them when their time comes, and make sure they arrive safely at their destination."

There had been no tremor in Soti's voice, no explanation demanded. It was her duty to obey. "You want me to protect Majest and Lunesta?"

"Not Lunesta. The third child, yet unborn. She is the one called upon."

"How am I to know when they need my protection?" Soti asked, curious.

At that, a white rabbit's foot had leaped into existence before her eyes, its knobby toes dangling in the lightless air.

"Take it," Komi advised, and the painted lines on his face had stretched with the movement of his mouth—something that occurred to Soti as oddly human. "It will signal you when either of the children is in danger."

Soti had taken it. It had not been as soft as she'd expected. "Forgive me, but can't you protect the Skylarks yourself? Why do you need my help?"

There had been many unspoken things between the deep-ocean shades of Komi's eyes. "If I want to prove my cause to the Highers, those who receive my gifts must survive on their own. Gods cannot interfere too deeply with destiny." There had been that human look again, something scratching out from beneath his immortal face.

"If I save them, aren't I interfering with destiny?" Soti had dared to ask, brave enough under Komi's gentle expression. "Am I breaking the rules?"

Komi's eyes had hardened again, authority drowning his voice. "You are not a god," he had said. "You are still flesh and blood. But you have been given the power to protect, to walk our skies with your human feet. I am asking you to use that power now."

Soti had bowed her head humbly.

And years later, as Komi had promised it would, the moment had come. The white rabbit's foot had gone black and swung like a compass, and Soti had torn across grit and sleet in the blind direction of the Skylarks' cottage. She had not made it in time—the danger had gone, and the children had sobbed against Maxine's muddy nightgown.

Soti would not let them down again, even if it meant going through her own nephew. The children were family to Dagur and Maxine, who had been a better family to Soti than her own.

Sira's son, however much he might have despised being witness to his mother's crimes, had never been someone Soti could have protected. But the Skylarks were noble, worthy of her protection.

When the light returned, bringing a chorus of birds and a playful breeze that tugged at the ends of Raizu's scarf, Letty felt lighter, too. She and Raizu moved briskly and easily through the snow, pressing eastward past the dead trees.

"Still no footprints," Letty said, shaking ice from her gloves. Even in the brightness of the morning, Cognito was still freezing. "Maji didn't come this way. Should we turn around again?"

"He might be behind us now," Raizu admitted. "If he took shelter last night, we could have walked right past him without knowing."

Letty felt deflated, but she was grateful for Raizu's apologetic honesty. He didn't try to placate her with hopeless optimism like Majest might have. He was a light, however quivering.

"Then, we should go back," Letty said. She crunched through the snow, not watching her feet. "He might be following our trail, and we could meet him."

"Good idea," Raizu agreed. "Do you want something to eat first?"

"Maybe once we get to— *Ahh!*" Letty flailed, her leg giving out as her foot crashed through paper-thin ice hidden beneath the snow. Cold seeped through her boot, soaking her sock.

Raizu grabbed for her shoulder. "What is it? Are you okay?"

"It's…water," said Letty, staring down at her foot. Despite the burn, she did not dare move. Her eyes unfocused, a shiver climbing up her spine.

"There must be a frozen creek under here," said Raizu. "The storm probably covered it. We'll have to find a way around it if we don't want to lose our toes."

Letty still did not remove her foot, or her gaze. She barely heard Raizu's words. All she could see was the water, gliding across the laces of her boot, hugging her skin. She had to force herself to step back to safer ground.

Raizu leaned forward to help, but Letty held out a hand. "Careful," she said, but didn't know why her voice wavered. "I don't want you to fall in because of me."

He said something in response, and this time Letty didn't hear it at all. A roar went off in both of her ears. It wasn't like she'd never gotten her feet wet before—but it had never been like this, full of mystery and possibility. For the first time, she was face-to-face with what might finally link her to the Power that had been promised to her by Komi.

Even as her toes screamed from the coldness, she found the idea of falling, letting the stream soak her hair and the fur on her sleeves, exhilarating. Empowering.

That's what I want, Letty thought, the words familiar.

Power.

It was the same feeling that had struck her at the mouth of a cave two years earlier. The same vast, ambushing command. It rose up under her skin, and she grasped at it, and she heaved.

The channels in her mind shot open with the kickback of a launched arrow. All her nerve endings lit, and for the first time, Letty saw more than darkness and an uncertain void in her mind—she saw paths that wound and twisted, and she saw the way out of them. She saw *light*.

Hands out in five-pointed stars, Letty traveled the paths. She felt for the way, bumbling and scraping against walls, unlocking doors—and then she was through.

In front of her, the stream rippled again.

"Raizu!" Letty cried in disbelief. "Raizu, look!"

Fingers curling, Letty watched as the puddle became hers. It spasmed and splashed, and for a moment, *she* was the mouth of the cavern and *it* the scared little girl.

Then, still flying through the paths of her mind, she felt something else. Something barbed and thorny along the walls. It tripped her up, stamped darkness behind her eyes.

Letty gasped. The thorny thing inside her hissed, stretching tendrils to all sides. It opened its dark mouth as if to speak, but Letty reeled back in horror, off the path, and the lights went out.

The water stilled.

Reality phased back into Letty's vision in hazy stripes of sun and snow. The darkness was gone, but its cold fingers lingered. *Maji never feels anything like that, does he?* For a moment, doubt overshadowed her thrill.

Then, Raizu broke the terrifying silence. "Letty, did you do that? That was amazing!"

Hearing the excitement in his voice, seeing the way his eyes lit like blue lanterns, a grin lit up Letty's face. He clearly hadn't noticed anything dark. Maybe she had imagined it.

"I did, didn't I?" said Letty.

"Now I feel like such an idiot," Raizu said, with a breathless laugh. "I said your Power wasn't possible, and then the stream starts dancing a jig."

"It's all thanks to you. I might never have looked at water the way I needed to without your help. What if I can move snow, too? Or ice?"

"Thanks to me? Letty, all I did was tell you I didn't know what I was talking about!"

"You did know, though," she said earnestly, looking at him. The sweep of his scarf, the ruffle of his hair. "I've known you for one day and I already owe you enough for a lifetime. What can I possibly give you in return?"

Raizu shook his head, going positively scarlet. "No way," he said. "I haven't even done the one thing I promised—I haven't found your brother. I have a zero percent success rate."

"We'll find him," Letty said. "Until then, you're my replacement brother."

Raizu grinned. "He'll be so excited when you show him what you can do."

"*If* I can do it again."

Majest might have brushed away her concern, given her the empty promise that *of course* she'd be able to. Raizu only gave her a small smile and started to turn back the way they had come before he realized she was still stuck and held out a hand.

Even Letty's darkest thoughts could not resist such a candle. She gripped his gloved fingers and followed him out of the ice. She was ready to find her way.

9

Over the gray curve of a rocky slope, Majest saw a familiar face beyond the trail of footprints, and he began to run. Snow flew up in white-caps behind him. "Letty! Letty, I'm here!" he cried.

She was here, too, getting closer and closer, followed by a stranger. Letty, hearing his voice and running, too. Letty, smiling like he hadn't seen in years.

They met in a flurry of fur coats and supply bags. Majest lifted Letty high into the air, twirling her in an enormous circle before returning her to the ground and crushing her into a hug. She buried her face in his chest, gasping and laughing. She felt weary but strong, as if her adventure had taken a great deal out of her and then pumped even more back in.

"I'm so sorry, Maji," Letty whispered. "I should've never been so reckless."

"As long as you're okay," Majest said into her hair.

"I shouldn't be okay— I would've died if it hadn't been for this woman who killed the bear that was attacking me."

"The bear that was *what?*" Majest listened in stunned silence as she explained, catching her words as they flew.

"*Vá*, Letty," he said when she finished. "I almost lost you, didn't I?"

"But you didn't," she said, and tilted her head to the stranger watching the reunion with an awkward grin. His boots kicked at the ground, hands worrying the ends of his sleeves. "Like I said, it's because of him."

"I—I'm sorry it took us so long," the boy stammered.

Majest glanced at him for the first time and then just as quickly fixed an embarrassed gaze on the ground.

"It's hard to keep a good pace in this snow, carrying all this bear meat. Not that I killed the bear! Did Letty mention that? I'm, um…I'm Raizu. Inertia pack. You probably…right, she said that already. Sorry."

Majest looked at Raizu and raised his eyebrows.

The boy took a breath. "It's great to meet you," he finished weakly.

He was the first boy his age Majest had ever met. A pack boy, no less. Majest knew many packs down south lived off bones and fear, but apparently, some of their members were delicate and neatly-groomed and stammered through every other word. Raizu was clean and bright, the periwinkle color of his eyes as refreshing as a breeze in spring.

"I'm Majest Skylark," Majest said, and smiled. "But hey, Letty said that already, too. Thank you so much for everything you've done for us."

"It's no problem," Raizu replied, his feet scuffing the ground. He dipped his head, the customary greeting between adults, though he couldn't have been older than eight birth-years. "Letty's told me a lot about you, and what you can—well, what you can do. With the, um, animals and rocks. It's all very impressive."

Majest's eyes flew to his sister. Had she really shared the secret that might have killed their mother? A pit formed in his stomach.

Letty cringed.

"So much for being careful," Majest said.

"He's not a threat," Letty replied. "He's a friend. He even helped me unlock my powers."

"You…" Majest thought his jaw might tumble to his feet. "What do you mean? You unlocked them? When? How?" His hands clamped around Letty's wrists. "Tell me!"

Letty had a round of giggles, then calmed herself. *"Well,"* she began. "Raizu and I were talking about you and your tree nonsense, so I told him about my message from Komi. He figured it out, the way Father figured out yours."

Majest turned to Raizu, his eyes softening. "How?"

Raizu looked startled to be asked. "Um, I guess I thought, 'what force can quench other forces?' and then I remembered that water quenches fire, and it quenches the ground, and I suppose it could quench the air if it wanted. It killed my parents during a spring melt back when we lived up by Great Bear Lake. Water's dangerous enough to do anything."

"I made water ripple!" Letty burst in and shook Majest's hands with her own.

"That makes *so much sense*," said Majest, thrilled. "*Water.* You're the most watery person I know."

"What does *that* mean?"

"I don't know!"

Letty thwacked him with a glove, grinning. "I have to start testing it," she said. "Practicing, like you."

"Maybe not on our drinking supplies, though, since we sort of need those to live, but…" Majest hugged her. "We could try melting snow. And any stream that comes our way is all yours."

"An entire stream? That's the best gift you've ever gotten me," Letty said, laughing.

"There's a river south of here," Raizu offered, his shy gaze still on Majest. "Back toward my camp. The water there moves so quickly, it won't freeze no matter how cold it gets. I, um… I could take you there, if you'd like?"

Letty's eyes lit up and Majest found himself drawn in by the offer, despite himself. He had the sense that this boy with his sunshine face and scattered raindrop words could grow into a valuable friend and ally. He knew the area, and he knew their story.

But Majest and Letty needed to disappear without a trace, and a pack in the center of the crowded southern forest would be a blood-red target painted in the snow.

Majest said, "Thank you for the offer, but it's best if we continue east."

"Inertia might be able to protect us," Letty argued. "We could give it a chance."

"We're a family," Raizu put in. He looked up at Majest from under long lashes; his eyes honest and warm. "We would keep you safe."

In his words, Majest heard all the things Raizu didn't say. He and Letty would never go hungry again. They would have shelter, and warmth, and a shield against the merciless winters. Above all, they would have companionship, as easy and gentle as the boy in front of them.

But it would be so simple for the enemy to find them.

"I'm sorry," said Majest, his heart heavy. "We need to find a hiding place where no one will ever think to search for us."

Raizu and Letty both looked like they might object, but after a few seconds, Raizu nodded. "I respect that. You'll be at an advantage staying off the map."

"If it's to keep us safe…" said Letty as both boys looked to her for a consensus.

"It is," Majest and Raizu said together.

"Then, I suppose we should head out, before I'm tempted to run off again and find Inertia myself. I'm freezing after all."

Majest almost smiled. "I don't think you have enough luck to worm your way out of *two* bear attacks."

"Luck? No. The power to explode snow in its face? We'll see."

Raizu grinned, staring at them as if to make the memory last. "Will you be off right away? You should take some of the extra bear meat with you."

"Absolutely not," said Majest. "Don't make our debt to you any bigger."

"Please," Raizu insisted, already kneeling and rummaging in his enormous pack. He held one icy piece of meat out, wrapped in thick linen. "You have a long journey ahead."

"Don't you need that for your pack?" Letty frowned.

"You need it more than they do," said Raizu, sounding more confident than he had before. "They tend to stuff themselves before winter anyway, so you're practically doing them a favor."

The meat was tempting, fresh, and right in front of him, so Majest took it with both hands. "Thank you. Seriously."

"Of course." Raizu's face went bright pink again.

And with that, there was no more to be said. They were strangers, about to part for good.

"Raizu," Majest said, "if we're ever back in the area, and there aren't murderers after us—would it be all right if we sought out your pack?"

"More than all right," said Raizu. "There's room, and we'd love to have you. Good luck out there. I'll keep an ear out for you."

"I hope you don't hear anything." Majest grinned. "We've got some disappearing to do."

"I won't tell anyone about you," promised Raizu.

Majest didn't think he'd ever seen someone look so sincere. "No matter who asks. It's a small world we live in. Maybe, I'll see you again someday."

"Hopefully in better times, right? That's what everyone likes to say."

An idea bright in his mind, Majest snagged his element, then summoned a stone from beneath the snow. Hands sweeping, brow furrowed, he shaped the stone into a sharp, flaring triangle. Another wave of his hand and he'd made a hole in the stone; a third, and he'd grabbed a sturdy twig and fastened it snugly into the opening.

It was an arrow.

"I noticed your sheath was one short," Majest said. He couldn't help but grin from cheek to cheek at the enchanted look on Raizu's face. "Thought I might start paying my dues with fixing that."

Raizu tucked the arrow in its proper casing, speechless.

"Thanks again for everything," Letty piped up.

"Of—of course." Raizu shook the shock off, the start of a smile on his lips. He turned his pointed feet south. "Good-bye, you two."

"Good-bye," Majest and Letty chorused, and waved as he started up the hill. Majest had a curious lump in his throat, as though Raizu had been more than a simple stranger. And yet, there he went.

When he was gone, Majest turned to his sister. "You thought he was cute, didn't you?"

"Who, me?" Letty wrinkled her nose. "Why?"

"Just a question."

"He's too old for me," said Letty, rolling her eyes. "I'm five birth-years. I need a little more time to think boys are foxes and pigs, all right?"

"I didn't need an answer that practical," Majest teased. "I was joking." His eyebrows waggled with mischief. "Pretty eyes, though. Almost violet. Like the edges in a sunset, just before night hits."

Letty elbowed him.

He laughed, unable to help it.

"Hey, if you think he's *that* good-looking, you can have him." She glanced to the hills, in the direction Raizu had gone. "I hope he makes it home okay."

"He will." Majest squeezed Letty's shoulder, and together they took the first reunited step of their journey. "And we'll make it to the Hudson Bay, too."

"We're getting a lot closer."

"How do you know? Do you think it's your power?"

"No, Maji— Look up."

Majest lifted his head in time to watch four arctic gulls pass overhead, wings flexing toward the spooling silver clouds.

"Gulls go where there's water," said Letty. "You taught me that."

"You're right," Majest told her as the birds' silhouettes gathered into one shadow in the sky. "They're on their way. Just like us."

As a rule, Seti expected unpleasant surprises, but he had never thought his aunt would be the one to come to him.

Yet here she was, sliding out from between a shield of trees, moving toward him with her nimble rabbit's tread. She called out a greeting, eyes wide and blue and so disgustingly innocent, it made Seti's stomach roil. He stared at the blood on her jacket instead.

Soti came to a stop in front of her sister's son, her expression worried. Worried for the Skylarks, surely—not this boy she barely knew.

They stood beneath an unstable ledge, which was littered crest to floor with loose rock fragments. Seti reached for his knife.

"Did you come to talk?" he asked. "I have nothing to say to you about those children."

Soti's expression pinched as she took him in—his face, his voice, his curse. "You'd rather fight?"

"I have orders to kill the Skylarks, and not even you can guilt me out of that."

"Orders from the Organization controlling you, I assume."

Seti bristled. "*Controlling* me? I'm just getting them off my back."

She dismissed the remark. "I have my own orders. Orders to protect Majest and Aletta."

At that, Seti sneered. "From the gods?" he guessed, and at the way she quieted, he knew he was right.

"What do they know, other than how to make the same mistakes for centuries? Good for you, helping them make another mess."

"The gods protect us," Soti snapped. She was on the defensive now, her fur jacket all fluffed out.

"The gods give out powers easily like rat bait, and then wait for evil things to smell and come knocking. Funny thing is, the gods never know what to do with the darkness at their door."

"This is all supposed to happen," said Soti. Her narrow jaw set in a level, unflattering line. "The gods have a plan."

"I'm sure." Something boiled beneath Seti's skin. He was still gripping the knife. "They're pathetic, and so is the Organization, and so are you. How about you all leave this land to rot?"

He shifted his eyes high above Soti's head, at the place where rock met sky. A boulder sat atop the cliff face, impassively observing the scene. Smaller boulders descended the slope below it. They were a fuse waiting to be lit— one push from the top would send them all tumbling.

Seti returned his gaze to his aunt. "Listen," he said. "If you want to help this country out, let me have the Skylarks. If I kill them, the Organization will lose its motivation. Its President might be spewing all sorts of rubbish about making an equal world, but I know who she is and what she wants. This could end here."

"It won't," said Soti. "What's growing behind the Organization's walls is more than one woman's orders. The Skylarks need to play this out in their own hands. That's why I'll keep them safe. Consider this your warning."

Seti saw the twitch of her feet, how they itched to flee. Any moment, she would spook, and he would be left chasing her again. That could not happen. This woman was heavenly power packed into frail bones. She could aim pebbles like missiles, slice bears clean through.

Seti had one chance to stop her.

Without giving himself time to think, he took a running start to where the cliff ledge sloped down to eye-level, racing from the ground to the top. In seconds, Soti was mouse-sized below him.

He barely had to tap the boulder. It went plunging down.

With it, came everything in its path.

Soti had no time to run; the violent shudder of the sky shackled her to the ground too quickly. The avalanche hit her like the heavens were falling, one crash after another.

Before the first rock hit, she thought of the Skylarks. Who would look after them now? Who would keep her nephew's knife from their throats? Who would carry out the gods' orders?

Soti fought to move, but the first impact of rock bowled her flat on her back. Pain raged up her spine, shapes crashed over her vision. She screamed, fighting to stand, but the stones kept pounding, merciless, pinning her legs, wrists, and chest.

You're making your mother's mistakes, she wanted to cry to her sister's son, but her voice shattered as the next stone cracked between her eyes.

Soti heard her skull fragment, watched the world go black. But in her mind flashed a single, familiar star. She grasped at it, clutched it with her last bit of consciousness.

I don't have time for this, she thought, before everything slipped out of reach. Everything except her star. *I have failed them. I have failed you, Komi.*

The star took off. Soti's stony tomb went still as the last of the rocks skittered to a stop. Somewhere above it, laughter rang out over the trees.

10

Letty startled from sleep when she heard her brother's cry of dismay. She lay slung in Majest's second hammock, her back throbbing, hair kinked. She sat up, finding her brother in the next tree over, wearing the expression of a very cross squirrel. Letty could almost imagine a furious tail snapping behind him.

"What's the matter?" she called.

Majest pointed to a branch beside him. Last night, he had secured their food bag to it. This morning, it was in shreds on the snowy ground.

"Oh, no," Letty whispered.

Red lines smudged the snow, letting them know the eight different directions their meat had been carried off in. Their water canister's lid had cracked open, a week's worth of sips dribbling into the ground. Even their handmade sack was ruined.

"Þetta er hræðileg," Majest said in their father's language. Whatever he'd said, it couldn't have been nice. "I should have tied it tighter. How did I not hear it fall?"

"You've always been a deep sleeper," said Letty.

Majest grunted and Letty could see his teeth grinding from here.

"We'll have to hunt," he said, already heaving himself out of his hammock. "There won't be anything left in the pack."

Letty felt sick. "All that meat Raizu gave us…"

"Wasted."

It was late in the season for caribou, but since there were paths nearby, they agreed to see what they could find. Majest used his element to help them down from their sleeping trees, and they rearranged the few supplies they had left, tucking them into safety until they returned.

"You sure I should come with?" Letty asked. "I don't know anything about hunting."

"I'll teach you," said Majest, sliding his slingshot into his belt. All of his motions were at full-speed, frustration at their loss churning off him. "Unless you'd rather sit in a tree all day."

"Not a chance. Though, I'm sorry if I'll slow us down."

"That can't happen if we're already going too fast." Majest grabbed for Letty's hand, towing her along as he began to sprint.

"What—? Hey!" Letty spluttered, barely managing not to trip. "Where are you going?"

"Here." Majest came to an easy stop in front of a tall fir in the ice straight ahead.

Letty still found it hard to believe trees hadn't always grown through frozen ground, and so many of Cognito's northern forests were less than a century old.

She tugged her hand free of her brother's and watched as he closed his eyes, his twitchy fingers running along the veins in the tree's bark.

"According to this guy, we just missed a small herd," Majest said. "A buck, at least four cows, and a few calves. We can catch up if we hurry."

"The little pine needles whispered that to you?"

"*No,*" said Majest, pouting enough that Letty chuckled. "I can feel the tree's memories. Things it has heard, or smelled, or sensed."

"Trees can smell?"

"I don't know how else to describe it."

Letty shrugged. "What direction are the caribou?"

Majest touched the trunk again, then started off in a new direction. "North!"

Letty did her best to match Majest's manic pace, knowing there was no point asking him to slow down when he was like this. "What about water?" she called after him.

"Keep an eye out. For drinking *and* practicing."

She had no complaints about that. The weather was pleasant today, the sun dipping around a blue-gray sky, but as the morning passed, Letty grew aware of her dry mouth, her grumping stomach. After a few hours, the silence broken only by birds' chatter and Majest's babbling, her whole body swayed with dizzying hunger. Imagining the red bear meat Raizu had given them yesterday was painful.

"Are we close to catching up?" she asked, clearing her blazing throat. "Can you ask another tree?"

Majest, who had been quiet for some time, put a finger to his lips and pointed at the ground. When Letty glanced down, she saw them—huge, round hoof prints stitching in and out of each other in wavering lines.

"How long have you been following these?" she whispered.

"I first saw the prints cross our path at the last clearing. They're fresh."

Majest's green eyes were glassy, knees bending and unbending. It was his same agitated energy from earlier, but now he had focus. His expression was almost excited. He pulled his slingshot out, loading it with a grass-bomb.

They trekked straight ahead until Majest, every step long and decisive, halted. Letty had already stopped moments before, staring in awe.

"Look," they whispered at the same time.

Several paces ahead, the caribou stood, dropped in against the winter backdrop like something from a dream. One bull, four cows, and calves—like Majest had said. Or rather, like the *tree* had said. Even at this distance, their size was stunning, their tapered faces towering high above Letty's head. They were graceful yet ugly, both enchanting and rugged. Letty was mesmerized by their bony legs, their bulging eyes.

Majest crouched down, raised his slingshot. The caribou were within range. One lucky shot, and their troubles were over.

Before he could fire, a hard *crack* split the air. A dead branch, weighed down by snow, had snapped on the ground at the center of the wandering herd.

Their heads bobbed up, muzzles buzzing with grunts of alarm. In an instant, they had unbent themselves from the snow and taken off, exploding outward into the trees.

"Go, go," Majest cried, tearing after them.

"Go *where?*" Letty demanded. "We can't catch them!"

But Majest was already flying. After a hard sigh, Letty followed.

The steady click of the caribou's ankles rose above the commotion as they fled, Majest's long legs giving him a blurry boost of speed. Luckily, these caribou were scrawny with winter hunger and lethargic under the gloom of the slow-moving season. By some absurd miracle, Majest managed to get close enough to the slowest one to take a shot.

His arms went up, practiced and polished, pulling back the leather-corded strings of his slingshot. He was in the impossible plane of adrenaline where stamina and hunger pangs no longer existed. Letty couldn't imagine how he thought he was going to aim at a moving target—but his arm pulled back, and the slingshot snapped.

The grass-bomb whistled through the trees, diving like a bird of prey. Its trajectory wasn't half-bad, but the young cow had swerved behind a cluster of trees, then disappeared over the buckling crest of a small hill.

A detonating crash sounded as the bomb overshot its missing target, landing in the trees. Letty stumbled to her knees, clenching her fists into the trembling earth. Sickly green smoke blew through the forest from the source of the impact, fast-moving and thick enough to drink.

Practically deaf and blind, Letty called, *"Maji,"* before choking on a wheeze.

Something pounded behind her, and she felt arms around her shoulders. She gasped, searching for clean air, and found it seconds later when Majest set her down in the snow.

"Sorry," he said. "I promise it's not poisonous, or I'd be dead a dozen times by now."

Letty couldn't reply at first; her breaths were sharp, her nose filled with the green smell of rot. They had ended up on the hillcrest the caribou had disappeared over, and the ravine below swirled as the smoke cleared. She saw something glimmering down in the thick of it, a bony figure wading up to its ankles.

"Water," Letty gasped.

"What? We don't have—*oh.*" Majest followed her gaze, and together, they watched their escaped lunch wade into a wide, glassy stream. Even from here, Letty felt thunder beneath her skin. Water. *Water.*

The animal bowed its head to drink, and Majest stood, more focused now. Letty, coughing the last of the foul smoke from her lungs, followed.

"Go," she whispered. "There's still a chance. I'll be right behind you."

Majest crept down the slope slowly. The caribou bent its head to drink, its back turned, moisture gathering in glassy beads around its muzzle.

Letty dragged herself after Majest, already imagining the rush of water over her skin, the cool liquid against her throat, the blue song in her blood.

They approached the stream together as the caribou waded deeper in. Its hooves cast ripples through the sluggish current. It seemed to have forgotten the danger, yet every step took the animal farther out of reach.

"I can't go in there," Majest said after a moment. "The waterproof oil is wearing off my boots. I'd wreck them. And my feet."

"You don't have any more grass-bombs?"

"One more. I'm saving it for an emergency. Who knows if we'll ever find more of the explosive power Mother had." Majest seemed frustrated, and Letty couldn't blame him. Catching that cow would have fed them for days.

"How horrible would I be if I tried tricking the caribou into letting me kill it?" Majest muttered. "No, I haven't mastered the caribou language yet. Do you think there are berries we could eat around here? How about tree bark? Is that rude to the trees?"

Letty barely heard him. She stepped forward, hooked by invisible cords. They pulled her to the water's edge. The river was so beautiful, and right at her toe-tips. It felt never-ending.

Komi's words rang loud in her ears: *While thought to be uncontrollable, you will have its strength at your beck and call whenever it presents itself to you.*

I'm here now, Letty thought, and the rest of the world blurred. *And I can control it, can't I? I can bring our meal back to us.*

"Can't I?" she asked out loud. The caribou's ears pricked; Majest turned his head.

She slid off her glove and dipped her hand into the stream. Her skin went numb, the locks on her mind trembling against their doors. Letty closed her eyes.

There you go, whispered a voice. *Like that.* It was the clawing dark voice from last time, trailing shadows over the bright paths of her element.

Letty gasped, and the voice vanished, leaving her alone in the labyrinth. But she had made it through alone before. She lifted her hand and water clung to it. It was *hers.*

She raised her arms higher, and the stream submitted, following her fingers. She was here; she was focused. She had the power to quench anything, and she did not want to let go.

"Now, fly up," she told the stream, refusing to let her focus break.

Nothing happened.

A betrayed sound came from her throat that was nearly a snarl. Behind her, Majest started to say something, but Letty ignored him.

"Fly up," she repeated, flinging her arms over her head. Majest made it look so easy, but something still held Letty at her mind's gates. *Why?*

"Up!" Her tone went dark and furious, and she felt it: that thorny creature returning. Maybe it had never left. She felt her body teeter, her voice not her own.

"Letty," Majest called softly behind her. The caribou tensed, ready to bolt.

A mad roar pushed forward from the back of Letty's mind, from wherever that black presence began, and its wave engulfed her.

Ride it out. Isn't this what you want? the dark creature asked. *To be like your brother? To be…in control? Even over him?*

Letty sensed the final release of her element. The last gate holding back the flood.

And yes—she wanted it.

"Up!" Letty howled, and she burst through.

The stream went up with a *whoosh.* Water flung backward, knocking Letty flat to the ground and soaking her through. It drowned the snow, decimated the sparse brush. The caribou lay still on its side, blasted against the shore. Dead, maybe, or dying. The entire section of stream in front of Letty was left gasping, drained, frantically trying to refill.

Darkness and light drained from behind Letty's eyes and she hissed as pain replaced it.

"That was a disaster," she said.

Majest was at her side, helping her sit. He was damp but not drenched, like he had jumped away from the blast in the nick of time. "Hey, hey," he said. "What disaster? You did it. You found your power, like Raizu said."

Letty rubbed her eyes with her red hands. "Well, it *hurts.*"

"That's what practice is for," he said. "I told you not to doubt yourself. Imagine all you could do with this."

Letty shivered, remembering the dark voice, the uncontrollable rage that had overtaken her. Majest didn't know about any of that. "I wouldn't get your hopes up."

"You caught us half a week of food, for starters," he said, gesturing to the caribou. He scooped a handful of water from a dip in the ground and slurped it down. "And we sure won't go thirsty, either. I'll fill the canister."

While he did that, Letty managed a weak grin. "You're out of luck if you want me to do anything other than nearly drown you."

Majest made a stern face at her. "Hey, now. It's only dinner you need to drown, unless you're calling me a sandwich."

"You *are* brown, white, and green."

"True," he chirped. "Now, come help me with our fallen friend?"

Letty rolled her eyes, unease finally softening into affection. "Sure."

They worked over the caribou as the sun sloped down, sitting cross-legged against the driest rocks and slicing the meat into strips before packing it in ice. They returned to their sleeping tree before sunset, with enough time to reassemble their packs and roast some meat for dinner. So much meat was stuffed into their bags, Majest joked he would be complaining of a backache before dawn.

Letty wanted to celebrate, but a strange worry still wormed in her gut.

Many long hours later, they set their sights due east once more, their hearts as full as their stomachs. And yet, Letty still worried.

Raizu Capricorn hadn't stopped smiling since the moment he'd seen the cliff-faces and protective hedges that meant home. He parted the branches to Inertia's camp and sucked in an earthy breath of air.

"I'm back!" he called. "With food this time and everything!"

Two dark-haired children flung themselves from the nearest cave mouth, barreling toward him. They wrapped their warm arms around him, hardly the size of newborn bear cubs. "Raizy," they squeaked. "Raizy's back!"

"Is he really?" A new face appeared from another cave and the slender figure swayed with laughter as it approached. "I thought you'd fallen down a rabbit hole."

"Kallica," Raizu grinned, squishing his closest friend in a hug. There was no discomfort here. This was home; this was family. "How is everything?"

"Arathiel's kids are annoying as ever," Kallica noted, shooing them away. "He got back two days ago with fresh fish."

"Enough for everyone?"

"Nearly."

"And our water supply?"

"Fine. It's always fine. Relax, will you?"

"Impossible," Raizu said. He tried not to notice the way Kallica held her elbow to her body, as if she'd injured it. Or the way she kept dodging his eyes. "Where is Rath now?"

"Our dear, most fearless leader is in the sleeping cave," said Kallica. She gestured to it, hair flicking her cheekbones as she turned. Short, black, coarse—typical Cognito hair, descended from an old-world native people. "Talking to Coda and Sylver. You going to check in?"

"Yeah, I'll be right back. Thanks, Kal."

The sleeping cave was the largest Inertia had, stretching far back under the broad-shouldered hill that surrounded the north end of camp. Packed wall-to-wall, it had enough space to fit Raizu's three dozen packmates—so long as they were comfortable breathing in each other instead of air. As Raizu poked his head in, the darkness came alive with murmurs and laughter. The only kind of darkness Raizu didn't fear.

"Arathiel," he called, wiping his boots off at the freshly-swept entrance. "Rath, you here? I made it back."

He received several greetings in response, an indistinguishable blur of sound. None of them were Arathiel, but he returned each wave and hello, stepping under the low roof.

"Hi, Raizu," said another friend as he made his way to the back. Impril, one of Kallica's sisters. "Good hunting?"

"Fantastic, thank you," Raizu answered, and remembered the twirl of Letty's hair, the freckles mapping Majest's face. "I, uh, brought bear meat for you all."

"You took down a *bear*?"

The echo from the voice came running down the long cave wall, and Raizu blinked until his eyes adjusted to Coda and her twin, Sylver, tucked in the farthest corner. Coda's big brown eyes shone in the dark; Raizu could almost see the puff of her hair dancing around her shoulders. Arathiel, who had spoken, sat on a fur blanket beside them.

"No, but I met a woman who could—in one blow," Raizu said, walking over and setting down his bags. "She was rescuing someone, and she let me have the meat."

"A matter of timing, then." Arathiel stood up gingerly, and Raizu took in the compact, lean form that was a mirror image of his own. The same bronze hair and round eyes. "Sounds like you've had some excitement, then, hmm?"

Raizu gave a meek shrug, meeting Arathiel's taller stance. His elder brother had arranged his features to look welcoming, but something in them faltered. His ankle looked wretched, too—swollen and violet. He refused to put weight on it.

"Seems like things have been more exciting here," said Raizu. "What happened to your foot? And Kallica's elbow?"

Arathiel lifted his chin. "You talk to your pack leader like that?"

"I talk to my family like that, when I'm worried about them," Raizu said. He tried to put force through the words, but his voice came out shaking and weedy. "Tell me, and I'll tell you about my adventure."

"You first," said Arathiel. "Sit down."

"Fine," said Raizu, and they sat together, shoulders brushing. The touch was cold despite the warm air around them. Arathiel's lower leg looked even more bloated all stretched out, and his eyes bored right through Raizu.

"I, um," Raizu began, but was interrupted when Kallica came in and plopped next to Coda.

"Hey," she said. "Sorry—I wanted to hear the story, too. There was a bear?"

Raizu almost smiled. Having her here made him feel better immediately. "Right," he said. "I was following fox prints, but instead, I ran into this woman who'd taken out a grizzly. The bear was attacking this lost girl. The woman ran off, so I ended up with the meat and the girl. I helped her look for her brother."

"Did you find him?" asked Sylver.

"Yes." Raizu thought longingly of the siblings. He wished he could have convinced them to come with him. "I gave them some of the meat and we parted ways. That's it."

"That's it?" Coda protested.

"Sorry." Raizu cringed at everyone's disappointed faces, but his lips would remain sealed on the details of the Skylarks' journey. He'd promised.

"Sounds like a bunch of bogus, Raizy," said Kallica. "No one would wreck a bear like that and then give it all away." She plucked a frozen chunk of meat from Raizu's bag and chewed off a strip.

Raizu almost rolled his eyes—only Kallica preferred her food raw.

"I believe him," said Arathiel. "How else would he have found all that meat? There's no way Raizu could kill a bear. He shouldn't have been in grizzly territory in the first place. Same goes for those siblings. Don't they have parents?"

Raizu's skin pricked in annoyance, but he responded in an even voice. "No, they're orphans like us."

"Rath, have you told Raizy about the Organization conundrum yet?" Kallica cut in.

"I was getting to it," snapped Arathiel.

"What's the Organization?" Raizu asked. "Is that what happened to your leg?"

Arathiel looked about ready to light something ablaze, but Kallica poked him, unfazed. "Get on with it," she said. "You don't have to be such a melodramatic—"

"*Okay,*" Arathiel said. "Yesterday after dawn, two strange men came into our camp. They claimed to be from something called the Organization, led by this *Lady President* they wouldn't stop spouting off about. Apparently, they're on a quest to wipe out powers—whatever that means. They want to restart the old world." Arathiel's voice held disgust. "They told us to join them. We told them to get lost. They beat us around a bit before they listened."

Raizu's head spun. Powers? *Oh, no.* "Did they say who they were after, specifically?"

Arathiel looked up for the first time and sighed. "Not *you*, Raizu, don't worry."

"But—what about where they're from? What they're doing?"

"I don't know. They mentioned the place of the Redwoods. Honestly, they didn't even seem to know what they wanted or who they were." Arathiel sneered. "Ridiculous."

Redwoods meant nothing to Raizu, but his chest still pounded.

"If you're really that curious, they did say one thing," said Kallica. "What was it? Oh, if we heard anything about someone called *Skylark*, we should find one of their representatives. They're supposedly *always watching*." She snorted. "Yeah, right."

Raizu's heart seized. *"No…"*

"I don't care how much they twisted my arm—*ha, get it?*—I'm not scared of those lunatics," Kallica went on, oblivious.

The Organization—they must be the people who killed Majest and Letty's mother. The Skylarks really were in danger, and they had no idea of the scope. Raizu did the only thing he could think of. He stood up and slung his sheath of arrows over his shoulder. "I have to go."

"Go where?" Arathiel demanded. "You just sat down."

Raizu, for once, didn't think—not of the consequences, not of the absurdity, only what a warning to Majest and Letty could prevent. The difference he could make for once. "Would you mind covering for me for another few weeks?" he asked cautiously.

"What?"

"I have to help someone—those siblings," Raizu replied, already calculating how much food and water he would need, enough to get him to the Hudson Bay.

"What siblings? From your story? Raizu, what on Earth are you talking about?"

"They're the Skylarks," Raizu said. Everyone blinked in astonishment. "And they need me."

11

ap-tap.

The rap of knuckles came against Shatter's chamber door. She stood up from the bed, setting aside her book, creasing the page she'd left off on. Shatter had never been taught to read, but she still loved books—the words and symbols were an endless, mesmerizing mystery. She thought of what her sister Sedona would say if she knew the Organization had books, and pictures, and *maps*. Their family had collected old-world treasures like that.

She would've come with me if she'd known. She wouldn't have looked so afraid.

The knock came again, more persistent this time, and Shatter shook herself of the memory. "Coming!"

It was probably Caiter, the mild-mannered scientist who had recruited Shatter from her home in Affinia. He had promised her a safe future. *A purpose.* Many of the Organization's members made Shatter's skin crawl, but Caiter's heart was pure honey. He'd gotten her on board in minutes, and she hadn't looked back.

Before Caiter, Affinia's last visitor had been Lunesta Skylark. She'd appeared like a sudden storm, thunder on her tongue as she'd spoken out about her deadly siblings, poisoned by power from an evil god. She had vanished, short hair spiking in the wind, and Shatter had never seen anyone called Skylark again.

But Caiter had come calling, and Shatter knew the world had awoken to Lunesta's warning. Now, Shatter would help save that very same world.

Shatter answered the door and was surprised to see not Caiter, but the President.

"Miss Shatter Seacourt," she said, her face calm. "May I have a word?"

Shatter blinked. The President never came to see her. "Of course," she managed. "Come in. Is there an issue?"

"An inconvenience." The President took a few slow steps into the bare room, boots clanking on the floor. Shatter had to look up quite a ways to meet the darkness in her eyes.

"What do you mean?" Shatter asked.

"It's the boy. Seti."

That got Shatter's attention. She thought often of the strange boy she'd led inside these white walls, miniature and porcelain, equal parts sinister and stunning—an antique toy soldier in mint condition.

"I'll cut straight to the point—his time is almost up," said the President. "According to the data the twins received from the watch, he's moving, but if he had caught the Skylarks, he'd presumably be sheltering, waiting for us to collect him. I assume he is still chasing. With his skills, this should have been done in a day."

Shatter felt her heart swell in her throat. She didn't know why, but she was drawn to Seti and didn't want to see Chami and Shayming toss him around again. Perhaps she thought under those unreadable smoky-gold eyes and stiff expression was something more than a machine. Machines, she had learned here, could be unmade.

"How long until you send the twins for him?" asked Shatter.

"I haven't decided, but I'm here to start organizing his replacement."

Replacement? Seti was the only one of his kind. The President had sent for him specially.

"I've sent recruiters to the north, to the packs this time," the President continued. "In the meantime, I want you to visit the laboratory and see if they can recreate the effects of Seti's curse—with more demon energy, like what we put into the watch."

Shatter swallowed hard. "What will happen to Seti?" she dared to ask.

The President shrugged, bony shoulders rising and falling. "Depends on what he's willing to do for us. Otherwise, I suppose we'll have to kill him."

"He could still find the Skylarks," Shatter blurted. "Any day now."

The President turned to leave. "Yes, he could. But why waste time waiting, with something this crucial to our mission? Report to the scientists. Immediately."

Shatter opened her mouth to reply, but no words came out. The door shut, and the President's metallic footsteps faded down the hall.

All Shatter could do was obey. She vowed, though, she would not give up on Seti. If the scientists couldn't create a better hunter, the Organization would still need him.

The laboratory wasn't a far walk, and soon after setting out, the door loomed ahead. Knowing what went on behind it, Shatter didn't care if it was unlocked—she knocked first.

A familiar face peered out. Caiter. He smiled when he saw her, but it was a weary, weathered smile. "Shatter," he said. "What are you doing here?"

"Lady President sent me to talk to you about a project."

"Another one? All right, come on in."

Inside, the Organization laboratory positively effervesced. The walls, the floor, even the pinched-tight faces of the scientists glowed with an artificial blue. The whole place felt as if it was underwater, from the domed ceiling that spun in a current of concentric circles to the gadgets that whirred and scientists who buzzed. It was dizzying to take in, even dizzier to imagine how the Organization might have acquired this place.

Caiter led Shatter between tables stacked with vials of rank liquids, all of which tossed her wide-eyed reflection back at her. Every scientist they passed had a frown.

One, a small boy with a mop of red hair, looked up from a pile of marked-up maps. "Caiter, I think I was onto something earlier," he called. "About the Hudson?"

Shatter perked up, but Caiter sighed in dismissal. "You should be working on your actual assignment, Ohanzi. I don't want you to get in trouble."

The boy faded among the hive of countless bustling strangers. Curious, Shatter peeked at as many workstations as she could. Were they working on enchanted objects, like Seti's watch? Collecting energy from the land? Fiddling with the technology piled high in the Organization's back rooms? Shatter would have loved a science lesson.

At last, they reached Caiter's table, full of beeping, color-spitting machines. Caiter sat in his plastic chair, propping his feet on the underside bar of the table.

"So," he said. "What's this about?"

"Seti," Shatter admitted. "She wants to know if the scientists could recreate his curse."

"The kid with the demon juice? Does anyone know how he got that way?"

"Not a clue," Shatter said, relieved. The less anyone could do about replacing Seti, the longer he might stick around—and the more time Shatter would have to learn about him.

"Hmm," said Caiter. "All we can do is try. I can look into…"

His words trailed off as another chair swung near them, and a man with unruly russet hair and the approximate body structure of a grasshopper dropped his elbows onto Caiter's table.

"Boo," he said, his eyes bugging out from under his round glasses. "Demon juice, you say? I've been working on something that might be on your grocery list."

"Malory," said Caiter, visibly startling. "You know the President doesn't like it when you start projects without permission."

Malory was exactly what Shatter feared about the laboratory. His bone-white grin and decades' worth of supplies had never seemed trustworthy. Even his voice made Shatter shiver, ricocheting too fast between her ears. He was supposedly brilliant, having taught most of the scientists here himself, but the way he radiated kept Shatter from standing too close.

"Psh," said Malory now, waving Caiter off. "Our President loves me. I bring her basement-grade projects screaming up to the rooftops, and I could take care of the energy-boost projects she gives me in my sleep. I dug up an old gift from my underworld friends, added a pinch of salt, and *voila.*"

He dangled a bottle in front of Caiter's face. Dark liquid sloshed inside it, and Shatter's skin crawled. "Demon serum, only fifty calories per bottle. Have you ever wanted diesel fuel for blood? You're welcome."

Caiter's mouth fell slowly open. "Is that…?" He leaned back to get a better look. "Where do you keep getting all this demon energy? I'm not sure using it on people is a good idea."

"I'm not sure sitting on your rump all day tapping on dead keyboards is a good idea, either, but yet here you are." Malory ignored Caiter's hurt frown. "Come on, think about it. We could make half an armada's worth of demon friends with this stuff. The gods would be wetting themselves."

Shatter shrank back, but Caiter only tilted his head. "Our mission is to get rid of dangerous powers in the land," he said. "Not create more of them."

"*Your* mission," said Malory with a sniff, and turned away. "There's unfinished business in other places. My places. Let me know when you're ready to hop aboard."

Caiter did not protest, just looked to Shatter with an apologetic stare as if to say, "What can you do?" No wonder he looked so exhausted.

Aloud, Caiter said, "Thanks for coming by, Shatter. Tell the President we'll work on her case, okay? I'll watch Malory."

Shatter nodded, though she couldn't quite manage a smile. Even as she made her way out of the lab, her thoughts spun, Malory's words and Seti's face pressed heavy against them.

There was nothing she could do now. Seti's fate was shifting sands, but Shatter's duties were a solid hill she could climb. And the other scientists, even Malory, were here at the Organization to climb that hill with her. At the top was the President's new, equal world.

Shatter straightened the collar of her shirt, setting her gaze straight ahead. She had to forget Seti for now.

If she could.

Weeks passed. Majest and Letty pressed on, inching closer and closer to the bay even as their feet throbbed with blisters. They didn't run into other storms or predators—it was just walking, endless walking, the repetition of footfall and snowfall, hunting and resting, *walking and more walking.*

The only change of pace was when they came across water. Then, Majest watched Letty's powers come to the surface, struggling against a feverish current. Though she faltered and twisted in the waves, Letty could hold onto her element, more so each time she tried.

"But I still can't control it," Letty often told him. "I can pick it up, but in the end, it goes where it wants."

She kept trying, pushing away the dark spark in her eyes, but Majest could see she was holding back. She feared whatever had taken her over when they had gone caribou hunting. Every now and then, she'd manage to lift drops into the air, paint timid ripples into the edge of a lake—but nothing more. She would not flex her new muscle, even while Majest dreamed of shaping valleys, moving mountains.

The days grew shorter as they traveled, winter stalking them with the lengthened nights. They had left the forest behind, trekking across stony plains that shone with ice as far as they could see. The terrain gave them more momentum but less protection, and less hope their destination might be waiting beyond the next line of trees. The horizon stayed empty.

Until one morning, Letty said, "I think we're here."

"Hmm?" Majest peeled himself from his thoughts.

"The bay," Letty said, even though the sky was blank ahead. "You know how I feel every river and stream in my chest when we get close?"

"Is it like that now?"

"More than ever. It's like I'm being pulled under. There's something—something around the corner."

"Around the corner?" Majest raised an eyebrow. "How about over this mountain?"

Together, they looked at the next slope, which gleamed in invitation.

"Let's find out," said Letty, and they clasped hands and ran. Snow flew, and the air turned their breaths to wheezes. It took some time, but soon, they reached the summit where the ice met the sky.

The top of the crest was high and cold, the world presented before them on a windswept platter. Wind whipped Majest's face, and silvers and whites smeared together on the slope below. At the horizon, earth and sky were one, a never-ending swatch of blue.

Except it wasn't the earth, and it wasn't the sky. There was the screech of birds, the slap of shoreline. The wind relented enough for Majest to blink properly. They had found the Hudson Bay.

Miles of waves pierced the low cloud cover, stretched over the distant curve of the Earth. The bay was the sky inverted, the clouds reflected. It took up Majest's entire headspace; it became all he could smell and see. He tasted salt, even from this high up. It was the kind of beautiful that drowned all things before it.

Letty quivered beside him, and Majest could not imagine what she must be feeling. "It's *huge*," she whispered.

"What did you expect?" he asked, and couldn't stop grinning. "A puddle?"

In Letty's eyes, he watched the reflection of white-caps, the foam and the blue. The darkness at the center.

"Let's head down," she said.

Careful not to trip on their own thrilled feet, Letty and Majest half-ran, half-skidded down the foothill, making their way against the treeless stretch. At this pace, it took less than an hour to reach the shore.

Up close, the Hudson Bay was overwhelming. There was no land on the other side, only trembling lines, ice floes, and the dark blue of his father's long-gone eyes. The call of the incessant gulls rang high and long and searching.

Letty ran right up to the water's edge. "This feels like home," she said, staring out.

Majest chuckled. "Not unless you're a halibut. Should we start looking for shelter?"

"Hold on, Maji, I see something." She pointed into the endless blue.

"What?" Majest asked, and when he leaned in, he saw it: a bump in the horizon, nudging the clouds. He thought he could make out the spikes of trees.

"Is that an island?" she asked.

"There aren't any islands this far north, are there? Father never said—" He stopped himself. His parents had never made a journey like this. Their words could not guide them beyond the forest.

"You've talked about making a rowboat to search for a home," said Letty. "The island can't be too far offshore, or we wouldn't be able to see it from here. We could go check it out."

Majest reeled at the idea. He had hardly considered what the actuality of making a boat would be like. He thought dizzily of his father's old stories, when he had sailed from his homeland in search of an end to the End. That ship had housed dozens, had whipped the wind and split the seas with its wood.

He swallowed hard. "I…guess. If we can find a few trees, I could try and carve something for the two of us."

"Don't look like that. It's a good idea," said Letty, nudging him. "And if we get too tired to row, I could help us paddle with my powers, maybe."

As if carried on the briny wind, doubt—uncharacteristic doubt—soaked through Majest. Letty wasn't ready for that kind of elemental task, and Majest didn't know if he was ready to toss their fate into the unfamiliar blue. They'd lived their whole lives between trees, the forest creating the wood for their home. They knew nothing of the Hudson Bay or its dangers. If they lost their supplies, there would be no replacements. If a storm hit, there would be no shelter.

But such doubts would not get them anywhere, and certainly would not make a future.

"Fine," Majest agreed, exhaling everything on that one word. "But if we get stranded out there and die, remember this was your idea."

"You can tell me 'I told you so' in the afterlife."

"Fair enough."

Seti looked on from the mountainside in disgust, staring at the figures on the shoreline below. He had taken too long chasing after Soti. Somehow, he had lost the Skylarks and spent the next weeks chasing his tail. And of course, by the time he'd figured out they were headed to the bay and had caught up, they were preparing to set sail out of his reach.

He could imagine the President's furious face at this wasted time, feel the pocket watch measure every useless second.

Now, Seti watched as Majest Skylark wandered the rocky beach with his sister and found two of the only trees for miles. Dumb, impossible luck. The boy lifted his hands, spending several minutes at it, until the smaller tree tipped. It crashed to the beach with a sound the waves immediately swallowed whole.

Seti should have swooped in right then, killed them where they stood. Ended this finally. But it was the first time he was witnessing the danger of the Powers, and he wanted to watch. Seeing Majest's element crawl through the air, carve through an enormous pine—it was uneasy, Seti could give the President that. But when Majest was done, he had an ugly rowboat and a pair of paddles, not a battleship.

It wasn't big enough for both of them, Seti realized.

Majest buried his head in his hands and shook it. Aletta patted him on the back.

Wasteful idiots. Seti curled his lip, but it soon turned into a smirk. These inexperienced children were supposed to be the enemy of the land? He wasn't sure who was the bigger fool: them or the President.

After moving the failed boat behind a rocky structure, Majest worked on the second tree for the next hour, the way he should've done in the first place. Seti didn't bother to interrupt. They'd be exhausted when this was over, and in no shape to row themselves anywhere.

Except once Majest finished the boat, they dragged it to the shore and got inside.

No. They're going to drown. Seti watched in disbelief. *One storm and that hunk of wood will be upside down. They won't make it across. They'll die.*

A slow smile took hold of Seti's face. All he would have to do is wait a few minutes, and the icy waves would capsize the Skylarks, eat them alive. Seti's aunt could not save them this time.

But Aletta Skylark seemed to think she could. She drew off her gloves, dipped one hand in the water, and began to move her arm in a slow pendulum rhythm. The boat drifted clumsily out to sea.

"Water powers?" Seti spat out loud. "She learned *that* in two weeks? Impossible."

The President had said *she* was the dangerous one.

Then Seti saw Aletta wasn't controlling the boat at all. Behind her, Majest plunged a paddle against the waves, body taut with effort, and rowed them forward. Aletta did not acknowledge this, but also did not remove her hand.

No matter how the Skylarks were moving, they were moving, and shrinking before Seti's eyes. Somehow, they kept up with the waves, and more than that—they made progress. They rowed on. Them and their damned luck.

Cursing, Seti leapt from his hiding spot and charged along the bank. He would take Majest's second, smaller boat. He would sail after them. He would catch up and ruin them…until he remembered he had no paddles. No element. His demon blood could not serve him here, at the mercy of the bay. The Skylarks could do this, but Seti would be dead.

I'll probably be dead anyway once the President gets her claws on me.

The failure overwhelming, Seti grabbed the pocket watch from his belt, flinging it to the rocks at his feet. Unharmed, it stared impassively back at him. He couldn't tell if its hands had moved at all, but he never could. Days would pass, but the clock insisted it had only been minutes. The hands were too slow. Just as Seti had been.

The children dissolved into the foggy distance. Seti picked up the watch. Despite everything, it ticked on.

12

Caiter decided it was far too early for this much talk of demonic injection. "Malory," he said, cringing out of the way of a vial waved in his direction. "Would you please be careful with that?"

"Why? It's harmless," Malory chirped, though he set the glass back onto his table. "Unless you touch it. Or ingest it. Or breathe near it."

Caiter frowned. "Have you moved since last night?"

Malory considered this. "I haven't moved in *weeks*," he clarified. "Weren't you taught not to stop anything until you're finished? Yes, shut up, you were. I taught you."

The President had agreed to let him work on his demonic serum in hopes of creating a Seti Sinestre who would actually listen to her. Caiter wasn't one to doubt his leader, but…

"When was the last time you slept?" he asked Malory.

"Seventy-six hours ago."

That explains a lot.

"Caiter, I want another animal for testing," Malory said. "If you're going to sniff around my desk and wag your tail, you could at least play fetch."

Caiter did not want to find Malory another animal. The last time he'd tested his serum on something—a stray silver tabby cat the twins had found gods-knew-where—the injection had caused some horrifying side effects. The cat's eyes had rolled back to their whites, mouth crackling with foam, the entire creature swelling like a balloon. The President had forced Malory to end the creature's suffering, but Caiter's suffering was still an open issue.

"I'll see what I can do," he said to Malory, and scooted out of range.

Caiter would visit Charan instead, the gentlest of the Organization's homegrown scientists. He had been one of the first to follow Caiter here, interested in chemistry and studious enough to learn its rules. Malory, on the other hand, was a bright-burning star hurtling toward the stratosphere. Spectacular, sure, but blinding at best and apocalyptic at worst.

Caiter set off for Charan's station but was summoned by a tall dark-skinned woman with gold loops in her ears. Her name was Nafuna, and she worked with the restoration of the President's old-world artifacts. She was interminably busy.

"Hey—the President told me to fix this," Nafuna said. "Looks like your kind of thing. Any idea?"

Caiter took a look. It was some sort of keypad, but twice the size of anything he had ever played around with. Not that he knew much more than how to attach wires together and hand them off to the twins to charge with their electrical magic.

"It looks like it's supposed to be attached to something else," said Caiter. "Sorry, I'm not sure. You might have to ask Malory."

"That's what I hoped you wouldn't say," said Nafuna with a sigh.

With another apology, Caiter carried on toward the opposite end of the laboratory. He found Charan's dark head bent over scraps of metal and a short page of parchment, reading with the kind of concentration that could bore holes. He looked up with a start when Caiter approached him.

"Needed a break?" Charan asked.

"Malory," said Caiter, and Charan nodded in sympathy.

"I don't know why you bother talking to him," Charan said. "As soon as he was finished instructing us, I was ready to never see that awful praying mantis face of his again. How is your project going?"

"Oh. Um." Caiter had nearly forgotten, and he burned with embarrassment. "I don't really know where to start. I'm no expert."

"It's a sleeping chamber, right? Don't the twins have the energy-sapping magic for that?"

"Sure, but I don't know how to design a machine that can keep someone unconscious without killing them."

"You'll need the plastic Malory showed us," said Charan, already grabbing for a notepad. "You could install tubes that keep the powder circulating through the air, which would make sure the person stays asleep. To keep them alive, you'll need an IV—you know, like in old-world hospitals."

Caiter didn't know. Charan's town must have had better history preservation than his.

Charan saw his hesitation and scribbled something else down. "Nutrients. Into someone's bloodstream, using needles. I could help you with the supplies, if you want?"

"That would be great," said Caiter, still sheepish. "I'm so late in getting started. Good thing the President never comes down here."

"I don't?" A dry voice said from behind Caiter's head, and he spun around in horror.

"Lady President," he stammered. "I wasn't—"

"I know you weren't." The President looked amused, the overhead lights like stars in her night-sky eyes. "Caiter, you usually do so well with your work. What's going on?"

"Malory," Charan said, and Caiter felt himself go red.

"*Malory.*" The President's eyes narrowed. "I came down here to check in on his serum project. I noticed Caiter wasn't where he was supposed to be."

Caiter's frown went queasy. As brilliant as Malory was, he was not someone Caiter would have trusted experimenting for the President. No one knew the first thing about him—why he was here, or what he wanted.

"I'm sorry if he's been a distraction," the President went on, "but he's making great progress. Malory has completed a serum that can give someone tremendous demonic abilities. This will help us track and kill the Powers much faster."

Caiter was appalled. "President," he protested, "don't you remember what happened to that cat? Do you want that to happen to one of us?"

"Yes, to an extent. We need someone who can bring the new world to our mercy so that we can fix it. Malory's new and improved substance will do that."

Caiter's stomach twisted further. The President trusted Malory, this unknown stranger—why? He wanted to know; he wanted a reason to trust Malory, too, instead of fearing he might wake up one morning missing an eye or a kidney.

"I know you don't understand, Caiter," the President continued. "Not everyone does. Shatter doesn't, either. It's all right. Just get started on that sleeping chamber." She folded thin arms across her chest in a gesture that should not have been as commanding as it was. "I will have use for it soon."

Caiter pursed his lips. No matter what he wanted to know, he was a servant of the Organization. He did not get to choose what he wanted. "Yes, Lady President."

Letty and Majest paddled until the sun lit up the frothy night, which was a welcomed sight after hours of uneasy travel. In the light, the island floated closer. Majest could see treetops and rugged shoreline, their silhouettes scratching the paint off the sky.

They traded off rowing and catching hour-long naps until they were both exhausted and cranky. Majest's arms felt like soggy tree trunks. When she wasn't paddling, Letty kept trailing her hand in the freezing water, her power trickling faintly out. Her fingers were redder than her hair.

"It's still so far," she said now, pulling her hand out and tucking it in her jacket. "I hope it's worth it."

"It will be if there are enough resources to make a home, and no one chasing us is stupid enough to do what we're doing right now," said Majest.

"You never know. Think of Father's stories—for so many, freedom only comes from risking the unknown. That's a good line, don't you think?"

Majest grunted in half-agreement, his eyelids dragging down. His knuckles ached from gripping the paddles so tight, the spray of the waves freezing on his cheeks. He could not imagine hours more of this.

A slight nudge rocked the boat, jolting him wide awake. It was subtle—barely a tap on the wood—but it was enough to send their food bag gliding.

"Did you feel that?" Majest inspected the water. Nothing but bay.

"Yeah." Letty leaned next to him, her pupils silver in the reflection. The boat lurched in disapproval of her added weight.

"Get back on the other side," Majest told her. "You're going to flip us over."

Letty sat down, rolling her eyes. "I'm sure it was just—"

The knock came again, adamant this time. It sent Majest and Letty sprawling into the middle of the boat. Majest landed with his legs twisted and Letty's hair in his mouth, and he untangled himself with a grimace.

"I'm sure it was *not* just a fish," Letty corrected.

"Someone down there doesn't like us."

"Can you see what it is? Can you try talking to it?"

"I only know forest languages," said Majest. "All I can do without practice is sound like a squawking idiot."

"You do that anyway," Letty informed him. "You should try—I don't want some sea monster trying to eat us. Squawk away."

Majest sighed. She was right. He cast a line into his element, snagging it toward him, exploding into its light. He thought of the languages he had learned and tasted them—bitter, soft, and tiny in his mouth: squirrels, lemmings, rabbits, and birds. All small creatures.

He tasted something nearby, too. Something with the same salty feeling as the Hudson Bay. It had a fuzzy presence just out of reach. He took a grab at it, but it slipped between his fingers.

"Letty, I don't think—"

Then his eyes cracked open, and he looked over the side of the boat. A white head poked up from the surface of the water and began to yelp.

Majest fought through the unfamiliarity in the tone. "Hello?" he tried. His throat felt thick and muddy.

"Hello," the creature responded, its voice distorted. "Hello!"

"What is it?" Letty asked, trying to see from her side of the boat.

"Good question." Majest leaned closer, straight into its enormous black eyes. It sure wasn't a fish or a bear. Clearing his throat, Majest attempted its language again. "Who are you?"

"I'm Donec," the animal replied. "I'm lost."

"It's a Donec," Majest told Letty.

"A *who?*"

"Seals like me should not be here," said Donec. "Too cold. Too much salt. I do not remember how I got here."

The only seals Majest knew of were the ones whose fur had become blankets on his family's beds. He did not mention that. "Humans shouldn't be here, either," he said, and had no idea if the creature understood his sloppy barking. "I'm not sure if we can help."

Donec made a low, terrible sound. "Feed me," he said. "Or I tip the boat."

"You're kidding," said Majest. First, Amitu wouldn't tell him where Letty was until Majest gave up his best nuts. Then, something had ripped their food bag to shreds without bothering to ask politely for a snack. And now, this dandelion fluff was threatening his life.

Maybe we are the superior species.

"Maji," Letty cut in, scooting close enough to see without wobbling the boat. "What's going on?"

"A little seal," said Majest. "He wants our food. He thinks he can tip us over."

"Give him a piece of meat, then, so we can keep moving."

"We can keep moving anyway," said Majest. "What is he going to do? If he touches the boat again, he'll get an oar to the head."

The animal glowered up at him.

"Can you eat seals?" Majest asked Letty.

"Don't you dare," she said. "He's a baby."

"He's *evil,*" Majest grumped.

Letty gave him a withering look. Before he could stop her, she had picked out a section of caribou meat from her bag and tossed it into the water. Donec's head bobbed beneath the surface and came up with the chunk moments later.

"Much obliged," he mumbled around his mouthful, and disappeared with a splash.

"Was that so hard?" Letty asked. "Now, let's go."

The boat lurched forward as if shoved by a god's hand. Majest and Letty were blown back against the wood floor as it took off at impossible speeds across the water. The boat had come to life—it was a polar bear now, an osprey, the heaving flanks of a wolf.

"What's happening? Are you doing that?" Majest cried over the roar, struggling to stay upright. He grappled for his packs, spray impairing his vision.

"No!" Letty protested, spitting hair from her mouth. "I couldn't do anything like this!"

"Then what—?" Majest heard soft, inhuman laughter coming from all directions. He peered into the water behind the boat to see Donec, of all things, shoving the boat along with his great white head. The bay churned and writhed behind him.

"The *seal?*" Majest cried. "Seals can't—they don't—" He looked to the skies and sputtered as if Komi had sent the super-powered Donec himself. Maybe he had.

"I'm dreaming," Majest said. "I'm dreaming, and the gods are playing practical jokes. Letty, wake me up before a fox builds us a new home and reindeer sew our clothes."

Letty began laughing, the sound blown away by the wind. Within seconds, she had Majest laughing, too.

"Who cares?" she cried. "We'll make it to the island in no time now!"

As a tracker, Raizu knew it was not convenient to be afraid of the dark, and his packmates didn't let him forget it. Yet he couldn't help the way he felt when the night swallowed the sun, terror a cold breath whispering over his skin. At any moment, some great beast could spring from the bushes and rip him to meat-and-cloth strips.

It was a burden that usually resulted in lanterns propped beside him while he slept and a grateful fondness for the stars. It was a burden that could not follow him here.

Tailing the Skylarks, Raizu had plenty of ground to make up. Now in the darkest hours of the year, stowing himself away at the first sight of every sunset was not an option. Majest and Letty were built of tougher stuff, stalking through the dark woods like they enjoyed the kick of the black unknown. If there were any hope of catching them, Raizu had to travel twice as fast, sleep half as much, and journey on even when the sun was gone.

After weeks of hurrying, the night that lay before Raizu was a still one. Usually, the wind blew and rattled the trees with its whistle, but the forest tonight was subdued. Spellbound. Not even an owl hooting in the distance. Just silence.

That was worse, somehow. As Raizu crept on, it became too easy to pick apart the quiet: the hinge-creaks of branches, the click-clack of distant elk. Once he started fantasizing about rolling into a ball under a tree somewhere, Raizu knew he had to get a grip.

"Logically, there's a slim chance of something wanting to kill or eat me," Raizu said aloud. Kallica had once told him to try talking himself through situations like this. "I'm too scrawny for a carnivore to want a piece of me and I have zero magical powers." He huffed. What was the matter with him? He never got this worked up hunting.

But this isn't hunting. This is life or death for real people.

Raizu sucked in an enormous breath, a futile attempt at calming his frayed nerves, and rechecked his bearings. East, still. He should have been right along the Skylarks' path.

What is it about those two? Raizu still didn't understand himself. *I barely know them, but I'm risking my life to tell them they're in danger. And not just that—they already* know *they're in danger. I'm only giving them names: Organization. President. Redwood.*

Maybe it was more than a handful of names that brought him willingly into the dark. Maybe it was the feeling that somehow, he belonged in their story. Or at least wanted to.

A branch crunched overhead, and Raizu jumped, his heartbeat loud in his ears. He realized a new, sickening fear: that even if he found the Skylarks, his cowardice would prove useless in their fight.

Panic got the better of him and Raizu stopped dead in his tracks. The world around him cranked louder. An owl hooted, the trees rustled, and Raizu grabbed for the sheath at his shoulder, wrestling his fingers around an arrow. Majest's arrow.

Sudden wind erupted. It buffeted Raizu's jacket around him, flipping his hair, creeping into his sleeves. He shut his eyes.

One foot at a time. He drew a hunting knife from his coat. He felt like a child, a weapon in each clumsy hand. *You'll be fine.* He tried to reassure himself and opened his eyes.

He had almost managed to convince himself when out of the black, a nearby owl swooped down to snag a squirrel a rabbit's-length away from where Raizu stood. Feathers exploded; the squirrel's shrill screech rang into the night.

Raizu took off in a terrified sprint, fumbling over the snow. Branches clawed at his hands, caught at his clothes and hair. But he did not stop, no matter what the night threw his way.

13

When Shatter opened her latest assignment, she found with dismay that the papers were all in the same jumbled writing as her books. The President had sent her the wrong files.

Cursing illiteracy, Shatter gathered the envelope and stood. She would have to return them and get her actual assignment—maps of the nearby towns and packs.

It was the last thing Shatter needed, on a day when Seti wore on her mind more than ever. She had tried forgetting him, but she knew the President had been making arrangements these last few weeks—with the twins and Caiter, and now with Malory, who drew closer to his delirious demon fever-dream with the President at his heels.

Before long, Seti would have no purpose.

Shatter moved toward the President's chambers on brisk feet, passing the laboratory, the scientists' rooms, endless closets, endless clutter. When she arrived, the door was locked. A keypad glared out at her, spitting the violet aura of the twins' magic.

Beyond the door, Shatter heard the murmur of voices and paused halfway into lifting her fist to knock. The President spoke, low and guarded. A voice for important matters.

Without thinking, Shatter pressed one ear to the door.

"…time to remove him," the President said. "After all these weeks, he has no excuse."

"But he still has value," a high-pitched voice answered. Shayming.

"We can't kill him like some bug on the floor," said Chami, her voice strained. "He's precious. A diamond."

They were talking about Seti, Shatter realized.

"I thought value depended on success," said the President in a sharp tone. "Therefore, he is a common jewel. A common jewel sitting at the edge of the Hudson Bay, the Skylarks lost."

"Maybe he has a plan," Shayming tried again. "Maybe he's waiting for the right time."

"Look at the screen," the President snapped. "You enchanted it yourselves. Unless Seti and the Skylarks are all enjoying the sunrise over the water together, he has *lost them*."

Shatter swallowed hard. They would kill Seti after all. She would never learn the story behind those gold ingot eyes. The thought made her irrationally queasy.

"You want us to kill him, then?" Chami's tone was taut.

Shatter remembered how the twins had showered Seti with praise; it had been their encouragement that had gotten the President to consider him.

But the President said, "No."

"*No?*" Shayming echoed, sounding just as stunned as Shatter felt. "But you said—"

"I know what I said," the President said, her voice a sheet of thin ice. "I have a plan for the boy. Catch him as you did before and bring him to me. I'll take it from there."

"Very well," Shayming and Chami said together.

"I also need a supply of your energy draining magic before you head out."

"For what?" Chami asked.

"I am not ready to disclose the project details. Get to it. We don't have much time."

"We'll take care of it immediately," Shayming said.

The door to the President's chamber swung open, nearly bowling Shatter over. She staggered backward, making an attempt to look as if she had just arrived.

The twins didn't even spare her a nod. Their eyes glanced off Shatter, and they walked down the hall—though it was really more of a *flow* than a walk.

Shatter, relieved, went through the now-open door, crushing her papers to her chest. The President's room was freezing cold, as usual.

"President?" Shatter called, finding her standing on the far side of the room, her arms folded. "Can I bother you for a moment?"

Midnight eyes lifted; hands smoothed down their spotless uniform. "Shatter," said the President. "Yes. What is it?"

"Someone delivered me the wrong papers."

"Oh." The President frowned, like she hadn't expected an issue so trivial. "Of course."

She moved to her desk, spidery fingers tracing the drawers. Seconds later, she handed Shatter a stack of colorful parchment.

"Maps of Cognito from our recruiters," the President said. "I need you to mark off the places we've visited and organize routes to the towns and packs we haven't. Give each recruiter three or four locations—whatever makes sense."

"I'm on it," said Shatter, dipping her head.

"Excellent. Off you go."

Shatter made her way into the hallway, the door closing behind her with a click. The last thing on her mind was recruiting routes. The President had a plan for Seti. He would not be killed after all. He still had a chance.

Shatter smiled the whole way back to her room.

Against all odds, Majest and Letty's rough wooden boat made it to the island shore—with the help of their unnerving heaven-sent seal friend, who had long since vanished.

"This place is amazing," said Letty, still trying to walk on the shore without wobbling on sea legs. "It's got to be a few miles across, right? Look—it has animals and everything." She pointed at a grazing rabbit, who shied away at the attention. "It's like a chunk of the mainland was scooped up and dropped out here."

"Don't get too excited," Majest warned, though the shine in his eyes was unmistakable. "We have to head inland and look for shelter. It could be dangerous."

"Oh, you're so stubborn. Can't we look around for longer than four seconds? Try it."

Majest, a sigh on his lips, stopped himself from rolling his eyes, and grudgingly glanced about the island. Tall evergreens blocked the view inland, standing guard to the trees beyond. Loose rock littered the stony coastline, where the tide spat out half-frozen froth with every push. Small animals shot through the outer trees, and birds argued somewhere deeper within.

"All right," Majest said after a minute. "I looked. I saw birds. Also, trees. Plenty of dirt. Let's go."

"Grumpy," said Letty, but grinned and followed him. She spared one last glance at the blue behind her, the lonely boat tucked into the rocks. She could have sat on the shore forever.

Past the first prickly evergreens, they found a tiny forest with only a dusting of snow. It was strange to walk over ground they didn't sink into up to their ankles. Majest was clearly at ease in the woods, and Letty felt it, too. She'd missed the bristle of evergreens, the sharp smells she'd grown up around. Trees had meant a roof over her head, even without a house.

"These pines are endless," said Letty. "We could make a home anywhere in here."

"And have the resources to do it," Majest agreed.

"Resources…wait." Letty put a hand out in front of her brother to stop him. "What about water? We only have a few days' worth left in the canisters. The bay has too much salt in it to drink."

Majest frowned. "You're right," he said, though he didn't seem too concerned. Knowing him, he probably expected drinking water to simply fabricate itself.

"Maji," said Letty, "this is a big problem. You can't just talk to the salt and ask it nicely to separate from the rest of the water. It's not a squirrel."

"I know." Majest didn't turn back. His attention was on the trees.

"So…?"

"Your powers might be able to purify the water, don't you think?"

"Donec the seal is better at using water powers than me. A *magical baby seal.*"

They kept walking, Letty's anticipation making her feet ache. They were so close—to a new life, or to the end of the line.

Something began to glint beyond the woods. White snow free of trees and tinged with other colors. Colors Letty had nearly forgotten—bright violets, yellows, and decadent reds.

"Looks like we found something," said Majest, squinting. "Come on!"

Letty followed as her brother swerved through the last trees, separating them from whatever lay beyond. Majest pushed back the branches, and together, they stepped through.

Snow-blind and breathless, Letty gasped. It was impossible, absurd—and yet there it was. Stone and wood buildings sat against one another, pebbly paths like speckled rivers between them. Large tables perched in the spaces between the buildings, each with baskets of brightly-colored materials and foodstuff. In the center of it all was a circular rock structure spilling endless crystalline water into a basin.

"What in the world…?" Letty felt her heart skip a beat.

"A town," Majest whispered. "Like the marketplaces back in Kartho. In the middle of the bay. *A town in the middle of the Hudson Bay.*"

Before Letty could stammer a reply, the sharp sound of someone clearing their throat jolted her attention to the right. A girl about Majest's age stood off to one side dressed in a fluffy, spotless jacket. Her hands, covered in rabbit-fur gloves, were on her hips. And her hair—it was whiter than the snow at her feet.

"Well, well," the girl chimed. "Look what the salt dragged in."

Raizu had known catching the Skylarks was a longshot, but it still took the breath from his lungs when he arrived at the Hudson Bay and found nothing. He had followed the trail exactly. He had gone due east from the clearing where he had reunited Letty and Majest. They should have been here.

But the shoreline stretched on for what seemed like light-years, without so much as the brush of a footprint, the echo of a laugh. Raizu had searched for hours and still found nothing.

They should have been here, but they could have been anywhere.

Had he gotten off course when that owl had scared him? Had Majest and Letty changed their walking pace, or decided on a different destination altogether? Were they farther along the shoreline?

Raizu reworked the route in his mind, running his hands through his hair. Ice crystals shook to the ground. Each possibility wove worriedly through him, racing in circles in his head.

Then, the worst thought of all: what if the Organization had caught the Skylarks already?

He picked up the pace, dread draining the blood from his face. He raced along the rocks calling, "Majest! Letty! Can you hear me?"

I didn't warn them in time. They wouldn't have seen the Organization coming. They didn't know the true danger. They never—

Raizu shook the thoughts off before they suffocated him. Majest and Letty were here. Somewhere. He took another look down the beach, his heartbeat hammering in his chest. Tall rocks closed off several sections of beach; there could have easily been caves or hideouts between them, shelter from the salty spray. There weren't any trees, except for two stumps in the distance. They were woody nubs against the endless shore.

That flicked on a light in Raizu's head. Majest could move trees. He might've knocked these two down to make a shelter. And minutes later, when Raizu knelt next to the stumps, he found the remnants jagged and snapped, not cut with an instrument. It had to be Majest's element.

The nearest rock formation wasn't enough space to tuck a home, but Raizu, his hope renewed, jogged up to it anyway. And sure enough, wood peeked out from behind it.

"Letty?" he called again. "Majest, are you here?"

He rounded the corner and realized the wood was not a part of a shelter. It was a hollowed-out trunk, edges shorn straight off. A rowboat.

A boat, with the same cut marks that had been on the tree trunks. A boat that looked new, the wood fresh and beaming. Had Majest made it? Why would he have left it here?

Raizu took a moment to stare.

Maybe they're coming back for it? Maybe it's not their boat at all, but who else could make a boat from scratch like this? There was another damaged tree—was there another boat? Raizu turned his questions to the endless waters of the Hudson Bay.

If Majest and Letty *had* gone out on another boat, they wouldn't have gone straight out. There was nothing there except water—treacherous and consuming.

A few steps to the left and a spot appeared over Raizu's vision. At first he thought it was the light, but blinking didn't clear it. Something was out there, only visible when he turned his body a certain way. A ship perhaps? An island? Hopefully it was not just a really big bear.

Whatever it was, he determined it was there, real as the sun in the sky. Which—he noticed with an upset stomach—was sinking again. His daylight was running out.

The boat behind the rocks seemed to call to him, posing a question. But it was beyond reckless, beyond *reason* to get inside it, fashion oars from the sparce wood leftover, and sail into the blue.

Raizu would never do it. He was not spontaneous. He was not brave.

Letty and Majest were brave. If they had seen this secret shape across the water, they would have taken the risk. Letty had never stopped looking for her brother, and Majest had never stopped looking for her. They would not have stopped now at the edge of the water.

But would he?

Seti watched the boy with the arrows roam across the rocks—the boy who was not Majest Skylark but was calling his name. This boy seemed older than the Skylarks. Desperation clogged his every step as he ran.

Seti crouched between the rocks farther uphill, pulling the last hunk of bread from his pack. It was stale and frozen, but it gave him the energy to sit and think. *At least this is something I can tell the President. A stranger who knows the children and is looking for them, too.*

Someone who had lost them, like Seti.

It was an opportunity for Seti to recoup some information out of this, bring the Organization a prisoner. It was *something*, when right now he had nothing.

A noise cut through the lulling quiet of the bay. A high-pitched *shriek*, a metal-on-metal grate that seemed to come from all directions. The boy with the arrows was far down the beach now, a scuttling bug over the rocks. He had not made the noise. No human could have.

Seti knew what the sound had been.

Already on alert for violet sparks and cat-eyed faces, Seti leaped to his feet. Above his head was the edge of the cliff that would take him off the exposed beach, where he could vanish into the pale plains of rock and earth.

He reached a hand to the surface above, but a booted foot kicked it away with a *crack* that sent him reeling. A woman chuckled and Shayming's noxious face appeared over the edge.

"Got him," she said, her stringy hair flying. "Chami, over here."

Seti reassembled himself into a crouch on the hard rock below as Chami stepped next to her sister and then he was seeing double.

"Seti, Seti," crowed Chami. "It's almost a good thing you did so terribly with this task, or we wouldn't have gotten to visit you today. What a fortunate misfortune."

"Terribly?" Seti echoed in disgust. "I've been tailing the Skylarks for weeks. I only lost them yesterday."

"Surely, you had a number of opportunities to kill the children these past weeks," said Shayming. "You refused to get your paws wet and now the Organization has lost the Skylarks. Where have they gone? The President is not pleased."

Seti did not particularly feel like telling the twins where the Skylarks had gone. "If this is such a simple task," he said, "why don't you fly around the Hudson Bay and kill them yourselves?"

Shayming and Chami laughed, as if Seti had told a joke. The sound was like shattering glass and sliced straight through him.

"You're precious," said Chami with a porcelain giggle. "Fly? You know we can't teleport anywhere we haven't been before. At least, not without help from a signal like the one in that watch of yours."

Seti would've loved to take a flying leap and smack the twins senseless, but any momentary satisfaction from that would be outdone by the psychic torture he would suffer for it.

"Fine," he said instead. "Then why are you here?"

"Is that any way to talk to two people who care about you, Seti?" said Chami, her eyes glimmering. "We only want to help you."

"Help me *how?*"

"We're taking you back to the Organization," Shayming said. "The President has new plans for you."

Seti's heart sank. He could not go back to that building and its empty white walls. He also could not fight off the twins in his exhausted state. When Shayming landed next to him and slapped a hand to his shoulder he was helpless to the crush of her fingers, the glow in her eyes.

After seconds of Shayming's psychic work, all Seti could feel was the cold rub of the pocket watch against his side, his body swaying. She drained him wholly, as much as if he'd walked the entire Earth.

His coat shifted and he saw the number on the pocket watch had changed: one hand on XI and the other on XII. The eleventh hour.

Shayming noticed the way his gaze traveled and snatched the watch from Seti's belt. A strange protective spark flared up in Seti's gut, but his arm could not move fast enough to stop her. Shayming frowned into the watch's circular face but said nothing, just slid the watch back through Seti's belt and managed a grin.

Seti tried to conjure enough energy to spit at her feet. Not quite.

"Are we heading back now?" Chami asked from on top of the ledge.

"Right away," said Shayming.

Seti could do nothing to stop her as she cradled him tight and the world began to blur.

14

The first thing Majest and Letty told the village of Hiding was that they meant them no harm. Majest could not have imagined how two cranky, bone-tired kids would have threatened an entire town in the first place, but with a name like Hiding, its people were in no mood to be found.

"We can't trust anyone," the white-haired girl had explained, though only after the Skylarks had explained their intentions. "Terrible things happen on the mainland."

"We know," Majest had replied. "That's why we're here."

"This place is harder to see and even harder to reach. You got lucky, making it here."

The girl's name was Sedona Seacourt, and she was seven birth-years old like Majest. She and her sister had paddled to the island a year ago, fleeing their home in the south. Because of what, Majest hadn't asked.

"You never know who might want you dead, who might know your secrets," Sedona had warned. Majest and Letty had exchanged a startled, uneasy glance. "This place tries to make sure they never find you."

Majest had tried to laugh, but it had come out strangled. "That's *also* why we're here."

Now Sedona led the two of them into the center of the town—a circling plaza wrapped around a stone fountain. This place was nothing like Kartho's crumbling buildings and desperate scents. It was so alive—and so anxious. Up close, Majest could see the settling lines in the buildings, the squeaking wheels of the carts, the faces peering from windows. They were all staring at him and Letty.

"I'm going to take you to see Vosile," Sedona told them. "He's our leader. The one who discovered the island."

"So, he owns the place?" The thought of meeting one of those suspicious stares head-on had Majest's gut tied in knots.

"Who else would have that much claim to it?" said Sedona. "He's been here longer than any of us can remember. Apparently, he was gone for a few years once, but when he returned, he brought life-changing knowledge with him, sent from the gods. He made this place a home."

"Gone? Where did he go?" Letty asked.

"I wouldn't know. I'm fairly new here myself." Sedona's voice dropped. "But from what I've heard, he hasn't been the same since his journey."

Majest and Letty side-glanced each other.

Sedona quickly waved her hands. "Oh, no, don't look like that! Vosile is wonderful. He fixed up the village, treated the ground to grow our food, brought the materials we make our clothes from, and secured our water source." She gestured to the fountain. "There's a freshwater stream that runs through here and Vosile connected it to the center of town for us."

"That's not possible," Majest said.

Sedona gave him a hard blue look. "I think you'll find that here everything is possible."

"Food can't grow in this climate," Majest insisted. "And the only water around here is full of salt. Next, you'll be telling me little birds weave your clothes and foxes brush your hair. Things aren't this easy."

"They were in the old world," said Sedona, guiding them toward a nearby house. "And Vosile has brought the old world here to us."

Letty looked intrigued, but Majest couldn't help a grimace. "We live in the present, not the past."

"We use the past to make the present. And Vosile knows a lot about both." Sedona gave him a look. "If you want to stay here, you'll have to talk to him. Are you interested?"

"Yes," answered Majest, his spirits lifting. "At least for now. Sorry. Thank you." He blinked at Sedona in the daylight, the sun slanting off her snow-bright hair. It almost hurt to look at her.

Sedona caught his eye and smiled. "If you've traveled as far as you say, Vosile will have to keep you." They reached the door of a quaint wooden house and Sedona pushed it open without knocking.

A small boy stood in the doorway beyond. Probably Letty's age, he had an open, refreshing face and his hair was an inky Cognito black that reminded Majest of Letty's adventure on her own with the black-haired woman who had saved her life.

"Sedona!" the boy said.

"Vari, hello," greeted Sedona. "Look what I found."

"Hi," said Letty, a smile budding. The boy's eyes traveled to her face with a burst of interest as she went on, "I'm Aletta Skylark—Letty—and this is my brother, Maji."

Majest almost objected to her revealing herself like that, but this place was far from the mainland. No one would know them here.

"I'm Vari. How did you get here? Where did you come from?" Vari's eyes stayed trained on Letty's face.

"A long ways away," Sedona answered, not bothering to elaborate. "We're here to see Vosile. Is he fit to talk?" Glancing at Majest, she added, "Vari is Vosile's caregiver. Although our leader's mind is strong, his body is growing frail, I'm afraid."

"He's fine," Vari said, almost defensively. "He's finishing eating."

"Of course," Sedona said. "Thanks, Vari."

Sedona led Majest and Letty to the back of the house. Vari's cheeks colored as Letty passed him. The place was cozy, overflowing with sharp-scented cedar. Majest felt at home here, among the familiar warmth of a cottage—the wood chairs draped in caribou furs, the rusting water vat, the dishes on the shelves. He hadn't realized how much he had missed it all.

"Sedona?" a hoarse voice called.

Majest turned to see a man sitting in one of the chairs. His hair was in wisps and his eyes were the same aging brown as the wooden walls. A face in this land could not be old—it was impossible—and yet this man's face was sunken and hollow. Cheekbones punched forward around his eyes, he seemed haunted by the sag of his beak-like nose, the creases of his chin. Majest could not tell when he had stopped aging.

"I found two visitors outside," Sedona told him, Vari peering behind her.

"What?" Vosile's face was animated at once, his eyes coming to life against the bland tug of his skin. He looked over Majest and Letty, his lips working. "Well, look at that."

"This is Letty," said Sedona, "and her brother, Ma—"

"Majest Skylark, son of Maxine and Dagur, brother to Aletta and Lunesta," said Vosile. "This is a strange coincidence."

"How do you know who I am?" Majest's knees quaked. How would anyone know—unless they were the ones who had killed their mother? Had he and Letty stumbled into a trap?

"Your names are all over the mainland," said Vosile, chuckling. "Good heavens, you two. Everyone knows who you are. Children of the elements."

"I didn't know who they were," Sedona said to no one in particular.

"Because you don't hear things like I do," Vosile told her. "I hear the words in the wind, through the trees, in the water and the ground we walk on. I am told the Skylark siblings and their powers are famous across Cognito. You have your elder sister to thank for that."

"Lunesta actually told people about us?" asked Majest. He didn't like the sound of that.

"Everyone knows about our powers, then," Letty said in horror.

"Powers?" Sedona interrupted. "Like Komi's?"

Majest reeled. To hear their Deliverer's name from another's mouth sent clammy, cold tingles down his spine.

"The three of you have Komi in common," Vosile said, unfazed. "You were gifted with two of the elements, were you not? Sedona and her wind powers are a third. Three Messengers."

"Wind?" Letty burst. "You met Komi? I thought we were the only ones!"

"My dream was about a month ago," Sedona said, looking a bit flustered. "Komi told me I have a duty to the gods—to be a Messenger. I discovered he gave me wind powers, though I can't do much with them yet."

"I have water powers and Maji has earth powers," said Letty. "Maji's amazing! He moves trees and earth and talks to animals, too!"

"Really?" Sedona's gaze shot up to Majest's.

Majest felt suddenly self-conscious. "It's nothing," he muttered, staring at his boots. "Just a lot of practice and stuff."

"Enough of this in my house," said Vosile, waving a hand. "I already know about everything you can do and I don't need to hear it again. I assume the Skylarks will be staying here. Why don't you show them around?"

Majest frowned. This man made him uneasy, all his knowledge with no proper explanation. He wished he could talk to Letty alone.

"I'm happy to play tour guide," said Sedona, her light eyes settling on Majest.

"Can I come?" Vari asked, rocking on his feet. "Vosile, will you be all right if I go with them? It shouldn't be long."

"What do I look like, an old man?" Vosile grumped.

Yes, thought Majest.

"I haven't aged since the world was a much younger place and managed myself long before you were born. *Go*."

Saying their thanks and good-byes, the four of them turned and shuffled their way out of the warm house. Outside, it seemed brighter, sharper, like the sun had narrowed its rays on the island.

"Don't pay him any mind," Sedona said. "I'll introduce you."

She turned to the town center and called to a tall man looking their way. "Rapple, can I talk to you?"

As the man approached, his face closed up. "Sedona, who are these people?" he asked. "The whole town is already sharpening their knives."

Letty's eyes widened, but Sedona just said, "Vosile approved of them."

"Oh." It was like a shift of the wind, the way Rapple's face changed. All suspicion blown away. "In that case, welcome to Hiding. I'm Rapple Ardyn."

Majest, bewildered, dipped his head. "Thank you."

Rapple nodded and held up one finger. "Hold on." He swung around to the village behind him, addressing the faces in the windows, the huddles of whispering bodies in the plaza. "Everyone!" he called and waited until all eyes were on him. "Vosile has approved of our guests! So, will you please stop lurking around here like you're waiting for blood to come spilling out of the sky? I know you all have things to do. Shoo."

Majest almost laughed at the villagers' sour faces as they moved on.

"It's fine," Letty said. "I wouldn't expect a warm welcome from strangers."

"Why not?" Rapple said. "Everyone's family here—they just need a little softening up. Like frozen meat. They're great once you thaw 'em out." He chuckled, then pulled something red and smooth from his jacket pocket and crunched his teeth onto it.

"Are you wasting apples again?" Sedona said. "Jay will skin you alive if the Souleias are short on stock because you keep sneaking some out."

Majest quirked an eyebrow. "Who?"

"Jay. He lives down the street," said Vari, standing dutifully at Letty's side. "Makes medicines and teas, and generally knows everything about anything. Sometimes, he helps out around here and sometimes he doesn't."

"I'd like to meet him," said Letty.

"No you wouldn't."

"Why not?" she asked.

"Because he's a crazy, blind freak," put in a new voice.

The group whirled around to see yet another young girl coming up beside them. "You know it's true."

"Sunny." Sedona sighed.

Looking at her, Majest thought she must be Sedona's sister. The curves of their faces were identical.

Sedona explained, "Jay might be prickly, but he's saved plenty of lives. The fact that he's willing to help anyone at all after what he's been through is enough to excuse a bad temper."

"One time I asked him if he had any tea for a sore throat and he nearly threw me out the window," said Sunny.

"Well, you try being blinded and tortured by your own father."

"You don't know that's what happened!"

"It's not like anyone gets close enough to ask. Besides, you know what Vosile says, and it's no wonder the kid doesn't trust anyone." Sedona crossed her arms.

Majest couldn't tell if Sunny was the younger sister or if Sedona just acted like everyone's mother.

"But he lives in *Raylea's* house," Sunny protested, as if that explained everything. "She was so happy to be our doctor. It's because of her Jay's even alive. You'd think she would've rubbed off on her little rescue before she died."

"What about the rest of the town?" cut in Majest, overwhelmed. "You've got a leader who talks to the gods, a blind doctor who hates everyone—what else? Merchants with inferiority complexes? A band of silent warriors bent on stealing food from polar bears?"

"I'm the town teacher," Sunny boasted.

"You?" said Letty. "You're hardly older than I am."

"In a few years, I'll know everything," continued Sunny as her sister rolled her eyes. "More than Jay and Vosile *combined*. Then, I'll have to teach the rest of the town what I know. For instance, did you know if you lick a block of ice your tongue will get stuck there?"

"You only know because you were foolish enough to try," Sedona retorted, though not without affection.

Sunny looked pointedly at Letty, who giggled.

"Anyway," Sedona continued, shifting her gaze back to Majest, "I suppose it won't do you any good to shout out any more names of villagers—you'll have to meet us for yourselves." She gestured to Rapple, who had drifted away across the pebbled road. "You know Rapple now. His partner, Acillia, is expecting their baby soon."

"What about them?" Letty motioned to a small house on the right, two faces visible in the open window. "They keep looking over here."

"Quell and Idyllice," replied Vari. "The Souleia twins. They grow most of our food. When I was little, they'd visit my parents and give us fresh fruits and vegetables. They're the hardest workers in the whole village and the nicest people you'll ever meet."

Majest had never heard of *vegetables* and he only vaguely knew of fruit as the berries that grew in rare patches back home. He wrinkled his nose but didn't ask.

"Quell and Idyllice," Letty repeated. "Those are pretty names."

"Aletta's a pretty name, too," Vari told her.

Letty's face turned an obvious red, glaring at him when Majest laughed. Maybe Letty thought she was too young to start thinking about partnership, but Vari clearly had a different opinion.

"Vari," said Sedona, not missing the exchange, "will you please go find Cydinne for me? I think she could furnish an empty house for Majest and Letty."

"Oh, sure!" Vari scampered off and Sedona turned to Letty.

"Sorry about him," she said. "Was he bothering you?"

"No, no," Letty hedged, giving Majest another sharp glance as he chuckled again. Her face was redder than the stolen apple. "It's quite all right."

Before Majest had time to comment, Vari was back. He had a tall woman with him that had the longest hair Majest had ever seen and small eyes against elegant cheek bones.

"Cydinne Floodleaf," she said, dipping her head. Majest knew it would only be seconds before he forgot her name—he had learned so many today. "I hear you need a house. Do you need your own or would a room in someone else's do? I know Minka's family is one short since her brother passed away, and Linus and Sharlytte's son moved out last month."

Majest remembered the stares of the villagers, their suspicion, their alienation. He didn't like the idea of staying with one of them, of forcing himself onto a stranger.

Letty said, "Our own house would be wonderful."

Majest was halfway through agreeing when an irritated voice came from behind him. "What are you idiots doing out here? Don't you know there's a storm coming?"

Everyone turned, startled, and found a short, scrawny boy in a dark shirt, arms crossed and eyebrows raised. He looked around eight birth-years old or sixteen old-world years, but his demeanor was that of someone much older. His hair was a dark mess of dull blue-black slate.

"Jay," whispered Sedona.

In the silence, Majest heard the faintest rumblings of thunder.

"It won't be a big storm," Sunny said. "I don't see any lightning in the distance."

Jay's scowl darkened. He already reminded Majest of Lunesta—so much aggression on such a young face.

"I don't have to *see* anything," he said with enough force that Majest felt the urge to step back. "Not in the waking world. But I know you all need to get inside."

"He thinks he talks to the gods, like Vosile," Majest heard Vari mutter into Letty's ear. "A prophet, seeing things in dreams before they happen. Like, actually *seeing* them. Nobody believes him, though."

Majest thought of his father's stories—prophecies and predictive dreams, spirits and psychic visions. His father would have believed Jay. Dagur had believed in everyone.

Jay made no indication he had heard Vari's words, but his face pinched tighter. "Are you planning to redirect the wind as a sort of talent show for your new pet guests, Seacourt?"

Sedona blinked. "No, I—"

"Then why are you still standing here?"

Now Majest understood what Sunny and Vari had meant. Jay was as stormy as the approaching rain clouds themselves. And his eyes—they were sightless and filmy, sure, but even beyond that, they seemed to repel any trace of sunlight. They were dark and distant, focused on something far away.

What can you ever really trust when something unexpected might throw you off of a path you think you have memorized by heart? How can you move forward when you can't see where you're putting your feet? Majest's thoughts spun.

"Would you quit your staring?" Jay directed his next snap at Majest.

For once, he was speechless. "I—I wasn't—" Majest faltered.

"Just because I can't see doesn't mean I can't feel your clueless eyes on me." Thunder crashed in the distance; the sun began to take cover. "Now, if you'll excuse me, my tea is getting cold. Enjoy the storm."

Spinning on one heel, Jay marched himself back across the town's center with surprising accuracy to a small house and slammed the door behind him. The loud sound mingled with the growing thunder overhead.

Letty turned to Majest and gave him a reproachful look—the same look she gave him when he ate the last rabbit leg or got mud in her hair.

"Sorry," Majest muttered. "I didn't mean to…offend him."

"It's hard not to," said Vari. "He likes to be offended."

"But Jay was right about the storm coming," Sedona said. "We'd better get inside."

As Majest stared in the direction of Jay's house, his father's voice rumbled in his ears. *"Sometimes dreams take us places we cannot find on our own. And there are some people, prophets, whose dreams take them so far from reality, they no longer see the world in front of them—only the future in their nightmares. The curse of the prophet is nothing but blackness."*

His father's stories were true.

Sedona turned to Majest wearing a peculiar expression. "You're lucky," she said. "Looks like your arrival was just in time before the downpour."

"Yes," he replied, staring up at the darkening sky. "Looks like it was."

bang rattled the Organization's headquarters mid-afternoon, sending Shatter's armful of maps to her chamber's cold floor. She gasped without meaning to, scrambling to pick up her fallen work. Her heart had to restart in the aftershocks of the sound. Horrified questions bursting inside her, she ran to her door, throwing it open to peer into the hallway.

Nothing. Only whiteness.

The idea that she had imagined the sound was impossible. Ignoring the fact that she had an assignment, that she wasn't supposed to wander around, curiosity grabbed her and propelled her down the hall.

Shatter went to the only room she imagined could have made such a racket. The door to the laboratory stood open, bent backward like a broken limb. Bright, anxious voices pooled into the hall.

Then, another quick *bang-bang-bang.*

"Malory!" a voice called. Caiter. "Malory, *stop!*"

Shatter entered the room to see Malory standing at the center of the laboratory holding an unsealed vial above his head. Foul smoke poured from its rim, as if something inside it had exploded. It shifted around Malory's face, rendering him ghastly. Several scientists hung back around him, refusing to step too close.

Except for one.

"Put the cover back on, Malory," Caiter insisted, his face a flustered scarlet. "Someone's going to get hurt."

Malory made a sound that was half-cackle, half-screech—it cracked glass. Behind his fogged glasses, his eyes were black pits. He already had a syringe in the vial, filling it with crimson liquid before holding it up to the light.

"Danger is the most important ingredient, Caiter," he said. "This is the perfect batch."

"If this is the one, why don't you put it down and fetch Lady President?" Caiter's tone was careful, cautious, a gently thrown stone trying not to ripple the surface. "She'll be thrilled you've finished."

"I think I get first dibs on my own work, thank you very much."

"We have to follow the mission—"

"I have my own mission," Malory growled.

Shatter stepped back and gripped the doorway as Malory pointed the syringe toward Caiter.

"And it requires a pinch of assistance."

Caiter edged backward. "What are you talking about?"

"You've been a friend to me, right? And revenge is my favorite cause."

"I don't—"

Malory took a careless step forward, syringe still aimed at Caiter's neck. His smile was all knives. "What do you say?"

"Malory, stop," Caiter stammered, his hands in front of him, pleading. No one else in the room moved. "The President wouldn't allow you to—"

"No!" Shatter's voice rang out from the doorway before she could stop it, echoing across the domed room. Every eye in the laboratory swung to her.

Malory leaned away from Caiter with a casual slide. "Shatter Seacourt," he said.

The sound of her name on this madman's tongue made Shatter instantly nauseous. She remembered when she had first arrived here, when Malory had been nothing more than an unpleasant disturbance. Now, he had his own gravitational pull. *Revenge?* Anyone with such a selfish purpose could drag the Organization right out of orbit.

Everyone was still staring at Shatter, whose face went hot under the glare of the lights. "You were all going to stand by while Malory injected Caiter with that stuff?" she called out louder than she'd meant to.

"Malory is our greatest advantage over the Powers," said a voice from the back. The crowd parted to reveal a cherry-haired boy with enormous eyes. He walked forward. "We can crush them with demon energy on our side. It's the first step to a new world like the old world."

Malory turned a charmed smile on the boy. "That's right, Ohanzi," he said. "How would you like to be the next Seti Sinestre? Minus the terrible taste in footwear."

Caiter had regained enough composure to step between them. "I won't let you test that serum without permission," he said. "What if it doesn't work? What if it kills—?"

"Do shut up," said Malory, and Caiter's face crashed. "I thought you at least would wag your tail and do this for me."

"I'll do it," said Ohanzi.

The room hushed all at once.

Caiter stepped forward. "Ohanzi, don't—"

But Malory's eyes already had a wicked black glow, and in an instant, he had Ohanzi's arm, too. The syringe went in, and then the serum, and then it was over.

At once, all murmurs were silent. Even the whir of the machines seemed soundless. The watching scientists had turned to ice—Ohanzi the most frozen of all.

The boy's mouth fell open with a pop.

A second passed. Another. Then, another.

"No…" Caiter whispered. "Oh, no, Ohanzi, *no!*"

The last *no* rang out and then Ohanzi was on fire.

The fire was inside him, not around him. It blanched his skin, steamed over his eyes. The boy crumpled to his knees, body in a violent forward arc. He screamed, eruptive and wretched, but it was not a human sound. Shatter did not want to watch, but curiosity made her.

Somewhere between his screams, Ohanzi's body began to change. Invisible flames seared him, skin burning crimson and then charcoal, his hair dissolving from his scalp. His eyes went white, then black, then unseeing. Claws and spines sprang from his fingers, face, shoulders—and what was left of his mouth foamed with blood. He became a monster, jutting teeth and body parts linked in all the wrong places.

Malory howled.

Someone vomited.

Ohanzi's mangled body fell to the floor, unmoving, a pile of ash.

"I told you!" screamed Caiter. "I knew he would die."

Except Ohanzi was not dead. His body had disintegrated, but in its place rose a dark, massive shadow, as if a black void had opened its mouth and swallowed the boy whole. The cloud rose, hissing and spitting. It was almost words—almost *"island,"* almost *"destroy."*

Shatter quaked as the shadow evaporated with one final, unintelligible wail. Ohanzi or not, it was gone, taking with it any evidence it had ever been.

For a long time, there was a horrified, shell-shocked silence.

"What have you done?" spat Caiter. His usual flustered appearance had gone through the roof with Ohanzi. The look on his face now was a dangerous sea of calm.

Malory, still leaning on his desk, gave a dreamy smile. "More than just inject demon energy into a human being," he said. "I *created* a demon. Gold star for me."

Horror-struck faces greeted him from all corners of the room. Shatter heard more sounds of vomiting and muffled whimpers.

Malory took up his vial of serum again, still half-full. "Who's next?" he asked.

With a sudden cry, Caiter sprung forward, hands slamming into Malory's shoulders. They tumbled to the ground in a flurry of wheeling arms and legs. The vial went flying.

"You can't do this anymore!" Caiter screamed. Other scientists rushed forward, pulling them apart. *"You can't!"*

Shatter couldn't do this anymore, either. "I'm getting help!" she cried.

She backed out of the doorway and bolted down the hall, searching for someone, *anyone*. Her stomach squeezed, threatening to pump her heart up and out of her throat. She had to stop several times, hands on her knees, her hair tangling down her back.

"Shatter," said a voice. Two voices.

Chami and Shayming materialized, a body slumped between them.

As if Shatter's heart could take any more today.

"Shatter," Chami said again, as Seti Sinestre struggled to keep himself upright in their grasp. "What's the matter? Shouldn't you be in your room?"

Shatter took a breath. She still saw Ohanzi's fire, heard the screams. "In the laboratory—there was—Malory is—"

From the corner of her eye, she watched Seti lift his head. Seeing him here took over her senses. It grew more and more difficult to remember what she needed to say, why she needed help.

"We'll report it to the President," said Shayming.

"It's an emergency," Shatter insisted. "Caiter is in trouble. Please."

"We. Will. Report it. Thank you, Shatter."

The twins kept walking, pulling the half-conscious Seti toward the President's room.

"Wait! Are you going to kill him?" Shatter blurted.

Chami turned her head back a fraction of an inch. "We hope not," she said.

Shayming glanced at her sister, her mouth tight. "What she means is that his fate is uncertain. As of now."

"I…" Shatter's mind reeled. "I understand. But—please send someone to the laboratory immediately."

"Yes, yes," said Shayming, waving her off.

"Say good-bye to Seti," added Chami. "This could be the last time you ever see him."

Shatter knew she shouldn't, but she let her eyes catch on Seti anyway. His head was bent over, his gold eyes invisible under the fall of his hair. He was so small. Defeated.

He didn't want to be part of the Organization, did he? He didn't want any of this.

Neither had she. Not Seti, not the scientists, none of it. They wanted a better world.

No more curiosity. No more meddling. Only the work I'm assigned.

Without her permission, a single tear slipped from her eye and fell to the floor.

Seti's surroundings came to him in shivery waves. The hard click of linoleum. The strain of Shatter's voice, a lighthouse in the fog. A knock. A whir. A white room. The pressure on his head easing, just enough to feel Chami and Shayming let go of him.

"The toy soldier returns," said a voice.

The world cleared, and Seti's eyes burned as the light of the President's chambers seared him. She stood over him, bony arms at her sides, pristine buttoned coat. "Chami. Shayming. You may go now."

"Go?" Chami sounded disappointed. "But what—?"

"Attend to the commotion in the laboratory. I give you my word you will hear of Seti's fate soon."

Chami made a soft sound, but as Shayming touched her sister's shoulder all she did was throw Seti one last glance. It looked like a good-bye.

As they made their exit, their feet made no sounds. Seti wondered if anything in this building even existed or if it was all a mirage.

Without the twins' support, Seti pitched to one side, leaning hard against a glass case. Someday, he would learn a way to counteract the effects of psychic magic.

"So," he rasped. "Bring me here to yell at me or to put a knife in my chest?" It made no difference to him. Though he did wonder if the President actually had the backbone to try and kill him for what he'd done—or what he *hadn't* done.

"You let me down, Seti," said the President. Her midnight eyes seared him. "I can't imagine what could have kept you from doing what I asked."

"Many things. One of them being that you asked murder of me. I prefer to kill those who deserve it."

"This was *not* murder. It was the first step to everything."

"You don't think I believe you're doing this for a new and equal world, do you? You're jealous of the other Skylarks. You couldn't *stand* how they were chosen for power and not you, so you created a phony army of psychopaths and old-fashioned gadgets to kill them under the disguise of some larger purpose because you're too much of a coward to kill them yourself."

The President's skin went white. "You...you said *other* Skylarks," she said. "You didn't just say Skylarks. Why did you say that?"

"I know who you are," said Seti. His head ached—this was such a bother. "Everyone knows about you, and everyone knows about the Organization.

They just don't connect the two together. I saw right through you, Lunesta Skylark."

The President's eyes flew into two wide moons. Seti could see it so easily after weeks of tailing Aletta and Majest. The angle of their noses, the crease between their brows.

"You thought you were so clever," Seti went on. "You thought you could grow out your hair and tumble into the arms of murderers, take out your little brother and sister without lifting a finger. You thought this was worth it. For *two stupid kids*."

"I did what I had to do," growled the President—Lunesta. "Their powers aren't natural. I had to get rid of them, don't you see?"

"Not really," said Seti. "You're a coward and a hypocrite. Employing psychics and planning to let your scientists use demon energy to make a more dangerous version of me?" Seti's words went molten. "Chami told me about Malory."

"I couldn't take any chances," said Lunesta, gasping like Seti had thrust a knife into her side. "Chami and Shayming found me crossing the forest alone and told me they understood me. They helped me find Malory, who I already knew about. He told me of a place far away, where the past lived on behind an ancient waterfall. It had laboratories, technology, everything. Malory had the demon energy, plans to keep the greenhouse working, ideas for weaponry, for claiming the place as our own—and I had to accept."

"You didn't," said Seti.

"It *was* too much for two children. You're right about that. I had to broaden my goals. This place, I knew, could restart the modern world. People liked that idea. They came to me."

"Because they think killing the Powers will somehow make this world the way it used to be?"

"Maybe they're right," said Lunesta, shrugging. "Everything has fallen into my hands so far. I rather like where this is going."

"You're disgusting," Seti told her. "You're selfish and incompetent, and you lie about every last motive up your sleeve, yet you *still* have the audacity to wonder why I refused to help you. If it weren't for this damned pocket watch, you never would have seen my face again."

"The watch," repeated Lunesta feverishly. "Of course. You never got to see how it worked, did you? I am sorry for that. At least you didn't dare see what would happen if you tried tossing it away."

Seti ignored this, glancing around the room for a way out. He found none.

"Are you going to kill me?" he asked.

"I'd like to," Lunesta said after some time. "However, it would be unwise."

"Why is that?"

"I'm quite certain I will have use for you and your watch later. You're of the old world. Perhaps you will become part of our new one, once the Powers are taken care of."

"And do you expect me to wait around here until that happens?"

Lunesta's mouth twitched. "I imagine you'd grow quite mad by then and turn me quite mad in the process. Perhaps you'd even escape, and I can't have that. No, Seti, I have just the place for you." She gestured to the glass structure he was leaning on.

He turned to look at it. It was the size of a large coffin, upright and clearly constructed by someone unfamiliar with glasswork. It had tubes and wires veining through it in reds and blues, buttons on its outer rim.

"Are you planning on incubating me like a chicken egg?" Seti asked.

Lunesta glowered. "Oh, you're no fun—you know all about these things, don't you? Never mind. I got the idea for a sleep chamber from a book I found here. Whoever owned this place before us must have written it, though the initial plan involved too much electrical nonsense. Here, we use magic. Chami and Shayming's energy-draining magic, to be specific. You are familiar, yes? No need for old-world chemicals."

Seti was fully alert now, his blood pounding. This was far worse than the thought of being held prisoner. Put to sleep, he would have nothing but dreams.

"You can't force me in there," he said, edging away from the glass. "Do you honestly think you could beat me in a fight? I'd cut you to ribbons."

"I don't *need* to fight you," said Lunesta. She took a few steps forward, steel boots clicking like a countdown on the floor. "One cry from me and in come Chami and Shayming and a force dozens' strong. I am their president and they are sworn to protect me."

She was right, Seti knew. One scream and the entire Organization would be on top of him; Seti would be killed within minutes.

Still, he said, "I won't go into that chamber unless you agree to my terms."

"And what might that be?"

"You'll actually let me out, for starters. Then, you'll set me free once the Organization has run its course. And it *will* run its course," he added, as Lunesta was about to protest. "Lastly, I want your word that you won't let anyone else end your life until I return. I'm starting to think I might want that honor to be mine."

"We could have accomplished so much together, Seti," said Lunesta.

"Is that a yes or a no?"

"The first, at least, I can promise." She looked almost hurt. "Despite how much I'd like to leave you rotting for a couple of lifetimes. Now get in."

"You are a child," Seti told her, crossing the room. When he swung the chamber door open, much harder than needed, he noted the tank of violet gas attached to it, the sickly aroma of ozone and sweat. Chami and Shayming had him *again*.

Lunesta followed him, towering over his shoulder. "And what are you?" she asked.

"Someone you're wrong about," said Seti.

"Someone I won't have to speak to for a very long time."

"We'll see about that."

"Good-bye, Seti Sinestre."

I'm going to kill you, Seti decided as the door closed behind him.

Chami and Shayming's energy coughed through the filthy tubes, wires sparking violet. Lunesta pressed a button and the prick of an IV needle jabbed into Seti's wrist. The air went gray and fuzzy—then dark, and Seti swayed backward, falling into nothingness. His senses faded, and he had only one thought: this was not the end.

16

The storm did not pass quickly.

Letty only had a few minutes to snoop around their new home before the pounding began, filling in the island's dips and valleys with slushy white. Thunder rolled its wheels overhead and lightning staked tree after tree. Majest cringed every time, as if he could feel the forest's pain.

They stood at the window, which was merely a gap in the wood with a thick curtain tucked into it. Letty thought, for a village so caught up in the impossible, they should have at least invested in some proper insulation.

The door swung wide, and in came Vari for the fifth time with a chest of extra clothes. He had been bringing in chairs and pillows and utensils from Cydinne for nearly an hour—all soaked, now.

"We really don't need three oil lamps," Letty protested. "You shouldn't be going out in this kind of storm."

Vari set down his box and stationed himself next to her. He wasn't standing any closer than Majest, but his presence was something different altogether. Letty watched a raindrop slide through the black hair curling at the nape of his neck and pressed her lips together.

"I don't mind," Vari said, darting off to stack plates into a cupboard. "No one's expecting me back home, and you can *never* have too many lamps."

Letty frowned as he returned to her side, their shoulders brushing. She wasn't sure how she felt about him butting into their new life here, despite his generosity and the warmth of his smile. Outside, the storm seemed to let up, going begrudgingly to the west in search of somewhere new to drown.

"We have thunder like this all the time," Vari said, his eyes on Letty's face. "You don't have to be afraid."

Majest made a terrible attempt to cover up a snort.

Letty scowled, reddening. "Afraid? I love thunderstorms. The more lightning, the better." She said it harsher than she'd intended, and not with complete honesty.

Vari's smile didn't even twitch. "I like them, too. Especially when it rains in the summer. Then we have more water to drink."

A knock sounded on the wooden door and Vari leaped to answer it. When Letty joined him, Majest behind her, she found Sedona's windblown hair and troubled face.

"What's the matter?" asked Vari.

"There was another boy outside," said Sedona, speaking mostly to Majest. "Rapple found him collapsed in the woods soaked straight through."

"A boy?" Majest repeated.

"You didn't take him to Jay's, did you?" asked Vari.

"If he caught a cold, he needs medicine. He felt like he had an awful fever," said Sedona. "It's not every day a stranger turns up here, especially when you two did just this morning."

Majest's eyebrows went up. "Is that why you came to us? Is something the matter?"

"He didn't look dangerous, just disheveled. We tried to wake him up and question him, but all he would say was your two names over and over again."

"I'm sure Jay loved that," Vari muttered.

"You should come see him," Sedona went on.

"I'm sure Jay will love that even more."

But Majest was already through the door, Letty following him into the soaked streets. Her thoughts were dizzying as Sedona pulled ahead, leading them to the house next door. Their boots sloshed against the stone paths, the sky sending its last wet regards.

Majest knocked, and Letty caught up in time to feel the whip as the door blew back.

An annoyed young face peered out. "Who is it now?" Jay snapped.

"Majest Skylark. The one who offended you earlier—uh, I'm really sorry. Can we see the boy Rapple and Sedona found? The one looking for us?"

Jay's sightless eyes narrowed in displeasure. "Oh," he said. "You. I had a dream you would come here, you know. Woke up with the worst headache."

Majest stared at him. "I—"

"Well, don't just stand there. Get in here."

The house was nowhere near as gloomy as Jay himself. It was clean, almost cozy. Fuzzy chairs were strewn across the front room in neat little pockets; miniature tables kept them company, including one holding an engraved metal box.

Jay gave Letty no time to stop and sightsee, feeling his way to the warm back hall of the cottage with irritated urgency. "I can't quite fathom what it is that makes you people storm into my house like I'm running an emergency room," he said as he went.

Majest made a face.

In the back room, there were no windows or lamps. The only light drizzled in from down the hall, flickering with the shadows of their movement. It was less clean in here, Letty noted, with tables draped in thick, itchy cloth and rows of bottles, plants, and sealed-tight powders. A heavy herbal scent penetrated the room everywhere and tipped-over liquids and teas stained the floor.

Letty was instantly overwhelmed.

"Your boy's over there," said Jay, giving a loose, approximate gesture to Letty's left. "And quit sniffing about before you breathe in something poisonous."

Letty turned to find an empty corner of the room, where a bed had been fashioned out of a few wooden planks. Someone lay there now, curled on his side, lashes twitching in feverish sleep. Though water had drenched his hair to a dark bronze, she immediately recognized the jacket, the laced boots, the sheath of arrows tipped onto the dirty floor.

"Raizu!" Letty and Majest exclaimed at once, rushing to his side.

"Mind the supplies," Jay muttered.

Majest reached Raizu first, kneeling on the floor next to him and putting a gentle hand to his forehead. *"Hímin,"* Majest whispered, his eyes huge and greener than ever. "How did he get all the way out here?"

Letty touched Raizu's cheek. It was like ice. "He must have tracked us."

"That's impossible," Jay said. "The island is only visible from shore if you're standing in just the right place. It's one of the ways we've kept it hidden."

"Plus, crossing the Hudson Bay is nearly impossible without a seal helping you," said Majest. Bewilderment rustled the freckles on his cheeks.

Behind him, Sedona and Vari fidgeted. Sedona stepped forward, demanding, "Majest, who in the world—?"

"M-Majest?" At the sound of the voices above him, Raizu blinked groggily, peeling long lashes apart. His eyes were unfocused as he stared up at Majest. "You're here? Really here?" He tried to smile. "I was so afraid you wouldn't—"

"Finally, he's making some sense." Sedona pushed past Majest to lean over Raizu. "So, you *do* know Letty and Majest? You're friends with them?" Her expression wasn't inhospitable, but it wasn't warm, either. "Tell them what you told Jay and I."

Somewhere in the room, Jay sighed.

At the pummeling of questions, Raizu's face went even paler. "Oh. Um, well—I came here to this, uh, island—it is an island, right?—and, er, I was looking for Letty and Majest, and I saw their rowboat—at least, I think it was their boat—if not, I stole someone else's, which was pretty rude—and it was on the beach, and—"

"*Stop,*" said Jay, cutting through the senseless story. "For the love of—if you all are done kissing awake your senseless prince here, would you kindly take him out of my house?"

Raizu shivered. "I didn't—if—I am *so* sorr—" He broke off to cough.

"What you should be apologizing for is sailing across the Hudson Bay during a storm. Look, I made sure you didn't get hypothermia, and since that's about all I'm good for, I think we're done here. Don't make me stand here and listen to what I already know."

Letty glanced at Jay with the uneasy regard she might have once given her sister. "You knew about Raizu coming here?"

"Of course I *knew.*" Jay glowered in Letty's general direction but didn't elaborate. Letty saw Vari roll his eyes in disbelief.

"I—I don't mean to be a problem," Raizu put in, his voice frail. His eyes looked glassy, and now he radiated nearly as much heat as a cooking fire.

"You're not a problem," Majest told him before standing up and whirling on Jay. "He looks really sick. You can't send him off without something to help him."

"I'm not a doctor," said Jay.

"But you have medicine," Sedona ventured.

"Not for strangers I don't."

"He's not a stranger," said Letty hotly. "He's our friend."

"No friend of mine," Jay said, but Letty's desperation seemed to soften his shell. He crossed the room, fingers running over the table of bottles until they closed around one filled with brown-green liquid. He held it out to Majest. "That should work well enough."

"This means a lot to me," Majest said, taking it. "We owe you—"

"Whatever, whatever, now *get out*," said Jay, the eye of the storm gone. His sightless gaze was a downpour over everyone in the room. "You Skylarks brought this burden on my village—now, get it out of my house."

A stab of resentment pierced between Letty's ribs. "We didn't bring Raizu here," she clarified. "He came on his own to find us. He could have died. He's not a burden."

Jay laughed once—a dry, miserable thing. "I'm not talking about Raizu."

Raizu had never been sick like this before. He put as much caution into his health as he did anything else. He stayed away from anyone who so much as coughed, didn't lay a finger on suspicious food even in the scarcest of winters, and kept up his hygiene no matter how much Kallica teased him. He dressed for the weather, and—up until recently—would have sooner cleaned Inertia's dirt floors for a month than go out in a storm.

How had the Skylarks already influenced him so much?

Raizu lay in an aching, dry-throated haze until the outside air hit him. Then he realized he was being carried and feeling was returning to his limbs. Not good feelings, though—flashes of boiling heat and icy cold. They raged through his body and nearly made him wish he could pass out again.

Nearly.

I have to wake up. He panicked. His senses screamed, veins catching fire. He tried to surface but could not break through. In desperation, he tried to fling his body, make it do anything, and he felt himself crash against something wooden. Starbursts of red pain erupted behind his eyelids.

Raizu gasped, waking with a start.

"Þakka himininn," came a relieved voice. "I was scared you'd never come around. Letty's been asleep in her room for a while now, but she was up worrying, too."

Majest. Raizu couldn't see him; he couldn't see anything but darkness, which tightened his already-aching chest. A sound came from his throat, words trying to form, but it erupted into a coughing fit.

"Don't try to talk," Majest told him. "Save your voice. Do you think you could swallow some medicine? Let me get a lantern."

Moments later, a dull light flooded Raizu's surroundings. He was in a small bedroom framed with wooden walls and a wide, curtained window. Someone had laid him on a bed, seal blankets snuggled up around him. In the corner of the room, Majest had a lantern gripped in his teeth, rummaging through a bag with both hands. The light jostled with his movement, casting strange, swooping shadows over the walls.

When he turned to Raizu and set the lantern on a side table, Majest was holding a small bottle and a damp cloth. He pressed it to Raizu's burning forehead, cooling its fire, though it did little to help the sopping mess of his hair soaking the pillow.

"Hopefully, this isn't poison," said Majest, popping the cap off the bottle. The bitter reek it emitted made them both wrinkle their noses. "It smells like the way Jay makes me feel."

With Majest's help, Raizu sat up, head spinning. He had to blink in pain a few times before he could see through the black pools of his vision. After a sip or two of the sharp medicine, he slumped back down.

"I've been…" Raizu managed, "looking…for you. And Letty."

"I gathered that," said Majest, sitting down on the bed next to him and crossing his legs. He put the lantern into his lap. "Why, exactly? I mean, certainly we have our charms, but you didn't have to *drown* yourself if you wanted to—"

"I had to tell you something," Raizu interrupted.

"What was important enough for you to come out this far?"

Raizu turned his head to see Majest on top of the blankets, looking intent. The lantern set off the green tints in his hair and lit up the planes of his face, making him look as if he were Element Earth itself, not just its Messenger. "When I got home, my older brother—Arathiel—told me about a group of people calling themselves the Organization."

"*The* Organization? That's a little pretentious."

"They told Arathiel they want to create a new world. Without… supernatural powers."

Majest's face tightened. "What do you mean?"

"It's led by some woman calling herself the President. One of her recruiters specifically told Arathiel they were looking for you—the Skylarks."

Majest's face fell like a fallen tree. "*That's* who is after Letty and I?" His voice trembled with a vulnerability that didn't seem to belong there. "How—how could they know? Letty didn't even know what her powers were until—" He swallowed. "Who—who is this President? Did your brother say?"

Raizu, who was usually the hysterical one, wasn't sure what to say. "N-no, he didn't know. Could anyone else have found out about your powers?"

"We kept it a secret in our family, but apparently, Lunesta has been telling all of Cognito about us."

"Lunesta?"

"Our older sister. She left shortly after we got our powers. She hated that we had them."

A long silence ensued before, almost absently, Majest reached over to pull the rag back up to Raizu's forehead where it had slipped down his face.

Then Raizu said, "Lunesta. She left because she was…*jealous* of you?"

Majest's gaze drifted toward the hallway. "I guess, but she had a problem with everything Letty and I did. Never mind that these powers are more trouble than they're worth."

There was something there, Raizu thought, though he couldn't place it. The fever had him practically thinking backwards. "Would Lunesta have thought you and Letty were more trouble than you're worth, too?" he managed.

Majest turned to Raizu with a start. "Wait. You don't think it's *her*, do you?"

A wave of fever took the world out from under Raizu. "What's…her?"

"Lunesta! What if she's leading the Organization? Quick, Raizu—what else did your brother say?"

Raizu fought to remember. "Something about…the place of red…?" No, that wasn't right. "Red trees, or the wooden red, or—"

"Redwoods," Majest finished, and he sounded numb. "That's where my parents came from. A group called the Redwoods. They used to live there, before they fled to the forest."

"That's what my brother said," Raizu realized in a rush. "The ones the President's parents knew—the Redwoods."

"*Ekki gott,*" said Majest in a voice like crackling ice. His hands shook as he swept hair back from his forehead. "My own sister. How could we have hurt her that much?"

"Don't worry," said Raizu, though he knew how lame the words sounded. "At least she won't find you here."

"*You* found us," Majest said dryly.

"I almost didn't, even though I knew where you were going. All things considered, it was a one in a million chance you ended up being exactly where I wanted to find you." He coughed. "I, ah…usually don't take these kinds of chances."

Majest stared at him. "That's what I don't understand. I barely know you and I already owe you more than I could pay back in a lifetime."

Before Raizu could respond, a burst of agony shot through his head in one long needle-like motion and he pinched his eyes shut, the rag falling down to cover them. Majest dutifully moved it back into place.

"I—" Raizu took a shaky breath through cracked lips. "When I heard about the Organization, I had to warn you. More than that, I—"

He had to break off once more to cough; this time a bout of foul-tasting mucus rose up in his throat. He forced himself to swallow it.

"You what?" Majest reached over Raizu's head to retrieve a water canister from the table next to the medicine bottle. He twisted it open and held it out. "Here, drink this."

Raizu sipped at the cold water gratefully until his throat stopped raging. "I wanted to help you," he rasped. He didn't say the rest of it: that he felt pulled toward the two of them, toward the unknown, toward adventure and purpose even at the cost of danger.

Majest blinked. Raizu couldn't gauge the feeling in his expression. "Help us," he repeated, the words sounding like a question. "After you already saved my sister, brought her back to me, gave us food, and traveled the whole of Cognito just to have this conversation, nearly freezing to death in the process." He shook his head again. *"Hímin."*

"I wouldn't be a bother," Raizu protested. "I swear, I can help with more than tracking. If there's anything that you want me to—"

"Raizu." Majest was laughing now, full and joyful. *"Hímin, hímin.* That means *heavens,* which means I'm speechless. You've got a fever. You don't know what you're saying. You don't want in on this, believe me."

"I do," Raizu said, hearing himself as if from a distance.

"And force me to owe you my life all over again?" Majest sighed, though the corners of his mouth remained turned upward. "I suppose I can't stop you, but honestly."

Raizu gave a tentative smile in return, his cheeks warm.

"It would be nice to have a friend out here," Majest told him. "Especially if Lunesta...wow. Yeah. I don't think I want one more thought about the Organization until I'm awake enough to properly freak out about it."

Raizu had to agree. "We should sleep," he whispered.

Majest made a move as if to douse the lantern. "Do you need anything?"

"I..." All at once, the thought of the pitch-black darkness made Raizu's chest seize. "Wait. Majest?"

"Yeah?"

Raizu felt his cheeks burn, and not only from the fever. "Can you leave the lantern on for me? The darkness and I...don't quite get along."

To Raizu's relief, Majest nodded, only one blink of surprise betraying the disbelief he must have felt upon hearing an almost full-grown boy was afraid of the dark.

"Sure," he said, and set the lantern on the table next to Raizu. It was not only bright, but warm—the kind of warmth that took away fear.

"Thank you," Raizu told him, and he meant it.

17

Only one day had passed since Ohanzi's ruin and Seti's disappearance, but already, everything had changed. The laboratory had been washed clean, Malory detained in the Organization's basement. Nafuna and Caiter had covered Ohanzi's duties. Chami and Shayming had disappeared back into the forest, out on another top secret order.

Shatter had stayed in her room, finding the white hallways a landscape too dangerous to forego alone. She hadn't heard of Seti's fate, or how Caiter was doing, or what the President's plan was now that Malory wasn't allowed anywhere near the laboratory.

What was worse was that Shatter had no appetite for going after those answers. At least, not enough to see the President about them.

Lunesta Skylark, Shatter thought, staring at the wall above her desk. She remembered when the woman had burst into her hometown, spilling tales of two monstrous siblings who wielded dangerous power like swords. The President had seemed so helpless then. Lost. *Young.*

Her name and plans stretched far beyond the Skylarks now. Shatter was proud to stand beside her. But with no Seti, a demon on the loose, and Malory's ideas scratched, Shatter was afraid the Organization had come to a standstill.

She wished there were something she could do. Something more than stare glassy-eyed at her new assignment: the maps Ohanzi had borrowed for his personal research.

Shatter followed the red lines of the recruiters, the blotches of towns and markets covering the southern pines of Cognito's woods. Ohanzi had sketched in his own path approximating Seti's journey using the twins' coordinates. Shatter traced that dark line now, until it ran into the edge of the Hudson Bay.

Chami and Shayming had found Seti there, not a Power in sight. If he had been tailing the Skylarks, they would have gone to the coast, too.

"They couldn't have disappeared," Shatter murmured, chewing on her thumbnail. "Seti wouldn't have lost them after all that. Not unless... unless..."

She had spent the last twenty-four hours trying to forget Ohanzi, but she remembered what he had said. *Destroy. Island.*

Sure enough, Ohanzi had drawn a small circle in the bay, just off the coast. Had he known about an island not on any Organization map? Somewhere not even the twins knew how to get to? Somewhere the Skylarks could have gone, with Seti unable to follow?

Shatter's thoughts raced, stirring up the curiosity she'd been pushing down for weeks. Ohanzi might have been on the brink of a discovery that could have changed everything. And now, demon or not, he still knew what the boy with the red curls had known.

If Ohanzi found the Skylarks, the shadows would take them, too.

It was strange for Majest to wake up without Letty beside him. For weeks, he had awoken with hair matted against his coat, pointy elbows in his ribcage. Together, they'd wiggle each finger and toe awake and find the strength to dig through their food sack.

This morning, Majest's hands were warm. His feet, boot-free, were toasty. His eyelashes weren't even trying to frost together. He was refreshed. Comfortable. Full. And the most novel of all: *safe.*

Maybe *safe* wasn't the right word, not with Lunesta and her Organization out there somewhere, but it was hard for him to worry too much with a roof over his head.

Somehow, this is all because of Raizu, Majest noted, stretching. The sunlight filtering through the window felt heavenly on his face as he sat with his legs dangling off the bed for a moment. The stranger with the arrows—he was the hero.

And he was gone, Majest realized, jolting sideways. The other side of the bed was rumpled, but empty. Majest listened, however he heard no wheezy breathing; the only noise was the gulls whining from the shore. As sick as Raizu was, he shouldn't have been going anywhere.

Majest rose, rubbing sleep from his eyes and shoving his feet into a pair of socks before they hit the cold wood floor. He moved down the hallway, stopping to glance into Letty's room—empty, too.

"Where are you two?" he called, skidding into his new kitchen.

"Here," said a cheerful voice.

Raizu sat at the wooden table, bundled into a blanket, his slender hands wrapped around a steaming cup. He grinned at Majest, his violet eyes bright. "Do you always sleep so late? The sunrise got tired of waiting and went ahead without you."

Majest exhaled. "Shouldn't you be in bed?"

"Sorry," replied Letty, coming in from the front room. She was carrying a basket loaded with colorful, round objects that looked like playthings, which she set in front of Raizu. "We woke up early to make tea."

"Tea?" Majest repeated, eyeing the basket. "That's not tea."

"That's a fruit basket," answered Letty. "Vari got it from Quell. The *tea* is on the table." She nodded to a pot across from Raizu. "Vari's been showing me all the different food they grow here, and some of it is really amazing."

"Vari was over already this morning?" he asked.

"We've been out since dawn," said Letty, pulling out what Majest remembered was an apple and taking a bite. "He took me to the market."

Majest's mouth twitched. He had been looking forward to discovering the village's secrets together. "Oh," he said. "He didn't have to do that."

Letty smiled. "It's awfully nice of him, I think. He's been such a good friend to us already."

Majest was about to retort that Vari's intentions were hardly those of someone wanting to be Letty's *friend*—and hadn't Letty been griping about Vari just yesterday?—when Raizu sneezed, and dragged his attention sideways.

"Are you sure it's okay that you're up?" Majest asked.

"My fever broke," Raizu told him. "I'm coughing a lot less, too. Whatever was in that stuff Jay gave you, it was practically magic."

"That's great. I'm glad you're feeling better."

"Thanks," Raizu murmured, staring down into his tea. "By the way, I told Letty about the Organization."

"Right!" Letty jumped up from her seat. "Is it true, do you think? About Lunesta?"

Majest shrugged. "Raizu wouldn't have known about the Redwoods if it wasn't. Those were Mother's people—Lunesta must have tracked their home down, wherever it is. It has to be her."

"At the same time, it can't be," said Letty, her face creasing. "How could Lunesta do something like that?"

"Jealousy is a bitter thing," said Majest, and both Letty and Raizu looked toward him in surprise. "How would you have felt if Lunesta and I had been chosen without you?"

Letty's eyes flashed. "I wouldn't have wanted you *dead*," she said. Then she dropped her gaze to her feet. "Besides, it's my fault, anyway. When Komi first came to me, he asked me to bring him my siblings and I only brought you."

Majest blinked. She'd never told him this before.

"I'm sure it doesn't work like that," said Raizu.

"Right, because you think we were born with our powers and there are no gods at all." Letty pulled another fruit from the basket, one that looked like a long, yellow nose.

Raizu shrugged meekly, tucking his blanket over his arms. "I really don't know."

He and Majest watched as Letty bit into her fruit, then reeled in disgust at the tough mouthful. "Skies, what *is* this?"

"You have to take the peeling off of bananas," came Vari's cheery voice. Seconds later, he strode into the kitchen, his hair a dark halo of static around the hood of his coat.

Majest suppressed a groan. Raizu arched an eyebrow.

"Oh." Letty frowned at the banana, peeling the top off to reveal a paler fruit underneath, which she began to munch on. "Thanks, Vari. Back so soon?"

"Sedona and Sunny wanted to check in on you," said Vari. Behind him, Majest could see the Seacourt sisters in the doorway.

"How've you been doing?" asked Sunny.

"Need anything?" added Sedona.

When no one immediately replied, Letty's eyes went to Majest and stuck there. *Organization?* she mouthed.

Majest nodded. If Sedona had Komi's powers, too, she would no doubt be a target for Lunesta's people. They had to tell her.

"Sit down for a minute," Majest said, gesturing to the kitchen table. "Raizu came to this island to give us news and you ought to hear it."

"Ith this goop callth Ognivashn," said Letty, her mouth full of banana.

"What?" said Vari, Sedona, and Sunny simultaneously.

"A group called the Organization," Majest clarified. "You're not going to like this."

One by one, Sedona, Sunny, and Vari filled in the remaining chairs at the kitchen table. For once, Vari was silent, allowing Majest and Raizu to recount everything they knew about Lunesta and her group—with the occasional interjection from Letty between mouthfuls of fruit.

Sedona was the first to speak when they were finished. "Your own sister did all this?"

"She must have serious issues," Sunny added, pursing her lips. "If she wanted you dead, she could have just thrown you off a cliff or something before she left home."

"It's not just about us," Majest insisted. "Maybe it started off that way, but from what Raizu's brother said, we won't be the only ones targeted for long. Not if she wants the land rid of Power and replaced with old-world technology."

"We won't let anyone near you," said Vari. "Right, Sedona?"

"As long as they don't let anyone near us," said Sedona.

"Never. We're in this together," Majest said.

"Good," said Sunny, and stood, brushing off her pants. "Now, how about we sit back and wait for the Organization to *never* find us?"

Everyone stared, and she snorted out a laugh. "Come on! People only see this island if they're in the right place, like us. We'll be fine."

Sedona leaned her cheek on her elbow. "Why are you the only one who isn't worried?"

"Because there's nothing to worry about. In fact, how about we forget this stuff and show your Messenger friends the ropes in town? They're completely out of place here."

"We're learning," Letty protested.

Sunny gestured to the bitten banana peel on the table. "Of course you are."

Majest couldn't help but smile. Sunny was right. Most of what the villagers talked about sounded like another language, and one in which neither his father nor his powers could've helped him with.

"Fine," said Sedona. "Want to come out with us?"

"Definitely." Majest nudged Raizu. "Are you up for joining?"

He ducked his head. "I shouldn't. I'm still not feeling the best."

"And if he's not going to be living here, it's not like he needs a tour," said Sedona.

Majest opened his mouth to reply, but Raizu beat him to it. "I would like to see the town," he said. "I thought I would stay and help Maji and Letty for a while. It takes weeks to get back to my pack—a few extra days here isn't going to hurt."

Majest smiled at him, and at the familiar use of his nickname. Something warm sprouted in his chest, right up next to his heartbeat. He wasn't sure if he fully trusted the Hiding townspeople yet—they were, for starters, something he would need to get used to—but Raizu already felt like family. The final piece to something he hadn't known was incomplete to begin with.

And for the time being, they weren't going to lose Raizu again.

"Can we tour tomorrow?" Majest asked. "We can take today to rest."

"That's…fine," said Sedona, eyeing Raizu with pursed lips.

"Sorry."

"Not a problem. Tomorrow then." Sedona got to her feet, towing Sunny and Vari with her. "We'll leave you alone now," she added, shooting a loaded glance at Vari.

He just grinned.

"Tomorrow," Majest said, the quiet afternoon already calling his name.

18

Raizu didn't think he'd ever had an afternoon like this. He and the Skylarks milled about at their leisure, Letty swapping supplies at Hiding's markets, Raizu trading childhood stories with Majest, wrapped in about three dozen blankets.

Night fell, filled with drowsy chatter and a meal of bread and fish—and a feeling between the three of them Letty described as "like a little family."

Raizu was inclined to agree. He slept easy, tangled in warmth and furs. He awoke with hardly a tickle in his throat.

"Tour today," Majest said through a yawn, the morning sun's rays flickering over them. His hair was charmingly tousled, eyes heavy but enthusiastic. "Time to see what else these islanders have up their perfectly-sewn sleeves. I'm still not over the yellow ban-nan thing."

"You and Letty didn't have much back in the forest, did you?" Raizu asked, watching with bemusement as Majest hurried around the room, trying to find a clean shirt.

Majest laughed. "Did you? It's a wonder we all grew to be the proper size, living off acorns and half-cooked rabbits."

"Our pack lives pretty close to the market. We get tea and clothes like this—though definitely not fruit baskets."

"I think Letty's eaten half the fruit on the island by now," said Majest. He finally located a shirt and yanked it on. "Her stomach's going to explode and it'll all come pouring back out."

"I'm not obsessed," protested Letty, appearing in the doorway and leaning against the wooden frame. She had her hair pulled back from her face with a thin cord, bringing out the soft angles of her cheeks. Raizu thought she looked older like that—until she stuck her tongue out at her brother. "If we're going to make this our home, I'm going to find out what I like to eat here."

"I liked the strawberries," Raizu put in, getting to his feet.

"They *were* delicious," Letty agreed, looking pleased. "I've never tasted anything that sweet before."

Majest grinned. "I'm sure they taste like the heavens having a dance-off in your mouth, or whatever. Should we get going? Sedona and Sunny are probably already waiting. This town gets up so early."

Letty and Raizu exchanged an amused glance.

"What?" Majest demanded.

"Nothing," said Letty, ducking as Majest swatted at her. "Do you think Vari will come with us today?"

"Oh, so now you want him around all the time?"

Letty blushed between her freckles. "*No*— I was just wondering."

"I don't think you have anything to worry about," said Majest.

"I'm sure he beat us to the Seacourts' house," added Raizu.

"Adorable."

"Vari's really nice," said Letty, pulling at her shirt. It was pale blue, made from the village's fabrics. In fact, she was dressed entirely in Hiding clothes, nothing remaining of the woodsy smell that seemed to cling to Majest like the sun to the sky. For her, it was as if it had been swept away the instant she'd washed ashore.

Letty stood upright as if she could sense Raizu's train of thought, taking her arm hastily off the door frame. "You're right," she said, "we should get going."

Majest smiled at her again. He smiled a lot for the burdens on his back, Raizu thought. It was strangely reassuring.

"All right, then," Majest said, and they took off into the chilled morning.

The Seacourt house was quiet and tidy—not quite like the cozy cottage Letty now shared with her brother and Raizu, but not like Jay's dim rooms, either. As she followed Sedona through the tall wooden door, sweet fragrance and walls of gray stone filled the room. Pots of herbs and violet wildflowers were arranged in pleasant swirls on every open surface, covering cracks in the walls. Wooden tables stood proudly in every possible corner. It was a challenge simply to get through the door.

Sunny greeted them with a mischievous grin. "Ready to go, newbies?"

"I am," chirped Vari from behind Sedona's coat. "I already decided what we're going to do today, Letty."

"Just us?" said Letty.

"We thought we'd split into two groups," said Sedona, finger-combing her hair. "Letty, Vari wants to take you to Quell and Idyllice's house to show you their garden, if that's all right." When her gaze sidled to Majest, it lit. "You can come with Sunny and I, but first, I have something here I want to show you."

"Where do I go?" Raizu asked tentatively.

Sedona blinked, and Letty got the feeling she hadn't even remembered the island's third guest. She was still looking at Majest.

"You can come with me," Majest told Raizu. "My sister gets Vari all to herself. Hope they can manage."

Watching Sedona stare at him, Letty almost retorted that she wasn't the only one who had to *manage* a new fan, but she settled for a raised brow.

"We're off, then," sang Vari, completely missing the exchange. His soft face was a map of excitement, as though visiting the garden was the most exhilarating adventure he could think of. He took Letty's arm and pulled her toward the front door. Letty barely refrained from *accidentally* knocking into Majest on the way out.

"Bye, Letty," Majest called as he shut Sedona's door. He made kissy faces at her until she was out of sight. Letty could see Raizu behind him, sighing to the ceiling.

Once outside, Vari let go of Letty's arm and turned to face her, his eyes dancing even in the frigid cold. "This way," he said, beckoning her toward a stone path.

They started off at a quick pace, Letty realizing her skin was prickling from more than just a chill.

"Quell and his sister, they really grow all the fruit here?" she forced out.

"Well, it sure doesn't come in with the tide!" Vari laughed, his breath billowing. "I know—everyone says plants can't grow this far north, and they're usually right. But Quell and Idyllice heat all theirs with lanterns."

"Don't plants need real sunlight?"

"When you're missing something, you've got to make do without it, right?"

He came to an abrupt halt next to a large stone house Letty recognized—she could see the open window and remembered two brown-haired heads peering out of it on the day of her arrival. *The Souleias.*

"This is it," said Letty.

"Hey, good memory," Vari said with a smile.

Letty tried to keep her face indifferent.

Footsteps sounded from inside, muffled noises on hard stone. When Vari knocked, a rather short woman answered the door, her hair twisted atop her head. She had the face of someone in her twenties by old-world standards, and calm winter-sky gray eyes.

"Me again, Idyllice," said Vari.

Idyllice's gaze was soft, almost doting. "Hi, Vari. You brought a guest?"

"Letty Skylark," said Letty, dipping her head.

"She's got powers like Sedona," Vari added, and Letty fidgeted as Idyllice looked at her in wonder. "She wanted a tour of the garden, if that's okay?"

Idyllice looked surprised. "Didn't Quell already put together a basket for you to show your new friends what we do?"

Vari ducked his head, going red. "Sorry. I didn't think you'd mind."

"I don't," said Idyllice with a laugh. "You're always welcome here. Quell could use the company and I could use a break from watching him spill potted soil all over himself."

"Is Quell here?"

"Downstairs. Making a mess. Come with me, both of you."

Downstairs? Letty wrinkled her brow.

Idyllice led Letty and Vari into the first door on the right. There was nothing in the room except for a large square door on the floor, which Idyllice yanked open, revealing darkness.

"The garden's down there?" asked Letty.

"It looks like a huge drop, but it isn't," Idyllice promised.

"The plants are safer from storms down there," said Vari, looking proud when Idyllice nodded. "The ground is higher here at the entrance, so it's easy to get inside."

Letty leaned into the blackness, seeing the flicker of candles from deep within it. As her eyes adjusted, she could make out a thin gray corridor, the sweet scents of living things.

"Go on in," Idyllice advised.

Vari didn't need to be told twice. He lowered his legs into the hole and slid forward with a short *whoop* and a push, landing audibly below. Letty could see the top of his head glowing, and he turned up to her with a grin. "See? Like jumping out of bed!"

Not allowing herself to hesitate, Letty sat down and scooted after him, trusting the fall. It was nothing like Komi's starry nothingness or her fall from the cliff—it was over before she could even make a comparison. Her knees easily absorbed the impact.

After a second or two of blindness, Letty's eyes adjusted; she saw the corridor sloping down in front of her under the arch of the low dirt ceiling. It led to a brightly-lit cavern, soft dust winking between the yellow glow of the lanterns.

"Amazing, right?" said Vari beside her.

"Idyllice, is that you?" asked someone else before Letty could agree. The voice was muffled, its owner somewhere in the cave ahead.

"And friends," Idyllice replied, landing next to Letty on the dirt floor and stepping forward. "Letty—Letty Skylark, that is—wanted to see the garden."

"Did she now?" The speaker stepped from the cavern, and he had Idyllice's soft face and eyes. "Sure she didn't come to see my prize-winning smile?"

"Quell!" Vari cried, running toward him.

"Hey, Vari," replied Quell. His expression was fond. "And welcome, Letty."

As she approached, Letty could see his fingers and the knees of his pants were black with soil. "Sorry I'm such a mess. Let me just..." He wiped a hand over his sweaty brow, but all that did was smear dirt over his forehead. "Nuts."

Vari, undeterred, said, "How are the bananas? Better than yesterday?"

"A little. They're not supposed to be in temperatures this cold, but we're trying everything short of knitting them sweaters."

Letty was intrigued. "Can I see them? The ones you sent over were delicious."

Quell wiped the rest of the dirt from his hands onto his already-filthy pants. "Go right ahead. Just don't knock anything over, okay? It's a bit crowded."

Letty nodded, and Vari beamed.

As she stepped fully into the cavern, the lighting changed, and Letty could see everything as if she were standing under the sun. The garden was as beautiful as she'd imagined. Rows upon rows of lush trees held on tight to winding trellises, while berries rested atop leafy bushes, rolled in every possible color. Lanterns laced the room in mesmerizing lines, radiating heat and painting silhouettes of leaves over every wall. The air tasted so fresh, it made Letty's eyes water.

"This is absolutely incredible," she breathed, reaching out to touch one of the plants. Its green veins were alive under her hand. "I didn't think beautiful things could grow in such dark places."

"Letty, come look at this," called Vari, breaking her out of her reverie. "Oranges!"

"Oranges?" Letty followed him through the rows of plants. Sure enough, bright fruit the color of early dawn rested on a fragile tree with leaves like pointed animal ears. Letty gasped, seeing the sun in a place where it could not reach.

"Those are my favorites," Quell said, coming up behind them. "In Vosile Masotote's tales, they used to grow in places so warm you could sweat from your ears without a jacket."

"And here I thought a summer day where you could feel your fingers was a victory," said Letty. "Where did you get all these plants?"

"Our family was originally from a lot farther south. They kept a seed bank after the End, and Idyllice and I brought it up here to grow."

"Hey, Quell! What's in here?" Vari was on the move again, poking his head into a crack in the wall, back in the farthest corner of the garden. "I've never seen this before."

"I wouldn't go in there," called Idyllice, even as Vari wriggled into the small space. "We don't know what's inside. Quell's been meaning to check it out, but—"

"This is so cramped," Vari said, his voice muffled. He was completely out of sight. "And *cold.* Has it always been this cold in here?"

All was quiet for a moment.

"Vari," Quell said, worry spreading across his face. There was no response.

"Vari—" Letty broke off her own call as an exclamation of shock and then a terrible, boiling screech came from where Vari had vanished.

It was a sound like the darkness had come to life. Shards of rock crumbled off the back wall, white teethlike chunks flying. Letty flung her hands over her ears. Quell ran forward, shouting, to the place where Vari had disappeared.

A second of struggle, and then Quell had Vari free. His face hit the light as Quell dragged him backward, and Letty nearly cried out at the sight of it. His eyes were open and black, pupils eclipsing every cell of white. His face was a hungry pit, his tongue lolled, and his arms and legs were frenzied. A line of foam trickled from his shining mouth and pooled in the crook of his neck.

Quell held onto him as he writhed like a caged beast, all sweat and saliva. Through it all, Vari screamed and screamed and *screamed.*

"Fetch Sedona and Jay," Idyllice said in Letty's ear. "Go. *Now!*"

Letty forced herself to look away, to remove the heels of her hands from her ears. She raced from the garden through the corridor, hauling herself into the Souleias' house. She did not look back, letting doors slam and winter air whip against her skin.

Vari's black eyes behind her own, she pounded across town to the beat of her heart.

"I have to hand it to you, Sedona," Majest said. "You know even more about this land than my parents did, and they practically traveled every corner of it."

Sedona smiled at the praise. "On Hiding, we learn so much about the old world from Vosile that there's hardly a point in living in the new one."

The four of them—Majest, Sedona, Raizu, and Sunny—were squished together on a large couch in the Seacourt house, cushions riding up between them. Sedona had told them Vosile Masotote's most famous stories of faraway lands across oceans and continents, boats and gadgets that whirred to life in places far out of reach.

"I thought Cognito was everything there—well, *everything*," Raizu said from Majest's left, their shoulders brushing. His head rested in his hands. "I thought the world started and ended with us. Now I feel like I've been living under a rock."

Together, they peered at what Sedona had brought out: a large sheet of thin, ragged parchment, unfolded to reveal a map exploding with color.

"This is what the whole planet looks like," Sedona told them, splaying it over their laps. "The land, the sea, everything in between."

"How could anyone have made this?" Majest asked in disbelief. "There's no way someone could travel enough of the world to know what every nub of the coastline looks like."

"No clue," said Sunny, tucking her feet under her. "But look—here we are."

She pointed at a large, water-dappled shape, and Majest recognized the ancient spelling: *C-a-n-a-d-a*. So much of this map he could read but not understand.

"I'm sure most of these places don't exist anymore," said Sedona, her voice almost a lecturing tone. She pointed, one by one. "Shanghai, Vienna, Buenos Aires."

"Vienna has a nice sound to it," Raizu murmured.

"Sparta is my favorite." Sedona, completely ignoring him, tapped somewhere in the center of the map. "Masotote told me a great kingdom used to rule there. I love to imagine what it might've been like, before the End. Don't you?"

Majest said nothing. She sounded like Letty, imagining a world that would never be shiny and new again—fantasies that would bring only disappointment.

"It's good to learn more about the people we came from," Raizu said, but Sedona only watched Majest over the bridge of her nose. Now that he thought about it, Majest couldn't remember her addressing Raizu all morning.

"Well? Majest?" she pressed.

Majest shook his head, giving her and Raizu both an apologetic glance. Raizu shifted, teeth working at his lip.

Sunny seemed to sense the deteriorating atmosphere and stood. "I'm getting apple juice," she announced. "Anyone want some?"

"No, thank you," they all replied.

"Your loss." Sunny exited the room with a tuneless hum, letting Sedona take her place on the couch. Sedona used the extra space to refold her map, avoiding Majest's eyes.

"I'm sorry," Majest told her. "The map is brilliant, just not my type of thing."

"I get it," Sedona said. "You're all about moving forward." She gave a wry smile. "I can understand that, I suppose. What's the point of the old world when it doesn't change what's happening in this one?"

Relief filled Majest's chest. "Exactly. The past isn't going to do me any good unless it shows me something that takes me where I need to be."

"Except it usually does," Raizu teased.

"I—oh, shut up," Majest said, elbowing him.

Sedona gave a reluctant smile and then an uncertain glance in Raizu's direction.

The noise of pounding feet cut off further conversation, and in flew Sunny, not a cup of apple juice in sight. Her hair was fluffed up, humor swallowed. Letty was right behind, her face ashen.

"Maji, please—you all have to come with me now," Letty insisted.

Majest rose to his feet. "What happened?"

"It's Vari," Letty said. "He's been possessed!"

19

"**N**ormally, I'd say *possession* is a considerable overreaction, but I have to go with the Skylark girl on this one," said Jay. He was leaning against the back wall of his medicine room, as far away from his guests as he could get. "Nothing else explains *that.*" He gestured to Vari, whose eyes were wide open and pitch-black, staring into nothing.

Letty swallowed hard against a foul taste in her mouth, remembering this room hours earlier: Vari snakelike and writhing hard in Quell's arms, the Souleias tying him to the makeshift bed in a bluster of voices and hands. Jay had actually invited everyone inside for once, blind eyes wide and horror-glazed. That terror had lasted for only a moment, but it had been like freezing rain on Letty's skin.

"Shadows!" Vari had cried in an underwater voice not his own. He had struggled against the restraints, gouging bloody gashes into his wrists and ankles. His back had arched upward, fingers curling like gnarled branches, claws scraping.

Letty remembered him gripping the wood of the doorframe, fingers aching and white. She had stood back while Idyllice had propped Vari's head up and Quell had murmured soothing words into unhearing ears, stroking Vari's hair until he had finally gone unconscious.

Now, Vari lay with his eyes open but unseeing, breaths coming in shaggy gasps. Jay moved around him, pouring this or that onto his tongue, and Quell and Idyllice stood worriedly by, along with the Seacourt sisters.

"You can really be possessed like that?" Letty asked. "I was only guessing."

Jay prodded one of Vari's arms. "Magic isn't all gods and singing animals," he said. "There's another side. Clearly, some sort of demonic force got a hold of Vari down in the garden. It's never happened here before, but I suppose there's a first time for every nightmare."

"How can you be sure?" said Majest. "My father would have told me if there were demons in our land."

"I'm with Maji," Raizu agreed.

"Thank you."

"Well, it's only because I don't believe in any of this stuff," Raizu amended. He stared at his feet, like he thought he would be screamed at if he met anyone's eyes. "There has to be another explanation for what happened to Vari. Could he have been poisoned?"

Jay sighed, though it was softer than the ones he'd fired at Majest. "No," he said. "I know what this is. I've seen it before."

"Actually *seen* it?" said Majest.

Jay didn't answer. He stalked over to a small table and snatched a water canister from it, taking a drink as if the conversation had parched him.

"Where did this thing come from?" asked Quell. "Is it still down there? My garden is counting on me. Every little apple and banana."

"My best guess? Someone summoned the thing," said Jay. "Which requires a certain brand of idiot to try. Demons aren't creatures you want to invite to lunch. Demons are not to be trifled with. They are restless and roaming and dangerous when summoned."

"I didn't do it," Quell said immediately.

"Of course you didn't. It's just using your garden to hide. Demons don't usually live on Earth. Especially without a proper human form, which not many of them have. So, they roam."

"How do you know that?" Sunny asked.

"I was raised in a place that taught its children these things. For us, it was not fantasy."

That shut everyone up fast.

After a moment, Sedona said softly, "We owe that knowledge for Vari's well-being. Thank you."

Letty stared at her. Her voice—gentle and kind; it was like a mother trying to swaddle a child. Something about her drive to prod and please everyone around her made Letty strangely sad.

Jay, clearly not feeling the warmth, either, flinched from the kind words like they'd struck him. "If you hadn't noticed, not much of Vari's well-being is left," he said. "All I did was drug him enough to sleep instead of scream."

"What does all this mean for the town?" Idyllice cut in. "And our garden?"

"I'm sure the demon is long gone from your garden after all this," said Jay. "Though, I can hardly say the same for the rest of the town. The thing could be near Haiti or taking a swim in the bay as we speak. Perhaps it's right in front of me and no one's bothered to mention it. Who knows?"

"Isn't it important that we find it and get rid of it?" Majest demanded.

"And will getting rid of it make Vari better?" Quell asked.

"If you have any idea how to find a demon and convince it to heal Vari, then go right ahead, because you sure aren't going to kill it," said Jay. "Or you could ask your god friend Komi, since he apparently cares enough about you to start a war over your powers."

"With everything you know, isn't there something you can do?" Letty asked.

Jay closed his eyes, probably more for dramatic effect than anything else. "I suppose I can keep Vari here with me, though he's not getting better with that thing still out there."

"That's all?" Majest asked.

"I've done all I can," said Jay.

Majest opened his mouth again, but after a warning headshake from Raizu, he closed it.

"Now, get out of my house before I collapse from the smell of all of you," Jay continued, pretending to examine his nails.

"The smell of *us*? Have you gotten a whiff of this room?" Majest grumbled, but made for the door all the same. Letty followed, catching a glimpse of the sour face Jay made after them.

Please, she thought, a silent plea in his direction. *Please keep Vari safe. Keep him out of the shadows, whatever it takes.*

Shadows.

Vari's screech rang in Letty's ears and she gritted her teeth, drowned out the shrillness of it with the crunch of her boots on the stone path.

That's what it's been ever since we left home—shadows and doubt. I thought Hiding was different. I thought we'd be safe here.

As Letty looked up into the sky, she saw a setting sun. Twilight had cast dark lines across the ground, stealing the light from under her nose.

Nowhere is safe.

"I still can't believe I'm doing this," muttered Caiter as he made his way halfway down the hall.

This was not one of the Organization's ordinary white halls; it was dingy gray and unused, back in the farthest, deepest corner of the building. It stank of metal and fear.

At the end of the hallway was a metal door rusted around the edges. Caiter pushed on its lever without a second thought.

This was all rather unlike him. He should have been physically afraid, coming down here, but his agreement to make this visit left him with more concern for his mental health than anything else.

No one with any brain cells rubbing together would do this willingly. And show sympathy *of all things,* Caiter's thoughts jeered. He ignored them.

The open door led him into a dim square room buzzing with the absence of light. The President hadn't had use for this section of the building until now. It was empty save for one guard standing at attention. He had mahogany skin and a shining bald head, eyes the same shade as the walls and not any friendlier.

"Caiter Mandle?" he asked. "I remember you. You shouldn't be down here."

"I came for a visit," said Caiter, kneading his fingers. "I'm a…visitor."

"Not for me, I'd imagine. The prisoner you brought down?"

"That's right," Caiter said, willing himself to remain composed. "I got special permission from the President. She wanted his side of the story, and I thought company might do him some good."

At this, the guard laughed. "I don't think anyone could ever associate the word *good* with that man. Suit yourself. First door on the left."

Caiter tapped his tongue against his teeth. *Why am I doing this?*

He waited while the guard chortled, snagging a key ring off his belt and handed it over. He jerked his thumb in the direction of a dark corridor to the right and said, "Stay on your side of the glass, all right?"

Caiter thanked him and hurried. This corridor was even filthier than the last and reeked of the smell of rust. His fingers fumbled with the lock on the door, everything in him screaming how terrible of an idea this was.

The door swung open, thrusting him into a sea of light. It was so intense, Caiter wanted to look away, but there was nothing else to see except the man sitting across the room. He was on the floor, knees to his chest, contemplating the ceiling. His dark hair, ruffled as ever, was the only color in the room.

He scrambled to his feet at the sound of the door. "Caiter!" he called. "I *knew* I liked you best. You wouldn't leave me here to rot."

Caiter flinched back as the figure barreled toward him, but the man stopped halfway across the room, face pressed against the glass barrier that split the room in two.

"Malory," said Caiter, his voice catching. He told himself he was not afraid. Malory was still a brilliant scientist and had *technically* never hurt him. "I didn't come to let you out. The President wanted me to speak with you."

"Oh." Malory's mouth protruded into a pout. "That's no fun."

"Everything you say will be reported back to Lady President," Caiter said. "So speak carefully."

Malory rolled his eyes. "I'm *terrified*. I suppose I'd better be on my best behavior, then, if I ever want to get out of here." He adjusted his round glasses. "Did Lunesta give you a script? Shall I recite the alphabet backwards? Which language would you like? Dutch?"

Caiter's jaw locked. No one ever addressed the President by her real name. "She wants to know about the demon energy you used on Ohanzi so she can figure out where he might be now."

"Oh," Malory said again, though this time his eyes lit up. He clasped his hands together. "Spectacular! I'd love to explain it to you, dear Caiter." He smirked. "Clearly, it's one of your favorite topics—got you hooting and hollering back in the lab, huh?"

"I'm not here to play games with you."

"That certainly ruins the session of charades I was planning for us later."

"Please—just tell me about Ohanzi."

Malory raised dark eyebrows. "Touchy, aren't we?" He chuckled, and Caiter felt it down his spine.

"Let me think, let me think." He pressed a finger to his lips. "Underneath all that demon razzle-dazzle, he should still have Ohanzi's memories, so there's that. But it's impossible to guess where he is without tracking his energy. A needle in a haystack, as they say. Too bad we can't just burn the hay."

"Then what—?"

"Not to sound too far up my own rear, but I put a *lot* of time and demon juice into that serum. Lunesta ought to appreciate this a bit more. I'd like to see her try and summon a demon."

"You *summon demons?*"

"Want to watch?"

Caiter refused to take a step back as Malory waggled his fingers. "Tell me about tracking him. Do you know how?"

"*Do I know how to make a demon tracker,*" Malory scoffed. "It's just magic, not rocket science."

"So…?"

"*So,*" Malory said, and winked. "Go see those nasty twins of yours and tell them to start up their demon watch tracker again. It's designed to track large concentrations of demon energy, so Ohanzi should show up. Simple enough?"

"You're actually helping me," Caiter said with disbelief.

"Why not? I'd love to know where Ohanzi spooked off to, especially since he believed Seti lost the Skylarks to some hidden island. If he goes after them, I want to hear all about it. Believe it or not, Lunesta and I want many of the same things."

Caiter blinked, watching Malory's face carefully. "You're *actually* concerned about the Skylarks?"

Malory splayed his palms in the air. "*Concern* is not the right word. Please tell my dear old friend Lunesta there's no hope in predicting the future, and no luck for those who do. She'll have to wait and see what happens."

"Fine," said Caiter. With reluctance, he realized his allotted time was running short. "I'll let her know about the tracker." He tried for a smile. "Thanks for the help."

Caiter turned to leave, heart thrumming. Soon, he would be back where he belonged. No more of this—

"Wait!"

"Yes?" Caiter whirled obediently, then cringed at the knee-jerk reaction.

Malory's face was open: eyes huge, hands outstretched. "You're really not letting me out of here? After all that?"

Caiter sucked in a breath. He was not supposed to show pity for the man who had nearly stuffed his veins full of hellfire. He wasn't sure why he felt pity in the first place. "Lady President wants you here until you decide to fight for *our* mission again, not your own."

"I told you—Lunesta and I, we want similar things. I have debts to settle, Skylarks to mow down, same as her. This place has the technology I need to make that happen."

Caiter's feet inched toward the door. He would not falter. He would not show compassion. Malory was hardly human; Caiter had to remember that. He had to.

Malory crushed his palms into fists. "I've done nothing wrong," he said. "I've given the Organization a valuable pawn for their board." He lifted his head, his eyes blazing. "Caiter, you have to let me out of here."

Caiter shook his head, remembering the syringe pointed like an arrow toward his heart. He had one hand on the door. "I can't," he said. "I'm sorry."

"Caiter, *please!*"

Caiter did not turn back this time. He pushed through the door, his teeth snapping in his skull when he slammed it shut. A howl of betrayal erupted from the other side. Caiter's skin crawled and his heart twisted at the sound, but he still walked away. His task was done.

20

Their cottage was pitch-black by the time Majest, Raizu, and Letty returned. Majest thought he almost envied Jay—at least Jay knew his way around the dark. Meanwhile, Majest tried to find the lantern and nearly knocked the fruit basket onto the floor.

"At least I found something to eat," he said. "You two want anything?"

"I'm fine," said Raizu from the table. His voice sounded strained.

"Letty?"

"All yours," she said.

Majest grabbed for a random fruit and took a bite. *Hmm. Apple.* He was grateful no one could see him when he dribbled a mouthful of juice down his chin.

"The lantern must have fallen over somewhere," said Raizu. "Just our luck."

"It's not like any of us are in the mood to read or play games," Letty noted. "Not with a demon on the loose. All I can think about is Vari."

"Then his mission is accomplished," muttered Majest, though he was sure his sister didn't hear.

"This is going to be a long night," said Raizu.

"Cheer up, Raizy," Majest told him, taking another bite. "The world's the same under the dark as it is in the light." Finishing his apple, he tossed the core in the direction of the waste bin, hearing it smack against the floor instead.

"Except you can't see what's lurking," Raizu said.

"Or where you're throwing. Are you going to pick that up?" asked Letty.

Majest fumbled for the apple core. "You know what we should do tonight?"

"Get to bed early?" asked Raizu.

"Better," Majest said. "We're going to go out."

"Out where?"

"To the forest," Majest clarified. "Night hunting. I used to do it all the time with our father. We can scope out the village, see if we find anything suspicious."

"With a demon on the loose?" Letty protested.

"*Because* there's a demon on the loose. Come on, if we're Messengers, we should use our powers to do something about this."

"Do we have to do something that involves a dark forest on an unfamiliar island?" asked Raizu. Majest pictured him with his hands kneading his lap, gnawing at his cheek.

"I won't let anything happen to you," Majest told him.

"Well, nothing is going to happen to me, because I'm not going," said Letty. "This is a stupid idea and I'm exhausted. I'm going to stay inside and worry."

"I could stay and worry with you," Raizu offered.

Majest found his shoulder and jostled it. "Not a chance. Come on—this is our first chance to have some real fun since getting here."

"Fun? I thought we were demon hunting."

"What's wrong with both?"

"Everything," said Letty.

Majest couldn't see her face, couldn't see the eyes that would give her heart away, but she sounded finished with the idea.

"I'm going to bed," she continued, and creaked off in the direction of her room. "Don't do anything Mother wouldn't have done."

"Mother would've loved this," Majest called after her. Getting no response, he left it alone—best to give Letty's flames space to die down on their own.

From across the room, Raizu exhaled through his nose.

"I hope that's a sigh of excitement," Majest told him.

"I'll go out with you," Raizu said, "but only if you agree we aren't looking for demons."

Majest's jaw nearly dropped. "You'd come out? In the dark? *Really?*"

"*Maji.*"

"Okay. We'll be safe," he promised before Raizu had time to change his mind. "You still have your coat on, right?"

Raizu made a nervous noise, which Majest took as a yes. "Then let's go!"

Raizu did not know what feverish lapse of insight had led him to agree to this. Each new step into the cold, empty darkness was like a plunge into ice water. He found the light of the moon, but the cloud cover seemed determined to not let it quite reach the ground.

Why was he doing this? Deep in his tangled stomach, he knew. He wanted to prove himself to the Skylarks. He wanted to prove he could be more than a coward.

"Raizy, you still alive over there?" Majest's voice cut through Raizu's worries. "We're not even into the woods. That's when the fun starts."

"What fun?" Raizu tried to keep his voice just as light.

Majest laughed, loud enough for Raizu to wonder how the whole world didn't hear. He grabbed Raizu's wrist, his gloved hand a pale flash in the dusk, and together ran. After a minute, the sound of Majest's thumping footfalls became reassurance, slowing the flurry of panicky thoughts and Raizu smiled, breathless.

They ran for what seemed like forever, then skidded to an awkward halt, their breaths coming in pants. Raizu put his hands on his knees, faint forest shapes moving against his vision.

"Fun," Majest repeated.

Raizu pressed his lips together. "How do you keep from hitting the trees?"

Majest started walking again. "*Hímin,* I don't know! They're awfully chatty tonight, but that's hardly any help when you can't see them." He chuckled, then seemed to realize Raizu was no longer following. "What's the matter?"

"We're going to get lost and I'm going to slam my face into a tree."

"No, you're not. I won't let you. And it's a small island—we'll be able to find our way back." Majest picked up the pace and Raizu had no choice but to follow on shaky legs.

What if the island is bigger than we think? What if the demon attacks us? What if we can't find our way back? Oh, or if—

"Hey!" Again, Majest's voice cut through Raizu's panic. "I think I see the coast!"

Raizu squinted ahead. "No way. It took me hours to get from the beach to the village. We haven't been out here that long." *Long enough, though.*

"It took you hours because you were frozen half to death," said Majest. "Maybe the island dips in over here. I don't know." He paused for a moment. "Do you hear that?"

Raizu listened, and sure enough, he could hear the gentle lap of waves as they touched the shore. "I hear it," he agreed. "Guess you're right."

"Of course I am."

Raizu smiled. "It's probably a nice view in the daytime."

"Letty would be all over it. Now that she's got her powers, all she wants to do is sit by the water. She's going to turn into a fish and then someone's going to catch her for dinner."

"You can't call her out on that when you're so in love with the woods, you want to be out here when you can barely see your hands in front of your face," Raizu teased.

Majest made a sheepish noise. "I suppose that's true."

"Are you going to help Letty train her powers? Or Sedona?"

"You think I'd be able to teach them something?"

"Sedona would love it, I'm sure, if her powers are brand new. She seems to like you well enough."

"Really?" said Majest. He sounded indifferent, and somehow, that was a relief. "I hadn't noticed. It seems like she takes everyone under her wing, doesn't she?"

Everyone but me.

They emerged onto the coast and Raizu gazed over the black water. A light glowed soft and faint in the distance. Raizu glanced up at the sky, but he didn't see the moon.

"That's weird," he said. "How can the moon be reflecting off the water if it's hidden behind the clouds?"

"What do you mean?" Majest leaned close over Raizu's shoulder.

Raizu pointed at the light patch in the water.

Majest went still. "That's not the moon," he whispered.

Raizu's heart knocked into his lungs. Majest was right. The white spot was floating closer and gaining features with each passing second. Its breath rippled the water, its eyes gleaming in the faint night. Its teeth were chips of ice, fur luminous and yellowed.

"Polar bear," Majest hissed, edging toward the trees. "First Letty and the grizzly, now this. What, do we smell like seals?"

Raizu ducked behind a rock, dragging Majest down with him. "Maybe it won't see us," he whispered. "They don't usually attack humans, do they?"

From somewhere in front of them, Raizu heard the slosh of water as the bear stepped onto the rocks. It reared onto its hind legs, sniffing, and Raizu saw its eyes. Lifeless. Blacked-out. *Wrong, somehow.*

No time to dwell on it. The bear had spotted them.

"On my signal, run back the way we came," hissed Majest into Raizu's ear. "Whatever you do, *don't stop.*"

"*Run?* You can't outrun a—"

"I'm not going to outrun it. I'm going to out-element it."

Raizu trusted Majest, even if he barely knew him, but he still half-expected his heart to give out when he heard the first warning huff from the bear's throat. "What's the signal?"

"*This!*"

Majest shoved Raizu back toward the trees; Raizu stumbled for a moment before pulling himself to his feet. There was no time to cringe at every cracking twig, no time to cower as the forest called out. Raizu ran for his life.

Now that his eyes had adjusted to the night, blurry tree-shapes loomed slow-motion against his vision and he swerved as best he could. Needles sprayed out at him, fallen branches rearing up. Fear was his only guide.

Soon, he heard something behind him.

"*No,*" Raizu gasped, the sound ripping from his chest.

"Raizy! Stop!"

Raizu did not stop, did not even slow down.

"*Stop!* It's me!"

"You told me *not* to stop," Raizu called back, his feet going numb in the tight leather of his boots. "Where's the bear?"

"I threw a tree at its face."

Majest's voice sounded fainter, as if he had stopped running. Reluctantly, Raizu slowed, then turned. It was like trying to reverse gravity.

Behind him, Majest grinned. Not a bear in sight. "See? Easy-peasy."

Raizu glared at him, panting. "Where did it go?"

"Somewhere back in the trees. I guess we'll have to continue our adventure elsewhere."

Raizu gaped at him.

"Kidding! We should let the town know. Come on."

Raizu shook his head, the night settling back over his skin. "I still don't think—"

A growl drowned out whatever else he might have said.

Raizu looked up, immediately wishing he hadn't. The blood drained from his face.

Looming over him, paws outstretched, eyes mere orbs in the shadowy moonlight, was the bear. It had a long red gash in its side, and it did not look pleased about it.

Not missing a beat, Majest stepped in front of Raizu and knocked him out of harm's way. Two steady hands snagged the slingshot from his belt and loaded it with something small and green, giving the bear no time for anything but a gurgling grumble.

For a moment, Raizu forgot his terror. He had heard that gurgle before. And those *eyes…*

Majest launched his slingshot, hollering for Raizu to take cover. Whatever he had released hit the ground at the bear's feet.

The explosion blew Raizu back into the dirt, his hands snapping over his ears and neck. He landed on his side, the breath knocked from him.

Instantly, Majest was at his side, pulling him to his feet. Raizu buckled against him as the world went whirling and green. His nose filled with smoke and pine and a bizarre sweetness that nearly sent him swaying back to the ground.

"Grass smoke," said Majest. "It might not kill the bear, but it'll give us a few seconds to get out of here. Stay close to me."

"If I were any closer to you, I'd be on top of you," Raizu wheezed, leaning on him.

"That's the idea."

Raizu closed his mouth to keep from coughing, gripping Majest's jacket tight enough that his knuckles throbbed in protest. The next moments were an agonizing crawl through green darkness, and just as Raizu thought his lungs might surrender altogether, the haze cleared.

The bear lay stunned paces away, covered in green powder. Foam crusted around its mouth, illuminated by the moon as it slid from beneath the clouds. When it saw Majest—the cause of its pain—it gave a feeble roar and tried to stand.

Exchanging a quick glance, Raizu and Majest darted off in the opposite direction, leaving the confused bear to stumble uselessly after them. Eventually, its footsteps faded as it gave up the chase.

Majest slowed, his eyebrows up, chest heaving. "Is that it?"

"I—I think so."

Majest laughed in triumph. "Ha! That was fun."

Raizu glared at him. "You do not get to use that word anymore."

They hustled away from the coast for long minutes before Raizu said, "You know, you don't owe me my life anymore. Without you, I'd be in stringy pieces."

"You think I saved your life?" Majest sounded surprised. "I'm the reason you were out here in the first place. I didn't even help you with your fear of the dark, did I? Of course not. You went out in the dark and got attacked by a *polar bear.*" He sighed. "I'm sorry."

"Don't be," said Raizu. "The dark is easier when you aren't alone. I'm—" He broke off, flushed a little. "I'm not so afraid when you're here."

"Aw, well, next time you want to throw things at bears you let me know."

Something kept Raizu from laughing along with him. "Didn't you think something was off with that bear? It had foam around its mouth, like Vari. The same dark eyes, too."

"Bears have dark eyes," Majest pointed out, but he sounded thoughtful. "You're right, though."

"Now we definitely need to tell the town," said Raizu. "Should we go right to the leader? Mosely… Vosely…"

"Vosile Masotote. Yeah," said Majest, "especially if he's expecting his faithful servant boy to come calling and no one's bothered to give him the news about Vari."

"Someone's got to start making sense of things."

"Vosile Masotote, it is."

21

Without Vari and Sedona's smiles stirring the atmosphere, Vosile's cottage was less inviting than Majest remembered. He had initially compared it to his family's home, with the same worn walls and rasping creaks of old chairs, but now, as dawn pressed into the edges of the night, it looked lifeless.

Majest knocked on the door several times, but no one answered.

"It's early," said Raizu. "He might not be awake yet."

"I'm not so sure." Majest, suspicious of the silence, pulled open the door with one hand. Inside, the room smelled of dust.

"You can't break into his house," Raizu scolded.

"I think a possibly-possessed polar bear is an exception."

"Maji—"

"Is someone there?" A voice rumbled from across the house.

"It's Majest Skylark," he called back. "My friend and I came to speak to you."

No response.

Raizu started fidgeting with the end of his scarf.

Hesitantly Majest added, "We're sorry if we woke you. It couldn't wait."

After another considerate moment, Vosile called, "Is this about the demon?"

Majest frowned. Someone had told him already? "Kind of," he answered.

"How's my Vari doing?"

"Jay is seeing to him. Well, metaphorically seeing to him."

Vosile didn't reply. Silence filled the space, and with it, disquiet.

"I suppose you'd better come in. First room on your right."

Majest and Raizu followed the wooden walls back into a fur-lined bedroom. And a bed drowning in caribou pelts against the far wall, sagging against its supports. Propped up in it was Vosile Masotote, who stared at Majest and Raizu from a blanket cocoon.

"Skylark," he said. "And friend. Vari told me they found someone else in the forest. Another body to house, another mouth to feed."

Raizu stared at the floor.

"This is Raizu," said Majest, perhaps too harshly. "He's helping us."

"O-only until we sort this mess out," said Raizu. "Don't worry."

Vosile frowned, eyes half-hidden under the tangled bushes of his brows. "In that case, tell me why you two have stormed into my house uninvited."

Unease filled Majest, feeling like it came from the cracks in the walls, the cracks in Vosile's voice. "Like I said, it couldn't wait—"

"If you've already said it, there's no need to say it again."

"I…" Majest clenched his teeth. "Raizy and I went out hunting and we found a polar bear on the shore. It chased us halfway across the island before it gave up, but it might still be around. We thought you should know."

Vosile's eyebrows shot up. "A polar bear hasn't found its way here in years."

"This one did," said Majest, frowning. Did he not believe him?

But Vosile didn't question the story. "We'll have to warn everyone to be careful outside. Thankfully, bears don't stay here long. They return to their seals and their ice, in places farther north."

"Right."

"That's not all, though," said Raizu. "This bear had foam around its mouth and its eyes were pure black."

"Ahh," said Vosile. "Like Vari."

Raizu shifted. "Yes. And it was almost as if…it came to shore only to attack us."

"If Vari's demon possessed this bear as well, it could have sent it after you. And if your story is true, you two are lucky to have escaped unharmed.

Demons are not to be trifled with. They are restless and roaming and dangerous when summoned. I would know."

At *demon,* Raizu's lip went between his teeth. Listening to the rest of Vosile's words, he looked plain startled—like he had heard them before.

For Raizu's sake, Majest said, "We might have imagined it looking like Vari. We were out hunting for clues, after all."

Vosile Masotote's lip curled and Majest thought he looked rather unfriendly for a village hero. "You should not have gone tumbling into the night after what happened to Vari."

"I had my slingshot with me, and my element," said Majest.

Raizu's face was wary. "If you don't mind me asking, how do you have so much of the same knowledge as Jay? He said almost the same thing about demons."

It clicked—those had been Jay's words of warning, tangled up and tossed out to his crowded back room. Vosile had used almost the same phrasing.

"In a village not too far from here lived a man who dealt often with demons," Vosile said, a note of caution in his voice. "His history collides with Jay's, whose collides with mine."

"You and Jay are from the same place?" Majest pursed his lips. "That explains a lot."

"But not enough," Raizu murmured too low for Vosile to hear.

Vosile's face was solid stone. "I hope you know what you've gotten yourselves into. That older sister of yours works with demons, too, and she will destroy you if you let her."

Majest froze. "You mean Lunesta?"

"Of course," replied Vosile. "Jay saw the Organization in a dream months ago."

"You *knew?*" A sudden rage pushed Majest's hands into fists. "You knew about the Organization, knew who Lunesta was and who we were—and didn't think to tell us when we arrived here?"

"We thought we could keep you safe," Vosile said. "We thought this island would be far enough from harm and didn't want to upset you."

"'We?'" Raizu cut in, something stirring in his gaze. "Who's '*we*'?"

"If you're plotting to hand us over to the Organization," Majest growled, "you've done a fine job of setting us up."

Vosile's face contorted. "Lower your voice, Skylark. Do not throw such accusations around."

"Then, why don't you tell us the truth?" Majest asked.

"You ought to show more respect for the man who brought this village to life. I know of the world as it is told to me, and my word is everything here."

Majest, about to hurl something back in reply, was cut off as Raizu stepped forward.

"You know of the world as it is told to you," he said, for once sounding unafraid. "Told to you by whom?"

Vosile shifted his glare to Raizu. "By the gods."

Raizu grabbed Majest's sleeve. "We have to go," he said abruptly.

"Go?" Majest turned to him, watched something flicker in his eyes. "Why? What are you thinking?"

"It's Jay," Raizu said, adamant.

At once, Majest knew he would follow Raizu—out of this house or anywhere on that look in his eyes alone.

Raizu said, "If we want to save this village from shadows, we have to talk to Jay before we listen to another word from this man's mouth."

"Raizy," Majest said again. "Do we have to walk so fast?"

Raizu was still gripping his sleeve like all might be lost if he let go, towing him through the dark village. Their breath clouded the air, fogging the pebbled streets.

"At least tell me what this is about," Majest continued. "I'm supposed to be the spontaneous one."

Raizu turned to him, determination clear on his face. This new determination suited him: brought out the upturn of his nose, the wideness of his eyes. "No one believes in Jay's visions," he said, "but everyone believes that Vosile speaks to the gods, right?"

"Sure," said Majest. "So?"

"*So,* Masotote has the town on his side because of his knowledge from the gods. They let him control Hiding because of it." Raizu's feet snapped against the stones. "But what if he doesn't actually talk to the gods? What if it's not his knowledge at all?"

"What do you mean?"

"What if it's Jay's?"

Majest nearly tripped. "That's a little far-fetched, don't you think? Why would Jay tell Masotote everything he knows? What would he get out of it?"

Raizu did not respond.

Majest realized they had reached the top of a slow-winding path in front of a familiar house with disapproving eyes for windows, a door like an open-mouthed yawn of indifference.

For the first time, Raizu hesitated. He gestured to Majest. It appeared he had come all this way only to realize he was afraid to take the last step.

Majest knocked on the door, Raizu's words replaying in his ears.

Raizu seemed to see what no one else could, uncovering the truth simply by shining his light. Never in all his life could Majest have pieced together what came so naturally to the boy with the arrows.

Jay's voice called through the door, scratchy with exhaustion. "Go away—some people sleep at this hour."

"Clearly not you or I," Majest answered. "We have to talk to you."

"Is that you, idiot Skylark? You are the absolute last person I want to not see right now."

"Look, I'm not your biggest fan, either—"

"I said no," Jay snapped.

Majest scowled. "What if we had life-saving information on how to stop this demon and you're turning us away?"

"*Do* you?"

"Well, no, but—"

Raizu cut him off, tugging Majest's arm. "Jay," he tried, "it's Raizu. This isn't some new Messenger drama, or anything to do with Vari. It's about you. You and Vosile Masotote."

To Majest's amazement, the door swung open immediately, like Jay had been standing behind it the entire time. He wore an off-white shirt much too long for him, some of his hair sticking into the air with static that crackled like the electricity in his expression.

"Can we come in?" Majest asked.

"Your friend can," said Jay.

"Just him?"

"It's too early for me to listen to a whiny Skylark."

"You've got to be kidding me."

"I'll talk," Raizu murmured, and gave Majest a reassuring smile. "Be right back, okay?"

"All right." Majest scowled at Jay. "But the next time we need you, don't expect I'll let you shut me out in the cold like I'm some stray animal."

Jay snickered, but there was no smile in it. "Please. No one really *needs* me, do they?"

Without Majest at his side, being alone with this stranger and his temper had Raizu's nerves at rigid attention. The house was dark, and Jay led him halfway down the hall before stopping in the middle. It took a great deal of effort not to barrel into him.

Jay turned on Raizu, propping himself against the wall. Raizu cringed, expecting a snap, but Jay's voice was light when he asked, "What is it?" His face was blank and open. "About Masotote, right? I stopped by his place this afternoon to tell him about Vari."

"R-right," Raizu said. "Do you…know him well? He said you were from the same village."

Jay stiffened.

Raizu was afraid he had overstepped.

But then, muscle by muscle, Jay relaxed again. "Sort of," he hedged. "He passed through my village around the time—the time I was escaping from my house."

Raizu did not know what to say.

"Masotote offered to take me across the Hudson Bay," Jay continued. "He was on his way back to the island after exploring the mainland and found me in the snow. Saved my life—imagine some dumb, blind kid trying to crawl his way through a Cognito winter alone."

Raizu imagined. He saw Jay even smaller and colder, gripping onto Vosile with the desperation only a child could have. He would have been shrunken and lonely and fearful, just like anyone else. The way Raizu had been as a child—and still was, half the time.

Even standing in front of him now, Jay was so small, so young in the planes of his cheeks and the curves under his eyes. Raizu wondered how many people in Hiding remembered that.

"You must be close if he saved your life," Raizu said.

"I guess. He's the only one who believes in my prophecies, so I don't talk much to anyone else."

"Do you tell him about all your dreams?" Raizu asked.

"More or less. He knows how to interpret them and put them to their best use." Jay sounded uninterested, but this was exactly what Raizu wanted to hear.

"Um, listen," he said. "Maji and I just came from Vosile's house. We found this polar bear that might be in the same condition as Vari, and Vosile… He told us almost word for word what you said earlier about demons."

Jay's eyebrows quirked. "Right, because he learned it from me."

"But he passed it off as something he had learned himself. It got me to thinking—what if this is something he's always done?"

"What do you mean?"

"I think he's been using your information to gain the favor of the town," Raizu confessed. "You say you don't talk much to anyone but Vosile, so maybe you haven't heard what the town thinks of him. Sedona implied that he's only in charge because the gods tell him how to keep the town safe. He claims he built this place from scratch."

Jay's brow wrinkled. "I didn't know that."

"Hiding would follow any order he gave, grant him anything he wished, because they think he has the gods' favor. If there are gods up there, they're talking to *you*. And he's lying."

That seemed to jostle Jay from whatever faraway place he usually dwelled in. His face, instead of contorting in anger, crumpled in on itself. He looked…*hurt*.

"Is that really what you think?" he whispered.

"Well…" Raizu swallowed. "That's—I mean, it's only an idea. I could be over-thinking things…but I don't really believe in gods anyway."

"No, you sounded confident there for a second," Jay insisted. "I didn't think there was a confident bone in your body."

"You aren't like me, right? You wouldn't sit by if someone's taking advantage of you."

"You don't know a thing about me," Jay said, but for once, his walls seemed to come down. "Or about Masotote. Yet here you are, when I haven't seen this in any dream."

"We could figure this out together, if you come back with us," said Raizu.

"Together?" Jay seemed unfamiliar with the word.

"If—if you want."

A long pause crept in between the two of them, both unsure of the stranger before them. Jay, illuminated in the starlight, breathed heavy, giving nothing away. And then, just as Raizu was about to offer him a way out, Jay nodded in agreement.

22

Majest did not ask Jay or Raizu what had passed between them, but he got the sense it was something big. He tried not to be too jealous. They made their way back to Vosile's house, where the man's intense gaze pinned them to the walls.

"More of this?" Vosile croaked. This time, he had not invited any of them in. "I have nothing left to say to you children. I cannot believe you'd waste Jay's time with this as well."

Jay did not respond. He was shivering under his thin jacket and Majest realized how small Jay was—the top of his head only came up to Majest's shoulder.

"I checked in with Jay because you claim to talk to the gods the same way he does," said Raizu with startling clarity.

Vosile's eyes narrowed on Jay. "Of course. The gods look kindly upon both of us."

"I don't think that's true," Raizu said, and Majest watched with amazement the way he met the challenge head-on, his lip barely trembling.

"Oh?" Vosile said.

"Jay's the only prophet here," Raizu continued.

Majest's heart skipped. Was he finally starting to believe in the gods?

"Everything you know about demons and the old world comes from him. He's been telling you his dreams since you first picked him up out of the snow."

177

Majest's jaw went slack.

Vosile laughed—a cruel, dry sound. "You're in way over your head, boy. Jay, tell him." It was an order, not a request. "There is nothing wrong with the sharing of intellect between two of the gods' chosen."

"Are we, though?" Jay lifted his head, blue fire in his eyes. "Because it sure would be convenient if you realized you could use my visions to your advantage."

"Come now, Jay," Vosile said. "What would possess me to do that, when the gods come to me, too?"

"Don't lie to me," said Jay, and though he was usually fuming, this was a different kind of anger. A personal one. "I thought if I let you interpret my dreams, you would use them to help the village. Not make them worship you."

Vosile's face twisted. "You'd make accusations against the man who saved your life?"

"No, but I'd make accusations against the man who *used* me."

"I was chosen long before any of you were born," Vosile hissed, trying to sit up. "I created this village, designed the houses that warm you, dug the canal under the fountain with my own hands—"

"And yet you can't get out of bed?" said Majest, starting to catch on. "Before Jay, you might have been around long enough to convince these people you founded the town, but Sedona said you got your real power when you returned to the island a few years ago with god-sent ideas for the town."

"Isn't that when you brought back Jay," said Raizu.

"It'd be the perfect opportunity to say the gods had chosen you. As soon as one of Jay's prophecies came true, anyone who doubted you would be proven wrong. Then, I bet you sat back and let the town pamper you until you forgot how to take care of yourself."

Vosile's mouth hardened into a thin, wrinkled line.

"I never knew," Jay hissed. "I thought Hiding had *always* treated you like this."

"Even if Jay had discovered what you were doing, you made sure no one would believe him," said Raizu. "You were probably the one who told everyone not to trust him."

Vosile said nothing.

Majest knew Raizu was right.

"I assume you didn't build this village, either," said Majest. "Was it like this when you found it, left over from the old world?" All at once, the island's illusion shattered into knife-sharp fragments. "Did you ever live in the old world? Maybe you went on that *journey* of yours to learn enough about it so you could pretend you did."

"Maybe when you found this island, you brought others here the way you brought Jay, promising a safe haven you built, claiming every building and path as your own," said Raizu.

"Has *anything* you've ever told the village been true?"

Vosile's face broke, vulnerable now. "The Organization," he said.

"What about them?" Majest demanded.

"Jay told me about their plans." Vosile's voice cracked, his eyes pleading. "I never lied about wanting to protect you. I still want to. And I believe…it was your sister who sent this demon here."

Majest blinked, shock freezing his anger. "You think Lunesta is responsible for the possessions?" He whirled on Jay. "And you knew about the Organization all along, didn't you? You couldn't have *bothered* to tell us?"

"I assumed Masotote told you," Jay snapped, his arms folded in defense. "As for your sister sending the demon, that's common sense. It'd be like telling you water is wet."

"The chances of a demon appearing from nowhere and targeting us are next to none," said Vosile, confidence dripping back into his voice. "Therefore, this one wants something. So does the Organization. Among other things, it wants *you*, Skylark. And if Lunesta can't track you, perhaps she sent out something that can."

"If that's true, why would the demon go for Vari and a bear when Letty and I are right here?" Majest heard his voice slope upward, peaking in pitch. "Why not attack us directly?"

"There is a reason."

"Of course there is," Majest snapped. "What is it?"

"You aren't able to figure it out on your own?" Vosile asked.

Majest slammed his fist into his other hand. "This is *your* village at risk. Don't you care for the people you've spent your life lying to?"

Raizu tapped Jay on the shoulder. "Do you know the reason?" he asked quietly.

"No," Jay said in surprise. "I have no idea."

Vosile sighed. "You see, children, you *do* need my help. Only I solved this mystery."

Majest clenched his jaw. "Tell us."

"All right." Vosile's hands lifted in surrender. "This demon can only attack in pure darkness."

Majest blinked. "Is that all? Are you sure?"

Raizu shifted anxiously beside him.

"The garden of Quell and Idyllice Souleia is underground, which would place it in utter darkness if not for their lanterns." Vosile licked dry, cracked lips. "When Vari stepped into the cavern in the wall, he covered the light source and ended up in blackness. Is that not when the demon took him in its claws?"

"That doesn't make sense," said Raizu. Majest expected a comment on the impossibility of demons, but he only added, "Last night the whole forest was dark. We should've been easy targets. But it went after a bear."

"What he said." Majest nodded, then squeezed Raizu's arm in reassurance.

Vosile gave him a withering stare. "The moon shines every night, even hidden behind the clouds. It brings light to the birds, the trees, the ripples in the water. But if the bear had been sleeping in a deep enough cavern, the moon would not have reached it. That would have given our demon an opportunity."

Majest, with great reluctance, shrugged. "I suppose."

"Then I can't feel too bad for not figuring it out," Jay muttered. "Everything's pure darkness to me."

"Whatever's out there, it's powerful," said Raizu. "What can we do about it?"

Everyone looked to Vosile.

Vosile cleared his throat. "I have told you all I know. It's up to you to find and remove the demon. I suggest you send a patrol out, or devise a trap, or—"

"Hold on." Majest felt his blood heating again. "After all this, you're asking us to kill the demon while you sit back here and watch? Absolutely not."

"I can't fight," said Vosile. "I'd be of no use."

"I can't, either, but I'm doing what I can," Raizu said.

"And he's not even from this village," Majest said. "You're a selfish monster, Vosile Masotote. Even if we killed the demon, I'm sure you'd find a way to take credit for that, too, lying here stagnant and useless."

Raizu stepped forward. "Maji—"

"I swear," Majest spat, "I will put an end to this. I'll destroy the demon and wipe that crooked smile off your face. But first, I'll tell everyone what a liar you are. You'll be thrown out to the wolves like the power-hungry rat you are."

Vosile laughed, a terrible, croaking sound. "You know, I like you, Skylark," he said. "You've got a lot to learn, but you have character. Now shoo, all of you—I could lie and say it was a pleasure speaking with you, but I need my rest."

"I don't get an apology?" Jay asked. "Not from the man who used me?"

"Not from the man who saved you," Vosile returned smoothly.

Jay looked as if he had expected that answer. He did not reply, just stepped between Majest and Raizu. Somehow, he fit there.

"Come on, then, both of you," Jay said. "It's way past our bedtimes."

A sterile glow flickered in stripes across the white ceiling. An electric computer screen running on magic. Both taken as Lunesta Skylark's own.

She squinted at the screen now, as she had been doing for days. Her vision felt pixilated, eyes gone dry and narrowed. This was an exercise in patience—a new skill for her as leader of the Organization. Chami and Shayming were precise, Caiter was efficient, Shatter was intuitive, but Lunesta was patient.

The map on the screen flickered. Lunesta shifted in her plastic chair, missing nothing. Her protesting stomach and drooping eyes did not matter. Any second could have been *the one*.

"Lady President!" The voice came from outside the room, its high pitch straining. "We desperately need to speak to you!"

Shayming. The twins had been floating around since they'd returned from their mission two days ago, waiting for instructions Lunesta did not have.

When Lunesta did not respond, Shayming spoke again with a voice that could have fragmented glass. "Has there been any change on the map? Is the screen working?"

"It's fine," said Lunesta. "It's tracking the demon energy, like Caiter said it would."

"I don't know why you're listening to Malory's advice," said Chami. "He almost destroyed the laboratory."

"Keep it down," Lunesta snapped, not shifting her gaze.

"Malory's got you believing his demon is going to find the Skylarks on some hidden island, doesn't he?"

"I believe in Caiter, not Malory. And Ohanzi *will* find them, wherever they are."

"Is the screen telling you that?" Chami's voice spiked up an octave. "Please let us in."

Lunesta stayed silent. Focused harder. The dots on the map didn't move.

"Ohanzi's theory does explain how Seti could have lost the Skylarks at the bay," said Chami. "If they had a way across the water and he didn't, they could have gone anywhere and Seti wouldn't have been able to follow."

Seti's name struck Lunesta hard. The twins had been trying to pry the boy's fate out of her since she'd put him to sleep, but she wouldn't share it. Not when she was still uncertain what Seti's fate meant for the Organization's future.

And so, the twins did not ask, not to Lunesta's face. But she could hear their words creep around the question, the thought crying out behind their teeth. *"Where is he?"*

Lunesta forced herself to blink. "What is it you two wanted, anyway?"

"We need to share the results of our mission," said Chami. "And…we would like an update on your progress, if you would let us see the screen."

Lunesta sighed. They weren't dropping it. "Fine. Come in."

She clicked a button on her desk and heard the door roll open behind her. Two pairs of light footsteps followed, and a twin came to hover over each of her shoulders.

Lunesta watched them take in the map: the expanse of jade pixels, mixed and matched with shades of snow and sky. Red marks dotted the screen here and there, and the largest of them sat near the top of the screen.

"Ohanzi?" Shayming asked.

Chami's eyes lit. "You found him."

"Unless there's another demon of that caliber roaming the northern woods. The other activity I'm seeing is much farther south. I'd like to think this one is Ohanzi. Are you able to get the coordinates, like you did with the watch?"

The twins exchanged a glance. "Yes," said Shayming, "but if it's not a place we've been before, we can't teleport there, like we did with Seti."

"This dot isn't in a place you've been before?"

"No. The coordinates don't mean anything to me."

"They have to mean *something*," said Lunesta.

"They don't prove Ohanzi's hunting the Skylarks, or that there's an island, or that the red dot is even Ohanzi in the first place. We could track Seti so easily because we had his starting position and knew the forest well. This, on the other hand, is uncharted territory."

Lunesta gritted her teeth. "Don't speak to me like that," she said. When the twins drooped, she added, "We don't know anything for certain, but I am hopeful."

Chami and Shayming ducked their heads.

"We have other leads," Lunesta reminded them. "Tell me about your mission. How did that go?"

The twins smiled again, catlike and delighted. "We found someone," they said in unison. "She wants to meet you. She'll be here soon."

"Oh?" said Lunesta, her gaze lifting. Behind her, Ohanzi's red dot crawled along just a step. "Excellent."

23

"Okay," said Letty, setting her cup of tea on the kitchen table. "I'm awake. Maybe… Tell me about every second of last night." She reconsidered. "Or, this morning. Or both. I cannot *believe* what time it is."

Majest and Raizu, sitting across the table and wearing yesterday's clothes, shared a conspiring look that made Letty's hands snap instinctively to her hips. "Come on," she prodded.

"Last night?" Majest said, feigning a wide-eyed look. "What do you mean? Oh, we were just kidding about all that. You can go back to bed."

"It's almost embarrassing how much nothing happened out there," added Raizu, in the worst liar's voice Letty had ever heard.

She pointed to the dark bags beneath her eyes. "Do you see these, Majest Dagsson Skylark?"

They spared her further shenanigans, and Letty listened as a furious retelling of the previous night was explained. Majest's fists clenched against the table as he shared Vosile Masotote's treachery, but Raizu's thoughtful notes on their unlikely ally in Jay eased some of the tension. They went back and forth over the polar bear and the idea of a demon that only attacked in darkness, passing ideas around. The two of them discussed things well together, and Letty didn't miss a beat.

"I want to say none of this makes sense, but it does," she said when they were finished. "I get why Jay would've told Vosile everything. He had no one else to go to."

"Maybe because all Masotote tells anyone else is to leave him alone," said Majest.

"Maji," said Raizu.

"Anyway, Vosile wants us to put together a plan to take out the demon. With no help from him, I might add. What do you make of that?"

"An incredible honor," Raizu mumbled, grinning into his mug.

"It's not funny," Majest insisted, thwacking him with a banana peel.

Letty sighed. "You can't *not* help the village," she noted. "Especially since this is our fault."

"I know," replied Majest. "I'm going to kill the demon."

"You mean *we* are."

"I don't know, Letty. I don't think your power is stable enough to fight with. And Raizy…"

"I'm completely useless," Raizu said, half-smiling. "Yes, I know."

"That's not what I was going to say," Majest protested. "I don't know if your arrows would have an effect on a monster like this."

"Who says our powers will, either?" said Letty.

"We need to be prepared before we try anything," said Raizu. "And we need to tell the rest of Hiding what's going on."

Majest leaned back in his chair. "Right. They need to know the truth."

"Do you think they'll listen to some guy they barely trust telling them their leader is a big, fat liar?" said Letty, doubtful. "They respect Vosile too much."

"They'll listen," said Majest, his voice dripping with confidence. Letty waited for him to argue his case, but he seemed content to fly toward the sun on optimism alone.

Letty turned to Raizu. "Put his feet back on the ground, please."

Raizu looked hesitant. "We have to try talking to them." He blinked shyly at Majest. "And I can't think of anyone better to lead the charge."

Majest tossed him a grin.

Letty made an exasperated noise. "Am I the only sane one in this house?"

"If Lunesta is responsible for the demon, then we're responsible for what it does to this place," said Majest.

"Fine. At least this means that killing the demon will stop the Organization."

"It also means the Organization probably doesn't know where you are," said Raizu. "If they did, they'd be knocking at our door, not sending something to track you down."

At that, a swift pound came from the front of the house.

All three of them went still.

"What a good omen," muttered Majest, but got up to answer the door. "This better be the fruit cart's new delivery service."

It turned out to be Sedona, her hair blown across flushed cheeks—like she had been running.

Letty tugged at a loose string on her shirt.

"Morning," Majest said. "Is something the matter?"

Sedona shook her head and her breath billowed in a whirling cloud around her. "Not at all."

"Good news, then?"

"It's a dream I had."

Majest's face crinkled. "Seriously?"

"I promise it's important. In the dream, I was running through the forest, but a gust of wind kept blowing me backwards. I tried to run through it, but it dragged me to the ground over and over. Do you know what that means?"

Three blank stares came from inside the house.

"Does it mean you shouldn't eat so much soup before bed?" Majest asked.

"Wind. That's her element," said Letty, still twisting her string.

"It could be her subconscious trying to tell her something," offered Raizu.

"Yes, that's it," Sedona said, her eyes burning into Majest's. "But in the dream, wind was holding me back."

"I, uh, don't think our powers are supposed to do that," said Majest.

"They will if I can't use them," said Sedona, her voice firm. "I've got a giant target painted on my back thanks to the Organization. I can't be helpless."

Letty leaned in, peering around Majest's shoulder. She knew too well what it felt like to be just out of reach of her abilities, the connection unstable.

"I haven't taken this power seriously," continued Sedona, "but Majest, you can use your element like a third arm. I want to be able to do that." She took a hefty breath through her mouth. "I want you to train me so I can help you fight the demon that hurt Vari."

Letty almost laughed out loud at the irony.

"Do you think she's been eavesdropping?" Majest asked.

"Sure seems like it," said Letty.

Sedona frowned. "What? Why?"

"We were about to call the town together," Majest said. "We want to defeat the demon, too, and we have a lot to say about it."

"Including a few mouthfuls about your leader," Raizu muttered, too low for anyone but Letty to hear.

"When the meeting's over, we should train," Majest went on. "We can work on your powers together."

"I'm in," said Sedona. "I want to do all I can."

"Good." Majest clasped his hands together with a loud *pop*. He swiveled to Letty and Raizu. "Raizy—you come with Sedona and I. We need to find somewhere to hold a meeting. Letty, go visit as many houses as you can—skip Masotote's, of course—and ask everyone to follow you."

"Why do I have to be the one running around?" Letty asked.

"Because you're cute, and people will listen to you," Majest said. "Bring the crowd to the center fountain. I'll take it from there."

Letty decided not to call him out on his bossy tone. There wasn't much that could get Majest to slow his plans when he was this determined. In his mind, he was probably halfway through the meeting already.

"All right," she agreed, "but remember we're a team."

"A team that's about to get a whole lot bigger," Majest said. He didn't wait for a response before grinning like a child and leaping for the door.

Letty had brought quite the crowd—Majest was impressed with the large turnout.

Sunny and Sedona had come, and so had Quell, Idyllice, and Rapple, though Rapple was nervous leaving his partner at home with a baby due any hour. Cydinne hadn't come, but Jay had. Majest didn't think anyone else would have expected him to show up to a meeting like this, but he was not surprised to see the tiny prophet leaning in at the edge of the crowd.

Sedona had suggested the use of a favorite spot of hers—a large, snowy clearing outside the village. It was exposed and treeless, surrounded on all sides by the woods. In a storm, Majest would have been the first target for lightning; he teetered over the crowd as he stood on a large boulder, hands splayed for balance.

He searched for Sedona, finding her at her sister's side. She was already looking at him and nodded when their eyes met.

It wasn't just Sedona—everyone was staring at Majest, waiting for him to begin. Suspicion darkened their eyes, restlessness shuffled their feet. They didn't trust him. Not yet.

"Hello," he called, cutting through the mutters. "I'm sure you're wondering what some boy of seven birth-years wants from you on this peaceful morning."

Still no encouragement, so Majest lifted his chin and smiled. "Don't worry," he continued, "because I'm actually closer to eight birth-years now, so that ought to ease your worries, huh? I left my calendar on the mainland, so I don't know my birth date for sure, but if you can forgive me that, we should be off to a good start."

If Majest had thought humor would release the tension in the air, he had thought wrong. The village held its stony composure. Raizu looked like he was trying to shrink into his coat.

"We're in grave danger," Majest deadpanned. "That's why Letty and I brought you here. It's danger we put you in."

The muttering died immediately.

"Not only that," Majest continued, his jaw tightening, "but your precious Vosile Masotote has been deceiving you for years. He has no intention of protecting you from this."

That capsized the quiet atmosphere. Wide eyes turned to wider eyes, the town stiffening together. Majest pictured them drawing imaginary swords.

Letty caught his gaze and mouthed, "Take it slow."

"You've got some nerve, dragging us out here to say things like that!" called a lanky, curly-haired man in the crowd. His hazel eyes were so vivid, Majest could pick them out in the distance. "Who do you think you are, Messenger?"

"Haven't you heard what happened to Vari?" said Majest, raising his voice over the rumble of the village. "I know you have. He's not the only victim of this demon, and if you don't hear me out, he won't be the last."

From off to the side, Jay raised a hand.

Majest looked to him in surprise. "Uh, yeah, Jay?"

When Jay spoke, it was warily. "This morning, a woman named Deras brought in her brother, Denrick, to me. She found him like we found Vari—legs going everywhere, screaming up a storm. She said his eyes were all black." Jay turned to address the town. "This demon isn't done here."

Majest's eyes widened. "Where was Denrick at the time?"

"In their back closet. He must have gone searching for something during the night."

"In the dark," confirmed Majest. "Everyone, we've figured out how the demon possesses its victims."

"Then you should have led with that," someone hollered.

Majest took a breath, willing patience into his words. "The demon can only attack in complete darkness. There was no light in the cavern Vari found and I'll bet there was no light in Denrick's closet. That's when you are in danger. You *have* to stay in the light."

The crowd faltered. Majest watched their icy faces melt and fall, one by one. Silence came until another voice broke through it to ask, "How do you know?"

Majest shifted his feet. "That leads me to my next point—Vosile."

"You can't accuse him of anything," said the hazel-eyed man.

"He's been lying to you," Majest said over another series of mutterings. "He didn't build this village. He doesn't *speak* to the gods. He only figured out how the demon attacks because he has an outside source giving him information."

"Vosile wouldn't lie," Sedona cut in, her voice apologetic but her eyes tight. "He gave us everything we have. We're only safe *because* of him."

"He's the one who told you that!" Majest insisted.

"Hold on," said Sunny. "What kind of *outside source* are you talking about?"

Majest turned pointedly toward the boy at the edge of the crowd. "Someone is here who can answer that question better than I can."

All eyes went to Jay, who stiffened under the pressure of their gazes.

"Every warning you get, every story you're told, every discovery that helps Hiding grow—it's all Jay's words. Vosile has been stealing his knowledge and prophetic dreams for years. He's the one you should be grateful to."

"Absolutely not," someone spat, and Jay's face froze. "That boy has given us nothing but grief. Did he put you up to this?"

"He's the one who wants to steal from Vosile it sounds like," another voice agreed.

Majest reeled. "No, it's—"

"How do we know Jay's not plotting against us?" a girl cried.

"Maybe he's the one who sent the demon," someone said. "If he learned so much about them from Masotote, maybe he summoned one to ruin us."

"Wouldn't surprise me."

Jay backed up, nearly tripping over a stone. Majest realized then that he was afraid of the village. They hated him. "Why would I do that?" Jay demanded. "I don't care about anything enough for that kind of effort."

Sunny shrugged. "I think he did it."

"The Organization sent the demon," Majest said, waving his arms. The voices continued—he wished he had the power to drown them out. "It's not after Hiding. It's after the Messengers!"

"The Organization did this?" Sedona's brow wrinkled.

"What's the Organization?" asked Quell.

"They're a group led by my elder sister, Lunesta," Majest said. "They want to wipe out those with supernatural powers. People like me. Letty. Sedona. Jay and Vosile both believe they've sent the demon to kill us. It's my fault for bringing Letty and I here. Therefore, I'm going to kill this demon and I won't let Vosile steal your loyalty any longer."

The people of Hiding stared at one another, their expressions curious.

Jay stepped forward in the silence. "I think you're done here, Skylark."

"Done?" Majest repeated. "We haven't solved anything yet."

"You heard me." Jay's voice was stern as he began to move toward the clearing's exit. "Listen to how much worse you've made things here. And just when I thought I might be able to trust you."

"You—*Jay*—"

But he was gone. Hiding would never hear a word in his defense. That had been Majest's mistake. He felt sick as the villagers picked up their feet and followed Jay out, accusations hot on their tongues, clustering amongst one another. Most of them gave Majest poisonous stares on their way into the trees.

"You should not have come here," said the hazel-eyed man.

"After we hear from Vosile, we'll be back," someone else spat.

In the end, the only ones who stayed were Letty, Raizu, and Sedona. Majest looked to them hoping, wishing…

When their eyes met his, fear filled him with dread.

24

“What?” Majest demanded, trying to ignore the guilty rash that crawled over him as he remembered the disappointment on Jay's face. He hopped down from his stone podium. “I told them everything, didn't I? Why is everyone so upset?”

Raizu's violet eyes followed the crowd out. “You gave them accusations with no proof,” he said. “You should have been more…tactful.”

“This meeting was supposed to be about fighting the demon,” said Letty, leaning hard on one hip.

“It was,” said Majest. “I told them to stay out of the dark, and about Vosile and the Organization. Now they have the chance to survive.”

“It's a lot to think through,” said Sedona.

Majest whirled on her. “What about you? Are you going to walk away, too?”

“I don't know what I believe, but I thought we were in this fight together. I thought you were going to train with Letty and I after the meeting.”

“That's true,” said Letty.

Majest let out a breath that deflated his entire body. “You're right,” he said. “I forgot about that. It might be a bit before we hear from everyone. Do you want to start training now?”

“*Now?*” Raizu went pale. “Shouldn't you go after the village before they come back here with torches?”

“They'll be fine,” said Majest. “They'll go talk to Masotote, and between him and Jay, the truth will work its way out. If our goal is to get rid of this demon, there's nothing better for us to do now than get some training in."

"But—"

Majest cut him off gently with a wave of his hand. "Sedona? Letty? What do you say?"

Sedona looked at Letty. Letty looked at Sedona. Hesitantly, they nodded.

Raizu made a worried, airy sound. He retreated to the edge of the clearing and sat down on one of the flatter rocks. His head went into his hands, mouth squishing.

"Don't make that face, Raizy," said Majest, taking off his gloves one by one and shoving them into his pocket. "Enjoy the show, okay?"

Raizu gave him a withering look.

Sedona, meanwhile, tried on a smile, shaking herself out. "Majest, could I pick your brain first? I can access my power, but I don't know the best technique to use to properly dig into it."

Majest was happy to change the subject. "What can you do so far?"

"Not much, but I can feel it there, in the back of my mind. I just can't seem to let it out."

"The key to accessing your power is focus," said Majest, recalling Dagur's earliest lessons. "True focus, our father taught us, happens when you no longer feel anything but your goal. It's hard to get a hold of at first—you have to find the doors in your mind and break them down."

"That's hard to understand, much less do," said Sedona.

"I'll say," muttered Letty.

"Can I watch you do it?" asked Sedona, stepping closer to Majest.

He grinned. "You don't have to ask me twice."

Three shades of blue eyes locked on Majest as he reset himself, furrowing his brow. The elemental passageways were old friends now, and they unlocked as he exhaled. He dropped his thoughts at the gate, entering his second home. When he flicked his wrist, a branch snapped above Raizu's head.

Raizu squeaked, then glared as Majest grinned and circled the branch around his head, cheekily writing his name in the air and drawing an enormous smiling face before tossing the stick away.

"Show-off," protested Letty, though she and Sedona clapped in appreciation.

Raizu smoothed his jacket back into place with a reluctant smile. "I think I'm flattered. Not sure yet."

"I'm going to try now," said Letty, bouncing in excitement. She closed her eyes like Majest had. Her brow creased into thick wrinkles, her mouth twitching in focus.

Do I look that ridiculous when I do it? Majest bit his lip to keep from laughing at his sister's pinched face.

The clearing was soundless and expectant as Letty concentrated. When her eyes snapped open, her expression was like something awakening from a lengthy slumber. She grunted, her arms bursting out in front of her, and then she howled. The trees seemed to cower at it. Raizu nearly fell off his seat.

Majest flinched, trying to keep the alarm off his face. He definitely didn't do *that*.

Sedona shot Majest a glance. Letty stared down at her hands like she did not know what they were, dismay covering her freckles.

Majest stepped toward her. "Letty, there isn't even any water around. Don't worry." He could nearly feel the heat radiating from her fingertips.

Letty glowered at her hands. "I thought I might be able to use what's in the snow, but I guess I'm not strong enough."

"It was a good effort," said Sedona.

"It wasn't," muttered Letty. "It was dry, and dead, and *nothing*."

"Only because you didn't have a proper water source," Majest repeated, though there was something about his sister's reaction he couldn't shake.

"I think I understand how it's done," said Sedona. "I never thought about going that deep inside my head to find my wind, but I'm sure I can. Mind if I try?"

Majest tore his eyes from Letty. "Go ahead."

"All right." Sedona mirrored Majest's stance. "Do I close my eyes?"

"I think it helps."

Sedona nodded, eyelids locking shut. "Here goes nothing," she said.

Majest hardly had time to register the words—after only a breath or two from Sedona's pale lips, Majest felt a ruffle in his hair, an uncertain breeze skimming his cheeks. It was only a tickle, but it was plain as anything.

"Did you do that?" he asked, amazed. It had taken him several tries to even sense his element, much less direct it.

Sedona did not answer. Majest watched her eyelids twitch as she moved through her mind's halls. He saw her jaw unlock, watched passageways open over her face. She was fighting through the same doors Majest had already burned to the ground.

Another gust of wind came, harsher this time. It whizzed around Majest's head, watering his eyes, dragging his mouth open. Raizu must have felt it, too, because he left his stony perch behind, joining his friends in the center of the clearing.

The wind grew stronger still, roaring until Majest had to put out his hands to keep his balance. For a moment, he lost hearing in one ear.

From somewhere, Letty gasped. She had, Majest assumed, expected Sedona's efforts to be in vain, like her own. The wind prospered and roared for several more moments until it faded into a quiet breeze, then dissipated altogether.

"Holy *skies*," said Majest, shaking his windswept hair back into place and staring at Sedona. "I've never seen anything like that before!"

"I knew I could do it," said Sedona, peach-cheeked and panting. "I needed a proper teacher to help me bring it out."

"I didn't do a thing," Majest said, and meant it. "That was all you. On your first try."

Letty sniffed, her eyes traveling up to the sky. "Yes, but you were the one to tell her how. Like you've always told me."

"And you've always listened," Majest assured her. "Maybe we could bring a vat of bay water up to the house for you to practice with. It's not your fault there isn't any out here."

"I know," said Letty. She managed a smile, adding, "Congratulations, Sedona. I suppose it's only fair. You're the oldest out of all of us."

Before Sedona could respond, footsteps sounded from behind them and Majest whirled to see Jay—of all people—hurtling toward them, his usual scowl nowhere in sight. He tripped a little as he ran, the first time Majest had ever seen his blindness get the better of him.

"What?" Majest asked. "Is there news?"

Jay took a deep breath, his exhale coming out as a shudder. His dark hair was in complete disarray and he had an angry red mark blooming on his temple, as if he'd struck something.

"Get over here," Jay said, his voice urgent. "The village is requesting to speak with you again, but you're not going to like the reason why."

Jay showed the three Messengers and Raizu to a large building behind the sparkling fountain. The place was a tall white glacier, paint chipping under the stress of the northern weather to reveal patches of gray.

A door creaked open, and Jay led them through a long, bleak marble hallway. They passed by doors left and right, headed for the back. The hall felt foreign and antique, the ceiling looming high overhead.

Majest stared up at it, wondering how old the building was. Definitely older than Vosile and his villagers. It might have stood tall before the End— but no doubt Vosile had claimed it as his own.

Raizu tapped his wrist. "What's the matter? You're making a face."

"More like *who's* the matter," Majest said.

Jay made a frustrated sound. He had one hand on the wall, guiding him forward. "Let the Masotote thing drop," he said. "At least for now. We're treading on thin ice—all of us."

Majest's stomach knotted. "I'm sorry I got you in trouble, Jay. I thought I was helping."

"So did I," Jay said.

"Isn't there anyone who believes us about you?" Letty asked.

The hallway reached its end and Jay drew in a long breath through his nose. "That's not important. I'm not important. It isn't about me. The village is going to be furious if you bring up your accusations again."

"Then, what do they want us to talk about?" Sedona asked.

"You'll see when we get there."

"Get where?" Majest cut in. "Where are we?"

"Village hall. Occasionally, Masotote likes to get someone to carry him in here so he can hold a meeting. It doesn't happen often."

"He's here?" Majest didn't like the sound of that.

"You'll see."

"Could you *please* stop being all mysterious? We're your friends."

"No, thank you," said Jay, and stopped walking. They had arrived at a large white door. Behind it, Majest heard voices.

"Watch your tongue this time," Jay warned and fumbled for the handle, letting them inside.

The room was massive and domed, chairs in orbit around a center podium. Everyone was sitting, holding a lantern in conversation. Their voices died down at the sound of the door opening, and countless pairs of eyes stared at Majest. Under those intense stares, he felt oddly small.

"I brought the Skylarks," Jay told the crowd. He sounded bored, but Majest didn't miss the tremble of his fists at his sides. "You can proceed with your business."

"Thank you, Jay," said—to Majest's horrified surprise—Vosile Masotote. He sat slumped into the center podium, bony chin jutting out as he gave Majest a hard look. His narrowed gaze was everywhere, passed throughout the room.

Majest forced himself to step forward. "What's going on here? Have you told them the truth yet?"

Vosile's mouth twitched. "We have sorted the situation out," he said.

"And?"

"And I have decided to keep you inside your house until the demon is gone."

Majest's hopes dropped. *"What?"*

"A near-stranger sneaking around the forest at night is a concern to begin with. The fact that you came back with a story of a possessed polar bear and a basket of lies about our village proves that such adventures may have, in fact, possessed *you.*"

"That's ridiculous!" Majest burst. "All of it is true. Raizy can tell you. He was there and so was Jay. We had you completely defenseless! You admitted to stealing Jay's prophecies!"

Raizu opened his mouth, but Vosile cut him off with a wave of his hand.

"You could get your little friend to say whatever you want," he said, "because *you* are a liar. And you have been listening to the worst liar of us all." He snarled the last few words at Jay. "How could you turn on your own leader like this—pretending my words are your own? I never should have brought you here."

"Really?" Jay's voice was cold, his walls back up. "Without my warning, you never could have protected our buildings from last year's blizzard. Without my knowledge of demons, you never would've figured out how this one strikes in the dark."

Masotote barely looked at him. "You were sent to fetch the Skylarks today, nothing more," he said. Then, his voice deepened. "You are not needed here any longer."

Jay flinched, then seemed to wind himself back up. "I can take a hint," he snapped. "We'll see how you do without me."

In seconds, the door banged behind them. Jay was gone, without ceremony. All hope seemed to follow him out.

Majest looked desperately around the room for any signs of sympathy, but familiar faces—Sunny, Quell, Idyllice, Rapple—all avoided his gaze.

"As I was saying," Masotote continued, dismissing Jay entirely, "Majest Skylark, you will be put under house arrest. The demon needs to be dealt with, but we will not have you in our way while we do it."

We, Majest thought. *There is no we.*

"The demon wants Letty and I," he said, shifting into the empty space Jay had left behind. "It's not going to stop until it finds us in the dark."

Vosile arched an eyebrow. "Correct."

"So, what are you going to do?" asked Letty.

Vosile stared her down with eyes like a vulture's. "What do you think we *must* do?"

An infinite moment passed by before the villagers turned to Majest and Letty, unblinking, unmoving.

Majest almost lost his calm. "Wait, are you planning on *sacrificing* my sister and I?"

The spell broke. Several villagers giggled. Even Masotote stifled a laugh with a cough. "I see you haven't lost your humor along with your common sense," he said. "Of course not. You'll be safe at home with your sister while we create our trap."

"Trap?" Letty interrupted.

"The gods have sent me knowledge on how to hunt this creature. I will have a building turned black, inside and out. We will block the windows and the cracks in the door and paint what we cannot cover. When the sun rises tomorrow, the demon will be looking for a place to hide. If it falls for our trap, we can send in forces to kill it."

Can you really trap a demon? Majest whirled to where Jay should have been standing. No one was there to answer his question.

"You can't know if that will work," he protested. "And you just sent away the one person who could have helped."

Vosile's eyes were ice cold. "Don't try to meddle any longer, Skylark. This is not your battle."

"Of course it is," Majest protested. "I'm the reason this thing is here."

"We want to try the trap," said Sunny. When Majest looked at her, she gave him a slow, knowing nod. "It's Vosile's idea from the gods. We have to test it."

Test Vosile's idea. It would be a chance to try out his own idea, wouldn't it? Is that what Sunny meant? If the villagers could not trap and kill the demon with the plan the gods had supposedly given him… If they were possessed, or worse…

All the same, Majest shook his head in Sunny's direction. He would not risk lives to prove the point Masotote was a fake.

"I'm the one the demon wants," he argued with Vosile. "No one else needs to fight."

"Foolish boy," said Vosile. "One child cannot take on the darkness alone."

"He's right," said Sedona. She held out a hand like she meant to put it on Majest's shoulder, but after a moment she let it fall. "I don't want you to be in danger. We can do this together."

"If I fail and the demon destroys me, I'm the only one who gets hurt," Majest said. "It will have gotten what it wanted."

"It wants me, too," Letty said, as Raizu and Sedona blanched. "You can't say that."

"I am the storm Jay foresaw coming to the village," Majest insisted. "I made the boat that brought us here. I put Sedona in danger and got Jay accused of treason."

"I'm just as much of this storm," said Letty, clutching at his arm. Her nails bit into the skin above his wrist. "I'm doing this *with* you. You'll die trying alone."

"No, I won't," Majest snapped. He suddenly felt sick—with Letty, with the villagers, and with Vosile most of all, risking his people to blanket his bed of lies.

Shaking Letty off, he stepped to the door and threw it open. "If anyone tries to stop me or confine me to my house, I would be glad to lock *them* in my house instead."

He stormed out and thunder followed him in the slam of the door behind him. The hallway that greeted him seemed swirling with life in the sudden darkness. Patterns on the stone warped in front of his eyes, scattering his vision.

Majest blinked until the hall shifted back to normal. His sternum rammed into his heart and his blood boiled hot, but for the first time since he'd stumbled across this village, he felt something other than the lull of Hiding's safety. He felt brave—himself again.

He burst outside, thoughts buzzing, and trotted down to the fountain. It glistened and swelled, the water sinking to the base only to rise again, then plummet.

Majest did not want to follow the same cycle. What was the point in hauling the truth up to the village if Vosile would only wash it back to the ground when he got there? Hiding had trusted him longer than Majest had been alive. The only way they would believe Majest was if he could prove Vosile's plans were faulty and follow his own—kill the demon himself.

Footsteps sounded behind the fountain. They were light, raindrop patters, barely there.

Majest balled his hands into fists. "I'm not going back to my house," he started, but when he realized who it was, the words died quickly.

"I knew you wouldn't get far," Raizu said. "You don't have a plan, do you?"

Majest swiveled to him, meeting his anxious expression with a slight challenge. "I have a plan," he bluffed. "I just got distracted."

"A distraction can cost you your life," said Raizu. His expression was unreadable as he scuffed at the snowy dirt with one boot. "I mean, not that you've ever had a problem risking your life before, but you might want to start preparing for the day when your refusal to ever slow down your own thoughts might be more harm than help."

Majest blinked. "Huh?"

"You rush into things," Raizu clarified. "Doing the right thing doesn't mean you have to do it without thinking."

"Are you telling me bravery is a weakness?"

"There's a line between bravery and recklessness. You and Letty love to cross it, which I already knew, but this is going too far. You won't prove anything by doing this alone."

"You were just as reckless as we were," said Majest. "You ran away from home. You crossed the bay on one of our boats."

"Because I had to sink to your level if I wanted to find you! You almost lost Letty on your way here. We all could have died crossing the bay."

Majest was stung. "Letty and I took care of ourselves and each other," he said. "You may have saved her life, but it's not because I failed to protect her."

"That's not what I said. You don't owe me anything. We've done enough for each other that none of that should matter."

"Great!" said Majest, throwing up his hands. "None of it matters? Fine. Now, if you'll excuse me, I have a demon to destroy and a village to save. I don't want to fight with you. Why don't you take Letty home?"

"No!" Raizu stepped forward. "Some things *do* matter. You matter. Throwing away your life for this—this *thing* isn't worth it."

"I'm not going to die."

"But you could."

"But I won't," Majest insisted.

"You don't get it, do you, Maji?" Any trace of the nervous boy who never angered is gone, the candle blown out. "You can't waltz your way through the world and expect every odd to turn into your favor just because you're trying your best."

"I do not *waltz*."

"There are things you can't do. This is one of them. If you keep digging your way through things with no second thoughts, eventually you're going to find yourself in a hole with no way to climb out."

"Oh, now I'm not waltzing, I'm digging. Okay." Majest stepped back. His next words made little sense, even to his own ears. "You'd pull me out."

Raizu's anger paused. "What?"

"If I dug myself into a hole, you'd toss me a rope, right? I'd do the same for you."

That twisted Raizu's confusion into a scowl. "Of course," he said, his voice shaking. "As long as you assume someone or something will be there to save you, you won't worry about it. You take everyone for granted. Me. Letty. Your powers."

"That's *not*—"

"But you won't actually *ask* for help? You have to be the hero and you're convinced nothing can stop you. Well, have at it!" Raizu's arms went up; the ends of his worn coat drooped around his wrists in defeat.

"Raizy," Majest tried, but he wasn't listening.

"If I can't stop you, then fine. Just don't ask me to watch you die." Raizu turned on his heel and stalked off, the air stirring around him.

Majest stood there alone, watching as the sun dipped low in the sky and the trees tinged yellow, and at Raizu as he walked away. No one else came to find him, despite all of Vosile's talk. Majest was left alone in the streets.

Maybe Raizu had been right. Maybe Majest always expected someone to pull him from danger but was too stubborn to ask for help.

It didn't matter.

I can do this.

I can do this.

I have *to do this.*

Desperation catching on his every breath, Majest raced out of town.

25

brush whipped, black spurting from between its weasel-hair bristles. It slapped against the panes of windows, oozed between the grooves in the walls. The building was surrounded by volunteers, who were spattering every unprotected grain of wood.

As they continued, the paint smacking and sloshing, the abandoned storage building began to reek. They had combined mud and natural dyes to create the black color after nailing boards and spare pieces of metal into any crack that might have let light in.

Their construction had taken all night and most of the previous afternoon, but it was precise. Hardly any black paint had been needed, in the end. Their nails and wood held.

"Looks great," one of the painters said, his coat stained with gobs of violet and brown.

"Brilliant," another agreed.

Someone choked on an inhale, letting out a stuttering gasp. Something frigid had punched through her, phasing through the wall her hand rested upon.

She struggled to speak. "It—it's *here*," she managed. "I felt it! The demon!"

They all drew knives from their belts, holding them awkwardly. They had their orders, but they all paused, eyes wide and doe-like.

"Go in," someone hissed.

"No, *you!*"

"We told Masotote we would—"

"I'll do it," said the girl who had felt the cold. She grabbed for the door handle, which seemed to freeze to her glove. "I'll lead us."

She pulled back the door. A slice of light meandered onto the bare floor, dust suspended in the glow. The girl lifted her blade and stepped inside.

The door banged behind her, though she had not touched it.

Everyone stared. There was silence, heavy and black.

From inside, they heard a hiss. A snap. A growl that might have been tangled words. Finally, a shriek with terror. It sent birds startling from the trees, made the fountain skip a watery beat, turned the fluffy heads of even the most apathetic clouds above.

Someone lunged for the door. He struggled to pry it open, as though something pressed it in from the other side. At last, it pulled open and the girl came tumbling out in a heap. Her eyes were black and rolling, tears wet and hot on her face. Her chest heaved for air.

"*Shadows!*" she screamed.

The man who had taken her out pulled his hat down around his ears, fixed the door with stony resolution.

"I'll be strong enough," he said. "I'll be next. Give me the dark."

Everyone wailed after him as he charged inside and soon, he was wailing with them. The crowd pulled at the door, a tangle of limbs dragging the man back outside. He was already half-possessed, lips beading with foam.

"We can't," a woman cried. "Skylark was right, wasn't he? This is impossible."

"But it's in there, isn't it?" someone snapped. "Pull yourself together. We have orders."

"Vosile's orders—"

They nodded, all of them.

Trembling and nauseous, they slipped through the door, but one by one, they reeled back, shrieking and covering their faces. Some eyes were black, some tear-filled. The dark was on their faces, slinking at their hands, throwing their arms to the sky without permission.

Cradling the injured and writhing, they abandoned the building, their brushes, their bucket of nails. It was morning, but everything was in shadows.

The dark could not be conquered.

Letty could sense something was missing before she even opened her eyes. She didn't have to let her gaze fall across the kitchen table or call out Majest's name to know he had not returned home last night. She had hoped she would hear him munching on something in the late-night hours, but the fruit basket on the counter was untouched.

She loved her brother, knew his heart was in the right place—but once that *look* flashed in his eyes and his dimpled smile, he couldn't be stopped.

Letty chewed on her lip. She had wanted to find him after the meeting, as Raizu had, but she had been swept into conversation with Sedona and Sunny, doing her best to work with the rest of the town. The people of Hiding had put Vosile's plan into action despite Majest's wishes and despite his disappearance.

Raizu and Letty had met up later at home—Raizu looking forlorn and spent, Letty with a discomfort in her stomach that squeezed up into her ribs.

"I tried to make him be reasonable," Raizu had told her, slumping into a wooden chair.

Your first mistake. "What did he say?" she'd asked. Though she hadn't known him for long, Raizu seemed like a steady light to keep her brother upright.

"I don't think I helped. I think he's still going to go after whatever's out there."

"Didn't you try to convince him not to?"

Raizu had looked embarrassed. "I hardly gave him a chance to get a word in edgewise, actually."

"You? Talking over Maji? I didn't think that was possible."

"I guess I got upset." Raizu had scratched his head with one hand, frowning. "I was…worried about him. But I stormed off. I'm sorry, Letty. I should have stayed with him or brought him home. I'm sure he must think horribly of me now."

"He wouldn't—I'm sure everything's fine," Letty had assured him, though her twisted stomach had said otherwise. "You did your best. We have to give him a little time."

They had done just that—more than that—more than a little time. The next morning, still nothing. No Majest.

Letty slipped out of bed, the wood floor creaking under her feet. She dressed for the day, tied back her hair, and pulled socks onto her feet. A few paces down the hall, she reached the room her brother had mocked the curtains in only yesterday.

She pushed open the thin wooden door. "Raizu?"

Raizu sat on the edge of the bed, his hair sticking out around his ears. He looked up when Letty came in, his eyes surrounded by dark circles.

"No sign of him?" Letty said. Her stomach did a flip.

"Nothing." Raizu's eyes were dark, more blue than violet today, as if their sunset edges had been swallowed by night.

Letty squeezed her eyes shut, thinking. "He went after the demon."

"I think so. It's my fault," said Raizu without hesitation. He snatched a pillow from the bed and took it into his lap. "I should have been there for him, but I tore him down."

"No," Letty said softly. "You said what you did because you care about him. All dreamers need to keep their feet on the ground. That's what he tells me when I don't let old-world stories rest. But he's a dreamer, too. His head's just in a different set of clouds."

That didn't help settle Raizu's expression. He picked at the frayed edge of the pillowcase. "I wish I hadn't left him on his own," he whispered. "I didn't even try to stop him. I'm weak and a coward, Letty. Don't tell me I'm not."

Letty's lip trembled. She didn't know what to say, so she sat next to him and leaned her head on his shoulder, the way she would have done for Majest. His shirt was warm on her temple, the silence holding them in place.

Until a noise broke it: a scream.

They were on their feet instantly.

"That didn't sound like Maji," said Letty.

"It sounded like *something*," said Raizu, already pulling on his boots. "We should go."

"Right," Letty agreed, and readjusted her hair. Then she realized something. "Raizu, really?"

"What?"

"Chasing the mysterious scream is your idea?"

He frowned. "What do you mean? If someone's in danger…"

"I mean," Letty said, "when it really matters, you aren't a coward at all."

They headed for the streets.

Majest knew he was predictable. The strings in his mind, the ends of his fingertips, the tread of his boots—they always reached for the same place.

And so, he found himself in the trees.

The harsh slant of the morning sun slashed through the heart of the forest and Majest ran, pushing branches away and kicking up mud. He didn't know how many times he had crossed his own path, how many rings he had gone around the island. He had lost count.

All night he'd been doing this, and he hadn't found anything but the erratic beat of his own heart. His throat ached from thirst, his lungs gasped at the frigid air. But he would not go home. Not yet.

Eventually, he had to admit the demon was not out here. It had probably returned to the village, to some other black place, and was nowhere near the trees where Majest had spent the night.

His entire body protesting, he had staggered back through the woods. The hike seemed to take hours, but eventually he could make out the gray, flat tops of Hiding's buildings through the thinning trees. It was early enough that most of the village would be asleep. No one would get in the way of his hunt.

As he ran forward, more impatient than ever, a faint pain-stricken cry got his attention. His blood chilled immediately. *Has the demon found someone else? Am I too late?*

He forced his desperate feet faster, the last of the forest behind him. He found the stone path that led to the fountain, the place where he had heard his doubts become words.

"There are things you can't do."

Irritated at the stab of guilt that pierced his heart, Majest turned away from the fountain and walked deliberately in the other direction.

This new path sent him toward several short, wide buildings clumped on the outskirts of town. They looked abandoned, unused—except for the footprints stamped in dizzy circles around the area. Someone had been here. Many someones. Recently.

A dark spot gleamed on the ground. Majest peered at it, crouching low on his knees in the snow. The rays of the early morning sun made it hard to see, but the spot looked wet, and black as Vari's possessed eyes.

Majest put a finger to the spot and drew it up to his face. When he took a sniff, he almost lost the food in his stomach. He flung his stained glove into the snow with a gag.

He saw it, then: a trail of black spots, crawling from his feet to the door of a boarded-up building. Wooden boards cut off the building's natural light, and more of the wet black dye filled in patches on the walls.

Majest came to a stop in front of it. This was it—the building Vosile had ordered be prepared to trap the demon. The nearby snow was flattened with footprints.

Majest was drawn to the building, found his bare hand on the door, the air seeming to pulse around it. Something pushed him, pushed his fingers, and the frame creaked open, nailed together wooden bits dragging on the ground.

Nothing leaped out at him. Nothing even broke the morning silence.

If Raizu were here, he would never have let Majest do this.

He went inside.

The instant he let go of the door, it crashed behind him and the light went out.

"No," he gasped. He would not be caught like Vari and Denrick.

The room buzzed with black; it smelled of the foul spots in the snow, hanging in Majest's nostrils like rotten fruit. There wasn't so much as a freckle of light.

He spun, his hands going for the door. There was no handle on the inside, only paint-sticky cracks he could barely fit his fingernails into. He pushed at the door with the force of his entire body, but it held. He was trapped.

"Djöfull."

Majest willed his eyes to go wider, to adjust, to find some scrap of light to see by. But the villagers had done a fine job of creating their darkness.

His breathing slowed, the hair on his neck on end. He reached for the knife in his boot. Nothing. It must have fallen out in the forest. With his last grass-bomb used on the polar bear, all he had to defend himself with was his element.

A lump rose in Majest's throat. He had sought this darkness out, but now, he was afraid.

The village wouldn't have been able to trap the demon so easily. It's not here. I'll be fine. All I have to do is find a way out.

He ran his hands along the wall, feeling for a loose board, a handle he could wrench open. Nothing but solid wood.

"Skylark," came a voice.

No—it was not quite a voice. It was something pretending to be a voice.

Majest gasped at the wicked scratch of the sound, forgetting his promise to be fearless. He staggered against the door.

"Who's there?" he called, his voice getting higher. "Show yourself!"

In response came a suffering hiss, like an animal wounded but not killed. Majest had heard the sound before, in exactly that same way—coming from an injured animal. The polar bear.

And now he knew what he was facing.

"You're the demon," he said, and let go of the door. He had imagined trapping this monster when he found it, but it had trapped him instead.

"O-han-zi," responded the voice, closer this time. The word was slurred to the point of being almost incomprehensible. *"I am Ohanzi."*

"Nice to meet you," Majest managed. "Surprised you speak human. I assume you know who I am."

"You are the gods' choice, and I was an accident," said Ohanzi's voice. *"It wasn't supposed to be this way. Lady President's scientists never meant for Power to drive out Power. I wanted an equal world, to melt away the End and the supernatural dangers that came with it."*

"So, it was the Organization who sent you."

"This is not the first time such experiments have cost a terrible price. Before you were born, the same madness that created me created others who spread far across the land—even

to this village. I once had family here, Majest Skylark. It is how I knew about this hidden place."

Majest choked on a breath. "Madness?"

"I thought my creator was like a god, but gods are weak. Humans are weak. Half-bloods like Seti Sinestre, who lost you are weak. And the Organization was wrong. It is Power that rules this land."

"I… Are you saying you're on our side? Who's Seti?"

Ohanzi laughed. *"It is* my *kind of Power that rules the land. Not yours. I am here to destroy you and rise above you. Above the Organization. Power seeks to rise. That is its curse—mine, yours, theirs."*

Majest's hope drowned before it could reach the surface. "Then come out and fight me," he whispered. "That's why we're both here, right? Power and Power."

In answer came a low gurgling noise. Majest saw Vari strapped to the table in Jay's claustrophobic house, fingers clawing at gnarled wood, seeking escape, to quench a thirst. He saw Letty, howling to the wind as water shed lifelessly from her fingers. It was all about Power. Everything.

An icy breath coated the room and Majest grappled for his element, trying to focus.

He was a moment too late. Darkness stabbed suddenly through his bones, carving out sections of spine, drinking from his veins. Majest felt nothing but cold as it overtook him, knocking his breath and body and heartbeat to the ground. The shadows devoured him—his hair, his clothes, the bright things he kept close to his heart. His family. His forest. Raizu, who had been right.

Majest was no longer just inside the dark but part of it himself.

The whisper at the edge of Raizu's hearing was an itch he could not reach to scratch. It grated against his earlobes, a near-silent scream. Something somewhere just out of reach was wrong.

"Raizu," said Letty for possibly the fourth time. In front of them, the fruit cart gleamed with dewy apples. "Did you hear him? He said the noise is Acillia, Rapple's partner."

"She's giving birth," said the man at the cart. He had familiar curly hair and hazel eyes—this was the boy who had taunted Majest in the clearing the day before. He didn't look quite so fierce alone in the light. "It's her first time. Can hardly blame her."

Raizu's ears buzzed. "That's all?" he asked. "I keep thinking I hear something…from that way." He gestured toward a stocky, ashen section of buildings.

Hazel-eyes raised a dark brow. "Funny you should say that."

"What? Why?" asked Letty.

"Those are old warehouse buildings to store housing material and the like. Usually, no one goes over there, but this morning, a team blacked out one of the buildings for Vosile. You know, the demon trap." He scratched at his neck. "They think they caught the thing in there, but everyone who went inside ended up possessed or in hysterics. They're regrouping at town hall with the victims."

The words stabbed Raizu's ribs. "Is everyone okay? Is—is anyone at that building now?"

Hazel-eyes shrugged. "I don't know. I've been boxing the Souleias' berries all morning."

Raizu squeezed his eyes shut until he saw spots. *There are no such things as demons. There aren't. This is a toxin, or an illness, or…*

Letty, giving Raizu a curious look, said, "Thank you for letting us know."

"No problem," said Hazel-eyes. "You know, I'm sorry about what I said to your brother. I'm sure that Jay kid was just manipulating him, right? I hope you find him soon."

Raizu saw Letty try not to stiffen. "Thank you," she said again.

The whisper scratched against Raizu's ears once more. His gaze tugged to the left, toward the storage buildings, his heart in his throat.

"Letty, we need to see what's going on over there," he said.

"Absolutely not," said Letty. "Did you not hear the fruit guy say they think the demon is in there? You sound like Maji."

"Exactly." Raizu heard the pressure of his voice, heard it crack. "If Maji heard about it, he would've gone there to fight."

"Skies, you're right."

"I wish I wasn't."

Fear making their feet crunch faster, they hurried through the cold village. The closer they got to the low-lying buildings, the more footprints they found.

"Maji's," Letty said, pointing to a line of familiar-looking marks. "That's the pattern on our boots."

The sight of them crushed Raizu's heart. He did not want to associate Majest with the hiss in his ear. He did not want Majest anywhere near this place.

They picked up the pace, Raizu's teeth finding their familiar position around his bottom lip. By now, his heartbeat had drowned out the whispering. It was in his throat, between his ears, behind his eyes, all he could feel.

The first row of buildings gave away nothing. They barely stood much higher than Raizu's head, smelling of mud and stone. Half of them were missing doors.

"Where is it?" Letty said. "Where's the trap building?"

Raizu was about to answer when the noise came again. No longer a whisper or a tickle—a terrible, shuddering groan. A shiver shot through Raizu's core. When he looked to Letty, her face was round with horror. She had heard it, too.

"Over there," she whispered. "Come on!"

With the next row of buildings out of the way, Raizu saw it: a building boarded up from roof to foundation, spattered in a black paste.

The instant fear in him was nearly hysteria. When the noise came again, Raizu could not help but whimper. There was a demon in there, wasn't there? He had fought so hard not to believe it.

His eyes lowered to the ground. The familiar footprints had gone right up to the darkened door and disappeared inside.

Letty made a choked noise.

"*Hímin,*" Raizu whispered. "I hope we're not too late."

Letty lifted her eyes at her brother's language on Raizu's tongue, like he was something she'd never seen before. Then together, they hurtled for the door.

"It's frozen shut," said Letty as she pushed on it. Her hand recoiled. Another long sound wafted from behind the wall. "It's so cold I can't touch it, even with my glove—"

"Here," gasped Raizu. He balled up his scarf, but instead of handing it to Letty, shoved it hard at the door. It swung open with a violent shriek.

At first glance, the room was empty. Wood, nails, shadow. No screams, no blood on the walls. Even the ghastly sound had vanished with the trickle of light streaming through the open door.

"I don't understand," Raizu stammered, still clutching his scarf. His heart had stopped skipping beats. For all he knew, it could have stopped altogether. "Where's—?"

"Maji!" Letty finished with a scream.

Raizu only had time to distinguish Majest's broken, lifeless body on the ground and let out a choked gasp before the door swung closed behind them, destroying any remaining light.

26

Blanketed in the heavy darkness, Letty couldn't see her brother. But she could feel him. Her hands were on Majest's cold face, stroking back his hair with trembling fingers. Time had been tossed aside, frozen by the cold blast that had smashed the door shut. For eternities—seconds—forevers—moments—there was nothing but Majest's body face-down on the ground.

Reality came back hard and the tears blurred Letty's eyes. She felt Raizu lean next to her.

"Is he breathing?" Raizu asked raggedly. "Is there a heartbeat?"

"I—don't know." With fingers shaking as badly as her voice, Letty tore off her gloves and felt for a pulse at Majest's throat. "I can't tell."

Leather squeaked as Raizu removed his gloves and took her place.

They held their rasping breaths.

"Nothing. I don't feel anything. *Letty.*"

A whisper pulsed around them. Letty's head swooped down and her thoughts spiraled.

"*Letty,*" Raizu repeated, grabbing her shoulders. "What do we do? He's dying!" The words were a hysteric near-sob echoed across the lightless walls.

Lightless. Whispering. This was still Vosile's trap—if they did not move, they could have three missing heartbeats instead of one.

"The demon," Letty gasped. She held her brother's lifeless body close to her, her heart's last stronghold. Majest would have wanted her to be brave.

Even braver than him. "If it's still here, we have to get outside. The door *closed* by itself."

She shoved Raizu upward, catching his hands and tugging. He made no objection about the demon for once, but he resisted her grip all the same.

"We can't leave Maji," he said, choked up and off-key. "I won't, not on my life. Help me lift him."

A hiss came from the back of the room.

Ignoring it, they bent down and gathered Majest in their arms, forcing him to slump upright between them. Their feet stumbled on the floor, but they held steady.

"We should take him to Jay," Raizu said, breathless and shaky. "Can you get the door?"

Another hiss, louder this time.

Hiking up her shoulders for leverage, Letty ran her free hand over the door, searching for a handle.

"I can't," she cried, staggering as Majest slipped in her grasp. "It won't open." She tried again, willing useless eyes to see, useless fingers to find *something* to pull. *"Help!"*

Something drowned out her cry—a gurgle. A snarl. A laugh. It sent a scream through Letty, buckled her knees at the familiarity of it.

Vari, in the underground garden. Lifeless eyes, lifeless cries.

Her hands and knees hit the ground. She felt Raizu lose what was left of their grip on Majest. They both tumbled next to her as the laughter grew louder, coming from everywhere—near and far and right over their shoulders.

"Skylark, you want power?" something snarled.

It wasn't too different from the dark voice that spoke between Letty's ears when she used her element. *"Let me show you what true power is."*

"No!" Letty howled, crawling toward Raizu, her elbows brushing the fur of Majest's coat. "Raizu, get up! Where's your bow?"

"I left it at home," Raizu cried, his voice cracked. "It wouldn't help, would it? It had Vari in seconds. Letty, I'm so sorry. You and Maji deserve so much more."

"Don't say that," said Letty. Out of all the times she had nearly died this past month, it seemed preposterous she should go without a fight, without a brother, without a drop of light. "Don't say that. Don't *say* it." She repeated and repeated the words as if she could will the truth away.

As they braced themselves, something rose above the hissing laughter—a sound high and commanding, whirring and grinding with Power.

Letty lifted her head and gasped. She hadn't heard this sound in so long, but as the roar of it filled her ears and folded itself over the darkness it was as if she had never lived without it.

"This is impossible," Letty breathed. "We're *not* dreaming."

She saw familiar lights wink under her feet, felt herself being lifted and carried high into space. The storage building buckled from existence, disappearing into the starry swirl of the heavens. Everything glittered indigo and gold.

"Letty, what's happening?" Raizu asked.

Letty realized in shock he was here, too, standing in the patch of nothingness next to her. His eyes were wild with starlight. "Are we dead?"

"No. We're in the realm of the gods," Letty breathed.

"We're *where?*"

"Aletta Skylark," boomed a familiar voice.

He appeared through the endless mist, cloaked and hooded in robes of starlight. The streaks of paint down his face took nothing away from the all-consuming universe in his eyes.

"Komi," said Letty, bowing her head low in respect. She wondered vaguely how to greet a god. She didn't have to ask him how he'd been, did she? "Why have you brought us here?"

"My job as Deliverer is to watch over my Messengers. I understand your powers have led to the rise of a great evil." He did not sound surprised.

"Yes," Letty whispered. "Our eldest sister sent a demon after us."

Komi's face was grave, almost human. "The one who created this demon has done so with expertise. This is no ordinary demon, able to be killed by mortals. It needs the gods' own element to assist—Element Light. Water and earth are not light, though they thirst for it. The sky has light but it is not light. Even fire, bright as it burns, is not light, and it is not fire's time yet."

"Then, are you here to help? Or…" Letty remembered what Komi had once said. "You aren't allowed to *interfere directly*, are you?"

"You are correct. I cannot," said Komi.

"Then what do you expect us to do? Why did you bring us here?" Letty wailed. "My brother was killed by this monster!"

"Wait." It was Raizu who had spoken, oddly calm in the quivering air. "You deliver elemental powers? I don't have powers, but I don't envy Maji and Letty for theirs. I don't even believe in the gods. Why am *I* here?"

"If believing is seeing, I imagine these stars might stir your mind," Komi said, and looked as amused as a god could. "I know who you are, Raizu Capricorn. You think you can walk alongside the Messengers? What do you think you can do for the Skylarks that they can't do themselves?"

"I don't—"

"Raizu's just as valuable an ally against the Organization as a thousand Messengers," Letty interrupted.

"Peace, little one," said Komi, holding up a hand. "I am not trying to offend. I have watched this boy fight to be wherever the two of you are. I have brought him here because he is a worthy vessel."

"Vessel?" Raizu squeaked.

"You will bring the light when I am unable to," said Komi. "You will drive out this darkness."

Raizu's hands went up, reminding Letty of the first time she had met him, wobbly and tongue-tied in the woods. "I can't be the hero," he said. "I haven't—all I do is—I mean—"

"You are the light," Komi repeated, and did not lower his hand. Its silver palm began to glow. "Come forward, Raizu Capricorn."

Raizu did not move.

Letty elbowed him. "Go!"

At last, on shaky pointed boots, Raizu stepped forward. There was no floor beneath him.

Somehow, Letty's future, Majest's future, the people of Hiding—it all was dependent on this ordinary pack boy who had chosen to tackle his fears over his cowardice.

Komi's smoldering hand reached through space, landing on Raizu's shoulder. The hiss it made was all four elements at once. Raizu shuddered.

"You are not destined for Messenger power," said Komi, "but you have proven yourself in other ways. You are the sun to grow the trees; you are the sun to warm the water."

"I don't understand," said Raizu.

Letty couldn't see his face now, from this angle.

"It will be up to you to use the light I give you. Because you are human and this is true godly power, you may only use it once." Komi released Raizu and stepped back.

Letty didn't know if it was her eyes playing tricks on her, but Raizu seemed to glow.

Raizu gasped, words breaking before they could form. He turned to face Letty, and his eyes were *definitely* glowing.

Komi bowed his head and Letty felt herself tumbling once more. The tunnel from the heavens propelled her downward, pushing the stars in reverse, flinging cosmic dust behind her. She landed on her feet in the black storage building, gravity landing with her.

Her body sagged as the hissing laughter returned. Majest still lay on the floor somewhere behind her, everything all dark once more.

"Letty," Raizu said. "Letty, are you there? Tell me that was a hallucination."

"It wasn't," Letty replied, and found her heart sinking. "If Komi gave you power, you've got about five seconds to figure out how to use it, or it's over."

"It took you years," Raizu protested, and she felt his breath on her neck. "Skies, it's all real, isn't it? Gods. Demons. And I'm supposed to do something about it. Why would Komi—?"

"You have to drive out the darkness, Raizu," insisted Letty. "You have to."

You can try, growled a voice in her mind. This time, it was not the demon. It was the voice that had flooded the stream during the caribou hunt.

She shook it away. "Concentrate. What do you feel?"

"Terror, mostly," said Raizu.

Letty could practically hear the pounding of his heart.

A wave of freezing cold rushed over her as the demon spoke from across the room. *"You dare to join your brother, Aletta Skylark?"*

Letty didn't reply. She held her breath, crouching low on the ground so that she could wrap an arm around Majest's ice-cold body, as if she could shield him from further harm.

"Lady Lunesta started this, and I, Ohanzi, will end it."

"You remember Maji's lesson, right?" Letty asked Raizu. "Focus. Let everything but this disappear."

"Letty, I'm not you, or Maji, or Sedona—"

"You have to try," she pleaded as the demon swept audibly closer. "Now!"

She heard Raizu clamber to his feet, heard how desperately he itched to turn and run. She could not help him—could only do her best to give him a chance.

Time. Raizu needed time.

"Why is Lunesta really doing this?" she called to the demon. "What's this *better world* she thinks she can create?"

Ohanzi laughed. It was not a human laugh. Thankfully, he took the goad. *"The Organization will not matter once I destroy you and their purpose alongside you. They are wrong about many things, but not this: Power like ours is for destruction."*

"Not if we have anything to say about it," growled Letty. "The Organization's destruction created you, and without you, they can't find us—so your time ends here. You and your shadows."

"You cannot fight the shadows. They consume everything."

"Except the light," said Letty. Her fear was gone.

"There is no light in this place."

"You're wrong," said Raizu loudly, and he came to stand at Letty's side. "Even in the darkest places, there are people who bring light—however, um, temporary their Power."

"You," cackled Ohanzi. *"You aren't a part of this, boy."*

Raizu was glowing again, and in that glow Letty could see the flaming violet smolder of Raizu's eyes, the silhouette of his shape.

"I don't want to be afraid," Raizu said, and for once, his lip did not tremble. "Not here. I'm so far from where I started, aren't I?" He glanced at Letty, then at Majest's body, and his fire softened, going rosy. "I might as well keep going."

Seconds were hours as Raizu raised his hands, totally focused. Letty saw a little of her brother in the set of his jaw, the steadiness in his reach.

"The light will drive out the darkness," he said. "No matter how dark our nights become, the sun will rise."

Letty could not be sure, but she thought his tone sounded hollow, metallic, familiar—and she thought she saw Komi's starry wings flash across her vision.

But then they were gone and Raizu was only Raizu.

His face shuttered, hands reaching farther and farther, as if toward the heavens. A stream of light burst from his fingertips, illuminating the building in a searing flash. Letty swept her eyelids shut, but even through their shield, the white-hot blaze blinded her.

Then came a scream, a bloodcurdling howl of agony. Letty swore she smelled burning flesh.

The room crackled. Sizzled.

Gentle, living fire licked Letty's hair, her face, her icy fingers.

When it died, she squinted. The flood of light was now a soft halo, blanketing just enough of the darkness to see. The air was silent. The building was empty.

Letty's heart quieted.

Raizu had doubled over, hands splayed over his knees, breathing with his entire body. His face gleamed with sweat.

"Did it work?" Letty dared to ask. "Is Ohanzi gone?"

Raizu swiped at his forehead with one sleeve, exhaling a breathy laugh. "It must have, because I feel like I'm going to pass out."

Letty rushed immediately to his side, letting him lean on her shoulder. His skin nearly burned her even through their jackets. No wonder this had been a one-time deal.

"You've saved us," she told him. "I'm so glad you were crazy enough to follow us across the Hudson Bay."

But Raizu couldn't squeeze out a smile. He wiped his eyes and said, "*Komi* saved us. He only used me so he could interfere without breaking the gods' laws. And it might as well have been for nothing." He looked to Majest on the ground, blurred in the fuzzy light. "He's gone, Letty. I couldn't stop it."

Majest. The last of her loving family. In the moment, she had almost forgotten.

Letty went to him, knees hitting the floorboards, and leaned her head on his chest. His body seemed to murmur, reaching for life, but he still had no heartbeat. Not even Raizu's light could have reversed that.

She put a hand to Majest's freckled cheek. It took what was left of her heart. "So much for Komi keeping his Messengers safe," she managed.

Raizu knelt next to her. She leaned into his warm arm as his eyes watered.

"Don't cry," she said before the first tear fell. "You saved the village."

"I don't care. Maji's dead."

Letty was silent. She had no words.

Behind them, the door creaked open and the room filled with sunlight. She and Raizu turned around and there stood Jay. Letty wasn't sure whom she had been expecting, but it certainly hadn't been him.

"Morning, you two," Jay said. "Thought I heard a racket." He leaned against the door frame, picking at the wood with one fingernail, then propping it open. "Is the demon dead?"

"Is that…why you're here?" Letty asked, bewildered.

"I was in the neighborhood. Thought I should try and clear my mind, since my village is probably going to exile me into the bay on a floating mat of logs. I came here to pretend I'm alone. Unfortunately, I have ears, so that didn't last long. The demon?"

"Raizu killed it," Letty told him. "We're okay, but Maji… His heart stopped."

"Let me see," said Jay, crossing the room with startling accuracy.

Raizu gave him room to lean over Majest's body.

Like Letty, Jay felt for a pulse. Unlike her, he did not seem concerned when he didn't find one.

"He's not dead," Jay said.

"What?" said Letty. "He's not breathing."

"Listen," Jay snapped. "I may be blind, but that doesn't mean you all get to be deaf. You heard me."

Letty's entire body went limp. She would not let her hope rise only to be dashed again.

"Don't just *stand* there," Jay pressed. "We need to get his troublesome heart working. There isn't much time."

"How do we do that?" asked Raizu.

"By getting out of my way."

They stumbled back in a daze, watching as Jay, surprisingly strong, gave a hard push to Majest's chest, one after another after another.

After only a few moments, Letty realized with embarrassment she was crying. Tears dripped down her face and off her chin, drowning out her vision until Jay and Majest became dark blurs in the welcoming sunlight.

She wanted more than anything to lean her wet face into the crook of her brother's neck, breathe in the evergreen smell that meant home. Let the warmth of the sun stir the top of her head where her hair had fallen out of its binding.

All she could do was let herself fall to her knees.

For a moment, she was years younger than the age she had needed to be. She could imagine herself back home, months ago, when "organization" had only been a way to sort her feather collection. There had been a time when she'd never thought she would need to know how to fight or even restart a heart. A time when gods had been legends and happiness had not. Now she needed to be strong, like her father, her mother, and Majest.

"Everything's going to be all right," she said, looking at Raizu. "The shadows are gone and we're going to be all right."

27

“You must have done something wrong, Jay. He’s not waking up!”

“Oh, he’s fine. Can’t you hear him snoring? He’ll be back to stomping around in no time like the gods’ gift to humankind you think he is.”

“You shouldn’t make fun of someone who almost died this morning.”

“I could make fun of you instead, since you almost died a few days ago.”

Majest could hear the voices somewhere above his head. He knew he had been dead, or was dying—hurtling into black space. He had tried to backpedal, keep his soul afloat, but he had lost ground for miles until someone had tethered him back to the shore of the living. His heart had returned, stronger than ever.

And now, he realized with sudden clarity, he was awake. More than that. His stomach was grumbling.

“I’m hungry,” he heard himself say.

He was on his back on a board of hard wood. The faint scent of blueberry stirred as Majest did, and he opened his eyes to see two dark shapes hovering over him.

“You hear that?” one of them said. “Our hero takes on a demon, gets the pulse ripped out of him, comes back from the dead—and the only thing he has to say for himself is that he’s *hungry*.”

“Sounds reasonable to me,” said the other figure.

As Majest’s eyes strained to readjust, the shapes became familiar faces. They belonged to Jay, and to Majest’s astonishment, Vari.

"Welcome back," Vari sang. He smiled as if everything about this was normal. "I just woke up myself. Jay told me a demon possessed me and you got hurt trying to save me."

"That's…" Majest's head ached. He tried to rub his eyes, but his arms might as well have been made of water for the absurd way they felt.

"Maji!" called a voice, saving Majest from responding. It was Letty, hurtling toward him. She stopped at his bed table, which Majest realized was the same one Raizu and Vari had lain on.

"Letty," Majest said, patting her arm to the best of his ability. "How are you?"

"How am *I*? How are *you*?"

"Great? Possibly?" Majest tried out a smile, but it only got halfway up. "Did I kill the demon?"

Letty and Vari exchanged a glance. Majest realized they were side-by-side, their hands clasped, and narrowed his eyes.

"Raizu killed Ohanzi," said Letty quickly, following Majest's gaze. She went pink with a blush but did not pull her hand from Vari's. "We found you in the storage building and got trapped inside with you. Komi appeared and gave Raizu a light power, and—"

"Komi *what?*"

"You Skylarks really *are* deaf, aren't you?" Jay muttered from across the room.

"I'll let Raizu explain," Letty said.

"Where is he?" Majest asked, confused for a moment. Then, with a sickening thought, he recalled their fight, Raizu's coat and scarf trailing behind him as he walked away.

"He's outside," said Letty. "Do you want to see him?"

Mostly, Majest decided, he wanted to swallow about six sandwiches whole. Was Raizu still angry with him? Was he angrier now that Majest had nearly gotten himself killed?

"You're not doing anything until you rest," Jay warned, marching over. He looked less irritable than usual and was only somewhat unpleasant as he added, "And eat."

Majest had no objection to that. He wasn't sure he was ready to face Raizu yet, anyway. "What are we having? Caribou? Rabbit?"

Jay snorted. "Soup."

"What kind of soup?"

"Vegetable."

"Vegetable?"

"Yeah, you know, sort of like lemming soup, except instead of lemming, it's got vegetables in it."

"It's really good," Letty added. "I promise."

Jay set to work, disappearing into the kitchen with Letty and Vari on his heels. Majest heard him snap a few times for them to get their noses out of his pot, but when they returned, Letty and Vari were beaming. Jay might not have been all-too gracious about accepting help, but those two were persistent enough to make the best of it. Perhaps now that the danger had passed, the people of Hiding would help each other again, too.

Except… Something didn't make sense.

"What happened to Vosile Masotote?" Majest asked. "I assume nothing's changed there."

Letty exchanged a glance with Vari.

"Masotote is dead," Jay said bluntly.

That took a second to sink in for Majest. "You're serious? How?"

Jay helped Majest sit up, then pushed a steaming cup into Majest's hand before he stepped back. "He heard about your death at the hands of his own failed plan and called another village meeting. He told everyone the truth about what he had done to you and what he did to me. He didn't apologize, but he said he could have prevented all of this." Blind eyes went to Majest's and bored through him. "Said he could have saved you, too."

Majest did not say anything. Something wormed its way through his stomach.

"Sedona took him home, and when she went to check on him a few hours later, she found him face-down on the bed, suffocated in the blankets."

Majest took a sip of soup. "I'm sorry," he said. "For starting this. I'm sure his death was a horrible shock."

Jay gave a lifeless laugh. "He was a *horrible* man and his greed would have gotten us all killed, if not for you."

"Does the village believe me, then?"

"More or less."

Majest exhaled in relief. "And you, prophet?"

Jay shrugged, scuffed one foot awkwardly on the floor. "Maybe, maybe not. Finish your soup."

When the last drop passed his lips, Majest felt lighter, well-oiled, like his arms and legs might swing on their own again.

"Can I see Raizy now?" he asked.

"Can you even walk?" Jay said.

"I don't know," Majest admitted. "I haven't gotten that far."

He swung his legs off the wooden bed and did his best to sit. The instant he did, his vision swarmed with black spots, his breath dying in his throat.

Letty was at his side in an instant before he could twitch another finger and let him lean against her shoulder. Gingerly, he set one foot after another on the floor, shifting his weight until he was in somewhat of a standing position. Letty teetered under his weight, and he realized he had a death grip on her sleeve.

"Are you sure you can walk on your own?" she asked. "I could go with you."

"No," said Majest through gritted teeth. "No, I need to do this on my own."

Before Letty could protest, Jay took a step toward the hallway. "Hold on. I have something you could use."

He vanished, then returned a minute later with two long wooden poles.

"What are these?" Majest asked, staggering forward to take them.

"Walking sticks. I, ah—used them back when I didn't know the area so well, to test the ground in front of me."

Majest raised his eyebrows. Jay sounded almost…embarrassed.

He didn't mention it, only tucked the sticks under his arms, leaning into them cautiously. He found he could take a step without Letty's help, and then another. "Perfect," he said.

"Just don't dent my floor," said Jay.

"Right," Majest said, and started for the door. "I'll be back soon. If I'm not, assume I've fallen over and Raizy's too mad to help me back up."

"Wait," Vari said just as Majest turned to leave. "There's something Letty and I need to tell you."

"No, there isn't," Letty said. "Not yet, anyway."

Now *that* was suspicious. Majest turned back to them, two children with their hands once again clasped. Though, he figured, he couldn't call them children much longer. They were six-birth years, true, but Majest was gaining on eight, and that was almost sixteen in old-world years. Letty would have been twelve—almost thirteen. They were nearly adults.

"What is it?" Majest asked.

Letty, crimson, looked at her shoes. "It's nothing."

"When I woke up this morning," Vari said, "Letty was the first person I saw. It was a relief, because…she was the only one I wanted to see." He looked at her, his eyes going soft. Majest, his stomach coiling into loops, knew that look.

And Letty returned it.

"Letty told me about what happened with the demon—how she had to be so brave," Vari went on. "How she had thought she was going to die. I asked her if she would be my partner."

Majest felt his eyes widen so much, they could have toppled out of his skull and rolled across the floor.

"Y-you," he stuttered. "You're *six*." He knew for a fact his parents hadn't been partnered until they'd been much older.

"I know," said Vari, cringing a little. "But I asked her, if in a couple years, if she were still interested—"

"And what did you say, Letty?"

"I said yes," Letty answered. "I know you don't like Vari, Maji, but this is my decision."

Majest pushed out air through his nose. He didn't dislike Vari. No matter how much or how often Vari irritated him, he obviously adored Letty. And if Majest's only protest was that *he* had forever been the one to guide Letty through the woods or wash the snow from her boots, that was an awful way of thinking. Letty was still so young, but she could wash her own boots and now she could choose her own path.

She had survived against the darkness when Majest almost hadn't. She was strong. Maybe even stronger than he was.

"All right," Majest said. "You have my approval. Take care of each other."

"Yes!" Vari cried, catching Letty around the waist and lifting her high into the air, the two of them twirling in a clumsy circle.

After settling back on solid ground, Vari turned to Majest. "Thank you," he said. "We will."

"Speaking of taking care of things," said Jay, "don't you have somewhere to be, Skylark?"

Majest glanced over, having forgotten Jay was still there—a ghost in his own house. He did not look pleased with the talk of love and partnership.

"Right," said Majest, gathering up the walking sticks. "I'm leaving."

"Good luck," Letty said, smiling with her whole face, the way she always did. "I know Raizu will forgive you. He was only angry because he didn't want to see you get hurt. He told me so himself. When you love someone, you try to protect them no matter what—that's what family is for."

Majest stared at her in wonder, wondering when she had gotten so wise. "I suppose we *are* family," he murmured.

"We are," said Vari, beaming.

"You, too?"

"You'll get used to it," Letty assured him. "Now *go.*"

Raizu was not hard to find. He wasn't like Majest—he wouldn't storm off into the woods when he had a bone to pick. He sat on the path to Jay's house, tracing loose patterns in the snow beside him. His coat trailed in the dirt, and his sleeve cuffs and knees were muddy. It looked as if he had been here a long time.

As he watched him, Majest's restarted heart nearly broke all over again seeing Raizu like that. This was his fault.

"Raizy?" He hobbled over on the walking sticks.

Raizu didn't look up. He didn't seem to notice he was no longer alone.

"Raizu," Majest said, louder this time. He lowered himself carefully down, setting the sticks aside. His weak legs went limp when they reached the ground and he had to prop himself up on his arms. "Can we talk?"

Raizu's head lifted. His eyes were blue and troubled, and Majest couldn't tell whether the sun was rising or setting inside them.

"I'm glad you're okay," Raizu whispered after a moment. "Jay said there was a chance you wouldn't make it."

Another lump formed in the back of Majest's throat. Two in one day now. "I'm so sorry for everything. I need you to know that."

Raizu squeezed his hands on the ends of his coat. He nodded but said nothing.

"Letty said you killed Ohanzi. That I should get the story from you."

"She said that? I don't know why she'd say that." Raizu stared at the confused lines he'd drawn in the snow. "It's simple—we heard a whisper. We found the building. We found you." His voice caught. "Then, Ohanzi found us."

"Letty said something about…a light power?"

"Komi appeared out of nowhere. Took us to a starry place." Raizu's voice was near-formal. "He gave me one chance to use godly light to get rid of the demon. He told me…I was the light."

"You are." Majest felt himself smile, however anxiously. "*Himin,* that's incredible." He nudged Raizu's shoulder. "Komi chose you. You can't downplay that."

Raizu shook his head. "If it hadn't been for me, you would have never been in there alone. If I hadn't yelled at you…" He broke off, his lip between his teeth.

Majest realized why Raizu was out here, sitting alone in the cold.

"You're not angry with me," he said. "You think this is your fault."

Raizu didn't say anything, just continued to bite his lip harder but the gesture betrayed him.

"Raizy, come on," Majest said. "You saved my life—*again.* I'm the one who was a stubborn idiot. I thought I could save Hiding, but it takes more than bravery to be a hero. It takes heart—light—and that's what you've got."

"No—no. I shouldn't have tried to keep you from going after Ohanzi. But I shouldn't have let you go alone. I just…just…"

"Just what?"

"Didn't want you to get hurt. I didn't want to have come all this way to lose you, lose the start of courage I've never had before, or the one who helped me find it." Raizu buried his head in his hands. "I'm sorry."

Majest felt his gaze melt. "Hey," he said. "Thank you. For looking out for me. How about we agree to call this the Organization's fault? They bring out the worst in all of us. They also bring the worst right to our doors and make us fight it to stay alive."

Raizu wiped at his eye with one hand. "That's true."

"And now, with Ohanzi gone, they can't find us anymore. Maybe Lunesta will decide we're not worth it—scrap her plans for good. We can start our lives over again."

That lit Raizu's expression. "On…on that note, there's something I need to tell you."

"What now?" asked Majest, grinning as he thought of Letty and Vari's declaration. "Don't tell me you're partnering with someone, too. Sedona? Sunny? *Jay?*"

"*Nooo*, but I decided I'm going to stay in Hiding instead of going back to Inertia, if that's of any importance to you."

Majest stopped laughing. "What? You're joking. You love your pack."

"I do," agreed Raizu. "But they'll have to understand that I belong here now, because I do. Being here, tackling the world with you—that's what I want to do." He gave a tentative smile, tensing, as though Majest might reject the idea.

Majest, however, had spent the last several days trying to forget Raizu had any other home at all.

When he didn't respond right away, Raizu continued. "For the first time in my life, I don't feel chained to my fears. My brother isn't coddling me or telling me how disappointed in me he is. Here, on this island, I can pretend to be brave until I learn how to do it for real. I can run through the woods at night. I can walk through the heavens. I can face demons."

"But you can't just…*leave*, not without telling your pack," Majest stammered. "I mean, I want you here more than anything—Letty does, too—but your family will think you're dead. They'll be worried sick—"

"That's why I'll go back to deliver the message."

"All that way? What are they going to say?"

Raizu shrugged. "We've had other packmates do the same. They find a home that's better for them, something or someone they love and they…" Raizu waved his hands in a shy gesture. "Leave. Maybe they're not usually the leader's brother, so I'll be the first."

"It's a long way back," Majest warned him, but the giddy grin that took hold of his face was impossible to tame. "I should come with you."

"Would you? You don't have to—"

"Don't be ridiculous." Majest was firm. "Letty and I would do the same for each other, and I know you'd do the same for us."

Raizu's face had a smile wider than all of Cognito's forests. "That would be—"

"Majest!" came a new voice. It was Sedona, running toward them, white hair flying. She came to a rushing halt at their feet, and Majest and Raizu split apart. "There you are! I've been looking everywhere for you!"

"What's the matter?" Majest asked.

"Why would anything be the matter?" Sedona beamed. "You saved the day, didn't you? The village is safe!"

Raizu turned red all over again. "It was Komi who—"

"We're having a celebration," Sedona explained. "As an apology. Majest, you were right about Masotote, right about the demon, and now we're throwing a party to celebrate the storm parting from our village. Music, lights, food, everything. What do you say?"

Majest leaned on one arm. "You're having a party to celebrate killing Ohanzi when it was my fault he targeted the village in the first place?"

"Don't rain on our parade," Sedona said, her hands on her hips, but there was affection in her eyes. "It's going to be amazing and you're coming."

"I never said I wasn't," Majest said with amusement. "We're honored to come. Right, Raizy?"

Raizu looked between them with a peculiar expression. "When does the party start?"

"Tonight," Sedona said to Majest. "And soon. You might want to get some rest for those wobbly legs of yours and wash up. Come down to the fountain in a few hours. We'll be all set up. I'm head of the party organization, after all."

Majest cringed at the word *organization* but held his smile. "We'll be there."

"Good," Sedona said, sounding as though she'd won some sort of prize. With a wave, she bounced away.

Once she was out of sight, Raizu turned to Majest, his eyes waltzing with mischief. "You know," he said, "I saw an old suit in the closet in our room. It's got buttons up the front and one of those old-world collars. Whoever lived here before us must've had good taste."

"You should wear that suit tonight, then," Majest told him, not understanding.

Raizu snorted. "Please. It would be too long on me." He smiled again. There was a lot of smiling happening today. "Sedona probably wants you to look nice. She seems to really want you there."

Majest shrugged, self-conscious. "Does it matter?"

"Wear the suit, Maji."

Majest sighed in defeat. Another smile, the thousandth smile. "Fine."

28

etty had never seen so much light tossed into the nighttime sky. Not just the white-gold of starlight, but scarlets and blues, pinks and violets. Sedona had managed to set the entire town ablaze. Streamers of merrily-colored paper twined between houses and trees; lanterns swung from branches, their frames dyed berry-red and blue. They sent color winking across Hiding's stone paths as children tumbled around, screaming in delight.

Someone had set up tables with plates of home-cooked food, brought from all of the townspeople. Caribou legs and rabbit breasts roasted into the dark, fruits and vegetables glimmered with sugar and salt, and bread that looked fresh enough to melt against Letty's tongue.

Behind the fountain, Rapple sat with his partner and their new baby, plucking delicately at the strings of a long wooden object in his lap. A soft note of music twanged out.

"It's pretty, isn't it?" a voice murmured in Letty's ear.

She whirled to see Vari, grinning and holding two cups.

"I brought you some grape juice," he said.

"Grape juice," Letty repeated, and took a cup. Vari's hand was warm where it brushed against hers. "Two weeks ago, I didn't even know what a grape was and now there's a juice of the fruit." She took a sip and was pleasantly surprised. "This is delicious."

"I know," said Vari, and slid an arm around her shoulders. "Quell and Idyllice had Nim from the fruit cart squeeze it fresh."

"Do they do this often?" Letty asked, leaning into him. She remembered the shock of his partnership proposition, the paralyzing relief she'd felt when he had gasped awake—when she had realized she felt the same way.

"They do," Vari answered. "Quell's got a special machine that squeezes the fruits to get the juice out. He made it himself. Sometimes, I go down there and—"

Letty giggled, cutting him off. "*No*, I meant, do they have celebrations like this often?"

"Oh! No, only on special occasions."

"Sedona sure outdid herself."

"The Seacourts aren't interested in doing anything halfway," Vari said. "They're dedicated to dedication, you could say."

Rapple began to pluck his strings again, in longer phrases this time. Melodies played chase with the breeze in streams of what Letty had only heard before, in lullabies and old-world rhymes—*music.*

Vari perked up. "Rapple's got his guitar."

"That's what that thing is?"

"It's an old instrument. Older than this village. His whole family can play."

Letty felt her smile blossom as the music played on. Rapple's head bent over the guitar, strumming to the beat of some unknown heart. It filled her ears with a strange, elated joy.

"We should dance," Vari said, nudging her shoulder.

Letty looked around, seeing couples young and old beginning to sway from side to side with the rhythm of the guitar's music. They smiled into each other's eyes, oblivious to anything else as they sidestepped and twirled.

"I can't do that," said Letty, feeling small.

"Neither can I," Vari agreed, not losing his grin. He caught Letty around the shoulders, tugging her closer. "But I'm willing to make a fool of myself if you are."

Letty laughed, her cheeks warm. She hadn't been this close to Vari before. He smelled nice—almost like sea salt. It was different than the pine and leather scents she had grown up with, but the newness was no longer frightening. She leaned in closer.

"Don't step on me," she said. "I still have all ten toes, despite this country's intentions, and I'd like to keep it that way."

"No promises."

Vari moved first. They swung in a slow circle, Vari's arms sliding around Letty's waist, her hands clasped at the nape of his neck. The ends of his dark hair were soft, like seal's fur. The music strummed on and sang between them, and Letty let it coax her feet forward, then back. Other dancers passed, hair tossing and lips stained with juice. Letty caught their laughter and let it fuel her own.

"We look absurd," Letty said as they spun, catching bemused looks from other couples nearby. "Like lumbering bears."

"The best-looking bears in town," Vari said.

Across the way, Quell waved, and Vari went out of his way to wave both hands back.

"Sure, sure," Letty said.

Vari touched their foreheads together. "I mean it. You look so pretty."

"You aren't too bad yourself, now that you aren't foaming at the mouth," Letty teased. She was suddenly conscious of how close he was, his face inches from hers. "The party is great and everything, but I'm just glad you woke up."

"I woke up because I wanted to see you again," he told her matter-of-factly. He pulled her even closer, and then they were kissing.

Letty, who had never kissed anyone before, let the moment fold over her, let it push her heartbeat louder than the thoughts roiling through her. She closed her eyes, got to her tiptoes on the light-dappled stones, and pressed her lips to Vari's. His lips tasted like he smelled—sweet as apples with a hint of the salty bay he called home. The kiss seemed to last forever.

When Vari finally let her go, she stepped back, swaying on her heels. Colors swirled; music surrounding them. Letty stumbled backward, dragging Vari with her.

"Would you two watch where you step?" snapped a familiar voice.

"Sorry, Jay," Vari said.

"Hmm." Jay stepped back, putting himself out of range.

"What are you doing here?" Letty asked him, honestly curious. "You don't seem like the partying type." Especially since he was at the very edge of the lights, alone and far from the center of the festivities.

Jay shrugged thin shoulders, lifted his blind gaze as if trying to find the moon in the sky. "Why is anyone here? It's a celebration. I'm here to celebrate."

Letty watched his face flicker with faint blues and greens. "Why aren't you with everyone else? Do they still not trust you?"

Vari shot Letty a look, probably expecting Jay's temper to rise, but Jay only sighed.

"It's not that," he said. "I can't tell where they put up the tables. The food. I wouldn't know where to put my feet without spilling juice everywhere. I'd probably end up causing injuries I'd be expected to patch up later."

And Letty, despite all the bitterness Jay had shown her, found herself sympathizing. Jay was capable of so much, but no matter his skill, his blindness locked door after door for him, keeping him out of the world he belonged in. If he didn't know something like the back of his hand, he didn't know it at all. Couldn't trust it at all.

Vari gave Letty another meaningful look, but she ignored it, staring at Jay as he pretended to stare at the ground.

"Hey," she said.

He didn't look up.

"Just because you've put up a wall around you doesn't mean you can't take it down. There are good people—people you can count on to help you. I know I have no right to know anything that happened to you, but—"

"It's all right, Letty," Jay said quietly. "I can't see any of the bad things, so they must not be there, right?"

Letty knew she had overstepped. "It isn't over for you," she finished. "They're not called happy middles—they're called happy endings. You'll get one. Promise."

Jay had looked up, jolted wide-eyed out of his misery, but Letty took Vari by the arm and let the crowd swallow them.

"Maji, you've been staring for half a song with your neck stuck out like a bird's—if you haven't found Sedona already, you're going to pull a muscle."

"I'm not looking for Sedona," Majest said, fidgeting to adjust the fancy coat Raizu had forced him into. It was soft and sleek, made of some foreign material that felt slippery against his skin. He couldn't decide if it was comfortable, but he had to admit, it looked good—it framed his body, but drew attention to the slopes of his shoulders and the length of his legs.

"Then what are you doing?" asked Raizu, both eyebrows raised.

Majest peered through the crowd, attempting to find the eye of its needle. Heads bopped in time to Rapple's music, lights spun, and the town dissolved any last memories of Ohanzi or the Organization.

"I'm trying to find Letty," he said. "She and Vari disappeared."

"Watching over her like a hawk isn't going to make you feel any better. She'll be fine."

"I know, but… We've relied on each other for so long that it feels like I'm cutting my arm off watching her walk away with someone else at a party that's supposed to be ours."

"Hey, you can't control the tide." Raizu touched his arm. "Why don't you try to enjoy the night? It's not like you're here by yourself. You've got me."

"Right," Majest said, quirking one corner of his mouth into a grin. "Shall I go get *two* cups of grape juice for the *both* of us?"

"Sounds like a plan."

The crowd parted and flowed, and Majest found the juice table, standing over a maze of cups with shimmering dark liquid.

"Hi, Majest!" Sedona appeared from behind the table, her hair pulled back from her face with metal pins. She had on a long cotton skirt that swished to and fro as she circled around to meet him.

"Nice party," said Majest. "Did you do all the decorating yourself?"

"Not *all* of it." She made a self-conscious sound, heat on her cheeks. "Sunny helped color the lights. We had to make new dye since we're almost out of old-world paint."

"Sounds like a lot of work for just a few hours," Majest said, impressed.

"It's what I like to do." Sedona paused, clearing her throat. "Juice?"

"Oh! Yes, please. Two."

"One for Letty?"

"Raizu, actually," said Majest, taking the cups she handed him. He sipped at one, delighted by the rich taste. "Vari took Letty to dance."

"They've been inseparable since Vari woke up. They're sure to be partners in a few years if they stay that way." Sedona flexed her fingers, looking down. "I wish all love was that easy."

"What do you mean?"

Under the party lights, Sedona's face turned an odd violet-red. "I actually…had an idea. For you. I was going to ask you about it—but I—" She broke off, her eyes jerking to the landscape in the distance, as if searching for a way to make her words come easier, or perhaps not at all.

Oddly enough, she seemed to find something in the distance and frowned. "What's going on over there?"

Majest followed her sightline, traveling beyond the party lights and into the dark, and then he saw it. Saw *him.*

A stranger stood at the edge of the celebration, just beyond the dazzle of the lanterns. He was tall enough to tower over the crowd and made no move to disguise himself or the soaking wet mess of his bronze hair. He simply stood, clutching a leather sack. Waiting.

"Do you know who that is?" Majest asked.

"I've never seen him before. But he looks…"

"Familiar," Majest finished.

As they watched, the stranger lifted his chin and bored two bright eyes through the crowd. Searching.

"He looks like Raizu," whispered Sedona.

Majest stiffened. How hadn't he seen it? The gold in his hair, even wet, the smooth angles of his face, the careful stance—the violet-blue eyes.

"Maji!" cried Letty, a blur of color as she crashed into him, Vari right behind her. "Do you see him?"

"Yes, I see him," Majest replied, untangling two warm hands from where they clutched at his waist, setting his juice cups on the table behind him. "Who is he?"

"I have no idea, but everyone's noticed him now," said Vari.

The stranger shuffled his feet as the ruthless, suspicious gazes Majest knew all too well landed on another surprise visitor.

The music stopped. Dancers halted mid-twirl. Every eye turned.

"Who are you?" someone demanded.

Majest forged his way through the throng, the others following. The crowd split apart like water and they broke through, stopping just a few paces from the stranger.

The man lifted his hands in surrender. "My name is Arathiel," he said. "I mean no harm."

Arathiel. Had Majest heard the name before? Up close, he thought Raizu could have looked into a mirror and found a version of this man staring back at him.

Where *was* Raizu?

He hissed the question into Letty's ear, catching her by the shoulder.

"I can't see him," she said. Majest couldn't, either.

"How did you get here, and what do you want?" Sunny demanded from somewhere.

The man cringed at the harsh voice, took a step back. "I've been searching for my brother," he said. "He's been gone for weeks. I tracked him to the shore, where I found a piece of his scarf washed in with the tide." He shifted his weight. "I rigged a few logs together and paddled out to see if I could find anything else of his, and eventually, I saw this island in the distance."

"You couldn't see it from the shore?" asked Vari.

"Not at all."

Good, Majest thought. By luck or fate, he, Letty, and Raizu must have been on the exact right sliver of beach to see the island's tree line, the spot Jay had talked about. Otherwise, it seemed, Hiding kept true to its name.

"Is he here?" the man demanded, water dripping from his hair. "Is my brother here?"

"I am, Rath."

Raizu walked through the parted crowd calmly, though Majest saw the indent in his cheek that meant he was chewing at his lip. He faced the stranger, eyes almost cold, and Majest saw it: brothers.

"Why did you come here?" Raizu demanded.

"Raizu," Arathiel breathed, and stretched out his arms in relief. He leaned toward Raizu, but Raizu leaned away. "Thank the skies you're alive."

"Why wouldn't I be?"

"You were gone for so long, I thought something must have happened to you."

"So, you came after me like I'm some animal you need to track?" Raizu didn't seem to register this conversation was happening in front of everyone. "You left the rest of Inertia alone because you think I can't take care of myself?"

"Don't use that tone with me," Arathiel said. "I risked my life spending two weeks in the forest on an injured leg to make sure you were all right."

"I didn't ask you to do that."

Majest had never heard Raizu speak like this.

"What do you want?" Raizu pressed.

This seemed to Arathiel a genuinely shocking question. "What do you mean? I'm here to take you home."

Majest went cold. He tried to catch Raizu's eyes, but when he couldn't, he forced himself into the conversation. "This *is* his home," he told Arathiel. "He belongs here now."

The muscles in Arathiel's face twitched. His gaze went to Majest with great reluctance. "I suppose you're one of the Skylarks."

"I'm Raizy's best friend." Majest crossed his arms. "He doesn't want to set one foot off this island. Not now, not ever."

"Don't you?" Arathiel said.

Raizu's eyes darted from Majest to Arathiel, and gradually, his expression lost its harshness. "I—I was going to live here," he said, and the words faded into an apology. "With Maji and Letty. Their battle against the Organization was something I wanted to be a part of, and even if the danger is gone, I want to stay. I'm valuable here."

"Your place is with your pack. Your only family. You're valuable there," Arathiel said.

Raizu's eyes were pained. "You don't need me."

"*We* need him," Majest put in, and had to physically force himself not to step in between Raizu and his brother. "He saved our village."

Arathiel's gaze hardened. He had Raizu's eyes, but Majest could not fathom seeing Raizu with such an expression. "He's my brother," he said.

"He's his own person."

"And I'm right here," said Raizu. "You can't just tuck me under your arm and take me with you, Rath. This is my decision."

Majest came up next to him and took his arm. "Tell him what you told me," he said.

Raizu nodded tightly, opened his mouth—

"We miss you," Arathiel interrupted, his voice stretching until Majest thought it would break. His eyes were more like Raizu's now—wide and endless. Convincing. "Kallica and the others are having a really hard time without you." He bit his lip. "They haven't been themselves."

Majest saw Raizu's resolve flicker. "Really?"

"Of course, Raizu. I've missed you, too. It's kept me up at night. I don't know what I'd do without you. You have to come back."

Majest narrowed his eyes. This was the same sort of manipulation Vosile had used. Arathiel wanted Raizu in a corner he could pluck him out of. Why couldn't Raizu see that?

Raizu hesitated, gave Majest a brief, desperate glance. "Well, I..."

"Don't go." Majest heard himself pleading. "Your brother can deliver the news to Inertia that you're staying with us. That way, we won't have to do it ourselves—you know, like we planned?"

Raizu turned to Majest then, away from his brother, away from the crowd. He looked torn, a page ripped right out of a book. "I thought I could stay," he said. "I didn't consider anyone else. But my brother came all this way to bring me home. Even found a way across the bay and to this impossible island. That means something, don't you think?"

Majest saw the glassy confusion in Raizu's eyes and knew he was giving in. "What does it mean?" he demanded. "That your brother can't stand to lose something he thinks belongs to him?" Majest grabbed the sleeve of Raizu's jacket. "What do *you* want?"

"*We* want you here," Letty chimed in, sure and fierce.

Raizu looked at the ground. "I'm so sorry," he murmured.

Majest watched the last of his fire go out. "What—Raizy?"

Raizu looked up, his blue eyes meeting green.

Majest tried to find that brave light he'd seen just minutes ago. Tried and tried and tried.

"Rath's right," Raizu said. "How would you feel if Letty ran off?"

"That's different," Majest insisted, shivering under his suit. "Letty and I only have each other. No—now, we have you, too. You said your pack would understand."

"I thought they would." The pools in Raizu's eyes swelled, leaking out the sides. Small tears. Unwilling. "I guess I was wrong."

Letty took hold of Raizu's other arm, locking him between her and Majest. By now, everyone but her and Sedona had lost interest, returned to the party.

"You can't walk away," Letty said. "The three of us, we're something special."

Raizu looked at her the way Majest might have. "You could come with me."

"That's not fair," she said. "This is our home now. We can't pack up and leave, not again."

"But I have to," Raizu told her, though he had turned to Majest. His voice was empty. "I was naïve to think I could leave behind my life the way you did."

Majest knew he had lost the fight, knew there was no way to save his heart from being wrenched out of place. Still, one last time he tried. "Please don't go."

"Enough of this," Arathiel said, and didn't even try to hide the dark, satisfied glint of his eyes. "If we leave now, we can make it across the bay before sunrise."

Raizu shook his arms free and wrapped them around Letty and Majest, head bent between theirs. "Don't worry. It's a small world we live in, right? I'll see you two again."

Majest buried his face in Raizu's shoulder. Those were the words that had first sent Raizu walking away through the forest—back to Inertia. And here they were again, at the crossroads, all three of them.

"Hopefully in better times," Majest managed to say. He tried to smile, to say something worth remembering, but couldn't. No words were enough, anyway.

"Don't worry about your supplies," said Arathiel. "I brought you a bag and a better bow. Come on."

Raizu nodded, slow and lingering. Then he turned around.

Majest only heard Letty's muffled sobs into Vari's shoulder and the sounds of footsteps fading as his first and greatest friend walked away.

It didn't take long before they were out of sight, swallowed by the night. Raizu had looked back a few times—of course he had—but he was gone now. Would they make it across the bay safely? Would Raizu be steady in the darkness, or would his fears return? Majest didn't know. Majest might never know.

"Majest," Sedona said, her voice catching. She'd run up behind him and touched his shoulder. "I'm so sorry."

"Don't," said Majest, finding Letty's hand and gripping it tight. He closed his eyes. "There isn't anything you can say." And it was true.

As if on cue, the party lights flickered once, twice, and then they sputtered out altogether. It was time to go home.

EPILOGUE

The Organization's corridors were silent. No shadows stirred across the white walls, nothing metal clinked across the cold floors, not even the electric whir of the laboratory interrupted the quiet.

Lunesta Skylark sat in her hard plastic chair, her spine stiff and unmoving. It had been almost three days since Ohanzi's red dot had vanished from her screen.

She turned her head, which made her neck crack in protest. "Chami. Shayming. Have you heard from the one who wanted to meet with me?"

The twins sidled over and said simultaneously, "Not yet."

Lunesta rubbed at the bridge of her nose. Even her face felt stiff. "Then without Ohanzi…" *Or Seti or Malory…* "We'll have to wait." *Again.*

"Lady President, don't be too upset about Ohanzi," said Shayming. "He was more of an accident than a plan."

He could have found them. Aloud, Lunesta said, "What are the scientists doing? Whether the Powers are in the bay or right under our noses, we're going to need a new tracking system. What we *need* is something to track *godly* energy—what do they have to say about that?"

"They'll work on it," Shayming said, patting Lunesta's back in consolation.

"Would you…?" Chami toed the ground nervously. "Would you consider bringing Seti back? If he's still around, I'm sure he—"

"No," snapped Lunesta, slamming a wall of ice around the subject. "Seti was a traitor. He is a last resort. I refuse to believe we are there yet."

"Yes, Lady President," Chami said.

A knock came at the door and the twins perked in interest. Lunesta wasn't expecting anyone.

"Unlock it," Lunesta said.

When Shayming did, the door blew back as though a hurricane raged behind it. Shatter stood in the entrance, her pale hair frizzy with static.

"There's a woman at the front door," Shatter said before Lunesta could ask. "The guard sent me. She's asking for you."

"The *front* door?" Lunesta was intrigued. The Organization's entrance was concealed behind a crushing, unstoppable ring of waterfalls—impossible to see or approach, unless you knew it existed. Few did.

"Show me," said Lunesta.

Trailing Shatter's light steps, she navigated the white maze, leaving the twins to watch over her room. No one else walked the halls or poked their noses into the light. It was as if the Organization was in hibernation. It didn't help that this was the first time Lunesta had so much as seen the door to the outside world in months.

It was a thick door, a solid metal wall of security. The waterfall in front of it rattled the walls, vibrating every movement. It took Lunesta several shaking moments to work her way through the padlocks.

"Last one," Shatter encouraged, her brow tense.

But before Lunesta could get the final combination, the door swung backward, a loud metallic hiss rolling from its hinges.

Shatter flinched.

Lunesta peered into the dark cave beyond the door. The waterfall's roar was all-encompassing. It even made it hard to see.

"No one's here," said Lunesta.

"She was," Shatter said, raising her voice to be heard. "Just minutes ago. She said Chami and Shayming sent her."

"I see. Then I have been expecting her." Lunesta took another look. "If she hasn't disappeared."

"I am here," said a cool voice.

Lunesta disguised the startled tremor that rocked through her. She squinted, but aside from a distant pair of stalagmites, the cave floor looked empty.

"Show yourself," Lunesta stated. "I am President Lunesta of the Organization."

The darkness grew a face, then a body. She was tall and formless, just a ribbon of dark water. She had inky hair and a too-small face, but anything beautiful about her was obscured by two pulsing red eyes.

"My name is Sira Sinestre," the woman said.

"Sinestre," whispered Shatter.

Lunesta ignored her. "I'm glad you came."

Sira did not blink. Her gaze was so intense Lunesta nearly shrunk back. It was as if something lived in her eyes, swimming in fire.

"You seek assistance for your sinking ship," she said. "I have come to offer it. For a price."

"A price?" asked Shatter.

"You can accept my help, or you can keep to your own path and destroy yourself."

"Name your price," said Lunesta.

"With these facilities, I will show you how to create an army that will bring an end to the world of the elements and put your Organization's world in its place. It will finish what I once started, and for you, it may do the same. And in return…"

Lunesta waited patiently in the cold gloom.

"In return," Sira said, "I will do as I wish with this new world."

PROLOGUE

A path split the trees of the forest as if it had fallen from the sky and landed there, subtle and alluring among the reaching arms of the evergreens. Morning sun filtered through to the ground illuminating the pebbles of the trail, though it couldn't really have been morning at all.

It was a dream. *What else could host such vibrant colors and shapes? In the waking world was only black, nothing but black. Here, there was brightness. Light. It was welcomed, even in this simple forest—peaceful and gold-green, the kind of colors that brought back distant, aching memories of a time when it wasn't only an unconscious mind that could witness the beauty.*

He found his feet, bare but warm against the smooth stone he walked upon. He marveled at the sight. He didn't think he had seen his feet in his dreams before, and the way his toes flexed and his heels kicked up off the ground, off toward his destination, fascinated him.

But where was *his destination? Usually, his mind could unravel its intentions to determine whether his dreams were fantasies or nightmares, and where the story should lead.*

This dream was different. Tangible. An uncertainty that pooled in the soles of the boy's feet until he felt as though he were swimming in deep water under watchful eyes. It made him certain this dream was no nostalgic meadow of blurry, long-forgotten colors and shapes. This dream had been sent from a higher power.

If this is supposed to be a message, I'd better keep walking.

Alight with decision, he focused unpracticed eyes on the trees ahead. He noticed with an almost comical abruptness that his arms were splayed out in front of him, as if feeling for the path ahead. He lowered them, embarrassed by the action even though he was alone. He'd forgotten there was no need for that here.

As he started down the pebbly path, a feeling of unease crept over him, winding around his thoughts with long, thorny tendrils. Something should have happened by now. A voice should have spoken to him by now or a scene should have unfolded to tell him what he was supposed to do.

But there was nothing but endless trees and the path of stone beneath his bare feet.

"I know you're there," he snapped, narrowing his eyes and whirling around, trying in vain to find anything out of place in the perfect greenness.

The silence that answered was bone-chilling.

"This is the part where you're supposed to give me a message," he said.

"Receiver." The word came from somewhere distant, like the trees themselves were speaking.

He relaxed. This was what he was used to. "This isn't anything like I've seen before."
Considering how much I've seen in the first place.

The boy shook the thought from his head. There was no point in bitterness when no one was there to hear it. He sighed, scanning the trees once more. The forest seemed darker now, covered in shadows.

"What is it?" he demanded of the skies, shaking his hair out of his eyes. "Another storm? You know I don't care for guessing games. If you want me to have this power, you might as well let me use it." He knew he was being unreasonable, but even in a dream, time wasted was time wasted.

The air grew colder. He glanced in irritation at the dreamland atmosphere above him and noted something passing over the sun, between the fog and the sky. Not a cloud, but a circular shape, a slinking silhouette.

The moon?

"Keep moving," the breathy voice whispered. "You don't learn by standing in one place, do you?"

He walked forward, muttering under his breath at how pushy the supernatural overseers were. Apparently, they were making him work for the message tonight.

In seconds, things began to change. The shadowy sphere drifted closer to the sun in a predatory threat, casting dark lines through the forest that twisted the blinding brightness into flickering golden shadows, like wavering candle flames.

The trees were moving, too—swaying from an invisible wind. They were starting to blacken and wilt.

Shuddering, he looked away. He was used to hearing and feeling destruction, but not seeing it. Whatever this message was, it did not hold hope. It held something darker.

With a mournful creak, the trees began to fall, roots buckling out of the ground and kicked out from under the trees. One by one, they collapsed, thudding into piles of coal-colored mess, their majesty stripped. There was no longer a living forest, only destruction.

The boy looked down at his feet to make sure they were still on solid ground. Luckily, the path of luminous stone remained intact.

Then the trees weren't trees anymore; they weren't even shadows. They were people, *faceless people, dropping to the ground like windswept ashes. A ticking sound as if from a clock filled the air and the boy could smell the acrid stench of blood and death. He knew that smell like he knew his village.*

He turned from side to side but couldn't find anything but the rising steam of burning, shadowy skin. Was this the message? Death? People died all the time. It was natural and to be expected. Humans always died, even in this new world where they were ageless. Why would the gods take special care in delivering a message of death?

No, there had to be something else.

"I get enough blackness in my conscious state," the boy grumbled, startled to find his voice normal amidst the chaos. "I don't need it here."

His exclamation must have triggered something because the shadows stopped falling. They froze, as if someone had turned them to ice. Everything was now calm and glacial.

He looked up to see the sun was covered in clouds. The sphere—perhaps it was really the moon, perhaps not; he could not be sure—had shifted to loom in front of a bright star, swathing it with gloom until only a faint ring of light was visible. It seemed the sun struggled in vain to return, pinned down and shackled.

"An eclipse?" the boy breathed, accustomed to the dark and unafraid. He had learned how to function without light and color.

The sudden sound of rushing water broke his train of thought as he was jerked sideways, pulled forcibly along by a current he could not see. And although he was startled by the change, he still was not afraid. He did not value his breath.

A river in the middle of the woods… How? I'm not even getting wet. Isn't this a classic Sender Darkbi mystery.

The boy lifted from the ground, elevated gently by the current. He closed his eyes as exhaustion overtook him. The Sender's dreams always drained the energy out of him. He wished—and not for the first time—that the gods would stop throwing their foresight at him so he could go back to ordinary sleep and not wake up with his eyelids weighing down.

At last, the river stopped flowing. It stopped moving forward and began to drop downward toward another plane.

He felt a lurch as he was dragged down into its watery depths. Soon, there was nothing but vertical space, extending forever into endless blurred shapes. Any last trace of a forest and the trees that had turned into victims was gone.

He held his breath and clutched his knees to his chest as he descended down toward nothing. The howling roar of water thundered in his ears, and he was finally grateful that he could see in his dreams, that he was not lost to the blackness and silence plucking his sanity from him.

This had to be part of the message: empty space, a wall of water roaring from it. He wished the gods could be less cryptic, less melodramatic.

As he fell, a voice rose up inside his mind. It was the same voice that had spoken earlier, the one he was accustomed to hearing. The words came faster now—urgent, as if he were running out of time.

"A wall surrounds that which must be broken," it said, its effeminate tone cutting through him, making him forget he was falling. "Those who seem to sleep are awakening and returning to their earlier schemes. You cannot see them, not even in your dreams. They have blocked themselves out."

"What does that mean? I don't have time for your riddles!" The boy gritted his teeth. His usual interpretational skills were less effective once the message foretold more than the coming weather. He did not understand the more complicated prophecies on his own and did not want to.

"While the enemy is emerging from sleep, the ones to destroy them must awaken," the voice replied. "The light can no longer destroy the darkness on its own."

A vision flashed in his mind of the eclipsed sun. "Is that all? The darkness? There has always been dark, with or without the light, awake or asleep."

"You must learn to fight in the shadows. You must learn to live through nights without sleep, fly with ease through the darkness like a nightingale until the sun returns and the larks can sing. Only when there is no more sleep and the four pieces align can there be peace."

He remembered a day long ago when a boy, who was slim and gentle with a tremor in his voice, had been the sunlight of their northwoods island village. He'd driven the shadow away from its den.

But the god had said light wasn't the answer to the darkness any longer.

And what was that about larks? Could it mean the Skylarks, Letty and Majest? If so, then who could be the nightingale? Was the golden brown-haired boy still the sun, even with his departure from the island? And four *pieces? Four of what?*

"Peace," the boy said, shaking off the questions. He hadn't the time to decode the confusing words.

Swallowing a metallic taste in his mouth, he continued, "Are you implying there isn't peace now? There hasn't been disturbances in years. There isn't any need for the elemental abilities of Komi the Deliverer. Everything is calm."

"You should know by now there is always calm in the middle of a storm," the voice murmured back, almost teasing. "The peace that rules now is nothing more than a sham of security, a false joy. Your people will find solitude in a different kind of light. Not the light of the sun, but the light of hearts capable of shining bright even through the darkness."

"Don't throw clichés at me. What does that mean?*" he asked again, frustrated.*

There was no one left in town to help him decipher the words, not a soul who knew how or wanted to try. It was only him. "No one's true heart ever saved anything."

"All conscious minds must be present. Everyone must awaken, even in the dead of night. The real light must be allowed to shine."

"Are you saying the danger isn't over?" He couldn't hear himself over the roar of the falling water.

"Awaken and shine," the voice said, fading away until it was only an echo, a mirage of sound.

"Come back," the boy demanded, but no one was there. Nothing but disappointment and distress of an unqualified Receiver, of an apathetic dust-laden sky.

Stifling a sigh, the boy gave up, reaching into the darkness to his arm, gripping his pale skin between his forefingers. He only had time to register the passing of the moon and the faint yellowing of a sunrise sky before his arm had been pinched red and irritated and he was tumbling awake.

Jay opened his eyes. He was back in his house in Hiding, a secretive island village just off the coast of the Hudson Bay. The vision was gone, leaving only emptiness, though the sights of falling trees and rushing water still hung on invisible cords in his mind and made him dizzy. Most of his dreams were images and shapes recalled from his four years of having sight, but when the Sender twisted the old images and spat them back at him in blurry kaleidoscope visions, he was lost.

He sat up, putting his feet on the wooden floor beneath him. Blood rushed to his head and the words from the heavens threatened to drain out reality. He knew he could not forget the vision as he had forgotten other dreams. If such words held the future for his people, he must remember.

"The enemy is awakening," he repeated aloud in a soft voice, his heartbeat pounding fast beneath his thin nightshirt. "The hero must awaken. All conscious minds must be present, even in the darkness; the real light… must be allowed to shine."

A deep breath. "Awaken and shine."

PRONUNCIATIONS

(In order of appearance)

Aletta (Letty) Skylark – Uh-LET-uh (LET-ee) SKY-lark

Komi – KOH-mee

Majest (Maji) Skylark – Muh-JEST (MADGE-ee) SKY-lark

Lunesta Skylark – Loo-NEST-uh SKY-lark

Maxine Skylark – Max-EEN SKY-lark

Dagur Sigurðsson – DAH-gur SEE-gurth-sun

SetiSinestre – SET-ee Sin-EST-ruh

Chami – SHAM-ee

Shayming – SHAY-ming

Shatter Seacourt – SHAT-ur SEE-cort

Soti Sinestre –SOH-tee Sin-EST-ruh

Raizu Capricorn – RYE-zoo CAP-rick-corn

Amitu – AH-mitt-too

Sira Sinestre – SEER-uh Sin-EST-ruh

Caiter Mandle – KAY-ter MAN-dull

Ohanzi – Oh-HAHN-zee

Malory – MAL-or-ee

Kallica – KAL-ick-uh

Coda – CODE-uh

Sylver– SILL-ver

Arathiel Capricorn – Uh-RAH-thee-ELL CAP-rick-corn

Nafuna – Nuh-FOON-uh

Charan – CHAIR-en

Donec – DOH-neck

Sedona Seacourt – Sed-OWN-uh SEE-cort

Sunny Seacourt – SUN-ee SEE-cort

Vosile Masotote – VAH-sigh-ull MASS-uh-tote

Vari Nyght – VARE-ee NIGHT

Rapple Ardyn – RAP-pull AR-din

Acillia (Cilli) – Uh-SILL-ee-uh (SILL-ee)

Jay – JAY

Raylea – Ray-LEE-uh

Quell Souleia – QUELL Soh-LAY-uh

Idyllice Souleia – EYE-dill-eece Soh-LAY-uh

Cydinne Floodleaf – SID-een FLUDD-leef

ACKNOWLEDGMENTS

I t's no secret this is a revised version of *Water & Earth* and the second time it has been published. After a few years of digging within myself and struggling to promote its unedited first edition, I made the decision to go back to the start and get the entire *Messengers* trilogy properly waxed and polished and re-published into something I could be truly proud of. I made the exact opposite of a mistake running into Brittiany Koren, the publisher at Written Dreams Publishing, at a local library event, and knew instantly WDP would become my baby's new home. To all of you who are here a second time, thank you, thank you, *thank you.* So much heartache and hair-pulling and passion has gone into this new draft, and it means everything that we can share it with all of you.

I can't go on without thanking my best friend and cover art designer, Sunny, for the use of characters like Lunesta, Shatter, Sedona, Jay, and more—so impossibly much more. Your reality checks, extra world-building bricks, and plot laser-vision turned this series from a childhood whimsy into something of grit and substance. Never forget Olives Tomatoes.

A canyon-wide shout-out to my parents, grandparents, aunts, uncles, and cousins for reading my books before they were edited and still loving them anyway. Mom, your seventh-grade students are fans I never expected to have, and I know they are fighting along against the Organization with me. Dad and Grandma, thank you for being my salespeople and promoters when my anxiety turns "would you be interested in my book?" into awkward, red-faced laughter.

Sammi, no one has ever made PowerPoints about my characters before, or debated so hotly about which *Messengers* character Logan Lerman would play in a movie adaptation. I still think it's Vari and not Maji, but I cannot love you enough for your laughter, enthusiasm, and support, so I'll let that one slide.

And lastly, endless love for the almost-real friends I've made over thousands of cups of apricot vanilla tea: Maji, Letty, Raizy, Jay, Sedona, Quell and Idyllice, Shatter and Seti, Caiter and Malory, and the dozens more of you who keep coming forward and introducing yourselves. A day without your annoying imaginary voices in my head is a day I don't ever want to wake up to.

If you read and enjoyed this, you are all Messengers of my childhood dream. Thank you.

ABOUT THE AUTHOR

A.L. Mundt has been putting stories to paper since she was just three years old. Admittedly, though, they weren't any good back then. A love for the sublime in the northern wilderness fuels the Messengers trilogy, as well as her day-to-day adventures. She is currently writing a new fantasy series. Aside from writing, she likes painting figure skating cats, pretending to be a pirate, and eating Spaghettios like it's 2005. She dreams of one day owning a pet squirrel named Daniel, visiting Eyjafjallajökull (and learning how to pronounce it), and recovering from a lifetime of having *Chicken Run* as her favorite movie. You can find her at @ALMundt on Facebook and @AuthorALMundt on Twitter, or visit her website at http://ALMundt. com.